D1711563

What the critics are saying...

"*Overcoming Abigail* is an atypical love story that will keep the reader engaged and enthralled until the final line" ~ *Angela Etheridge of The Romance Reader's Connection*

"*Mr. Mabeuse* has written a really extraordinary story. The sultry bohemian lifestyle of the "Big Easy" mixes perfectly with the steaming hot love scenes."

"...if you do enjoy reading D/s I would defiantly tell you to get this book. It really might be more of an eye opener then you think, it definitely was for me." ~ *Raven Jackman of Romance Junkies*

"*Dr. Mabeuse* has penned a tale of love and BDSM that many are sure to enjoy. I recommend this book to fans of BDSM stories and those who enjoy a historical setting. *Overcoming Abigail* is a keeper." ~ *Susan White of Coffeetimes Romance*

Elliot Mabeuse

Overcoming Abigail

ELLORA'S CAVE
ROMANTICA PUBLISHING

An Ellora's Cave Romantica Publication

www.ellorascave.com

Overcoming Abigail

ISBN # 1419953133
ALL RIGHTS RESERVED.
Overcoming Abigail Copyright© 2005 Elliot Mabeuse
Edited by: Shannon Combs
Cover art by: Syneca

Electronic book Publication: June, 2005
Trade paperback Publication: December, 2005

With the exception of quotes used in reviews, this book may not
be reproduced or used in whole or in part by any means existing
without written permission from the publisher, Ellora's Cave
Publishing, Inc.® 1056 Home Avenue, Akron OH 44310-3502.

This book is a work of fiction and any resemblance to persons,
living or dead, or places, events or locales is purely coincidental.
The characters are productions of the authors' imagination and
used fictitiously.

Warning:

The following material contains graphic sexual content meant for mature readers. *Overcoming Abigail* has been rated *E-rotic* by a minimum of three independent reviewers.

Ellora's Cave Publishing offers three levels of Romantica™ reading entertainment: S (S-ensuous), E (E-rotic), and X (X-treme).

S-*ensuous* love scenes are explicit and leave nothing to the imagination.

E-*rotic* love scenes are explicit, leave nothing to the imagination, and are high in volume per the overall word count. In addition, some E-rated titles might contain fantasy material that some readers find objectionable, such as bondage, submission, same sex encounters, forced seductions, etc. E-rated titles are the most graphic titles we carry; it is common, for instance, for an author to use words such as "fucking", "cock", "pussy", etc., within their work of literature.

X-*treme* titles differ from E-rated titles only in plot premise and storyline execution. Unlike E-rated titles, stories designated with the letter X tend to contain controversial subject matter not for the faint of heart.

Overcoming Abigail

Chapter One

Darkness slid out of the swamp and slowly enveloped the house as Abigail sat unmoving at the window, watching the night fall but hardly seeing it. She was listening, but not to the songs of the frogs and the crickets as they sang outside in the deepening dark, but to the voices of the Doctor and her father as they conducted their business in the other room. She didn't listen to their words because she already knew what they were saying, but rather to the sound of their voices as they rose and fell in tedious negotiation. Her father was giving her to the Doctor, handing her over as if she were a chattel, paying off his onerous gambling debts by trading away his only daughter to a stranger. She didn't want to hear the words.

She paid no attention to the servants who came in and lit the kerosene lamps, nor did she acknowledge Old Barrows, the Doctor's butler, when he brought her a glass of wine on a silver tray. He set it down on a table to her right and silently withdrew. She sat there and watched the shadows beneath the ancient trees, the moonlight in the hoary swags of Spanish moss that hung from the branches. She was numb, she was not here. She was so far removed that it was several minutes before she realized that the conversation had ended.

She felt rather than heard the Doctor come into the room, just as she heard the front door close, her father depart.

"Well," he said. "That is that."

From outside, she heard the groom call to the horses, and the wheels of her father's coach as they began to roll down the cobbled drive to the main road. She had hoped that the Colonel would at least come in to bid her farewell, but as usual, she had expected too much. There was to be no goodbye, no show of affection. She should have known he would just leave her there, eager to be done with her, eager to get back to his cards and whiskey.

"He's gone?" she asked dully.

"Oh yes," the Doctor said, "He left your things in the hall. I'll have Barrows take them up. He seemed to be in quite a hurry. I'm afraid his sudden departure has upset you."

She turned away from the window, not wanting to see the coach leaving her behind.

"I'm sorry." The Doctor's concern sounded genuine. "I'd hoped to make this transition as easy as possible."

Abigail moved away, trying to keep as much space as possible between the Doctor and herself. Her humiliation was now complete. There was no way to pretend now that her father had felt anything for her, that he had made this unconscionable arrangement at any pain to himself.

Still, Abigail had her pride, and she held herself erect even as she felt the Doctor come up behind her and stand so close that she could hear his breathing and smell his cologne. He reached out and took a lock of her auburn hair which had escaped her severe bun and ran it through his fingers. It was an impertinent and possessive gesture, and he had intended it to be. She was his now and he was sampling the merchandise. She held her breath.

"You do understand what has taken place between your father and me? You understand your new status?"

Abigail's fingers knotted nervously in her dress. "I wish you wouldn't touch me like that, Dr. Trier. I'd been led to understand that you are a gentleman, sir, and that you treat a lady with respect."

He stepped back and smiled, then reached down and took a thin cigar from a humidor on the desk. He made a show of lighting it , twirling it in the flame and drawing on it, and she saw his face illuminated in the orange flare, brooding and imperious, his dark eyes bright with cruel amusement. He was a well-made man, lean, with powerful shoulders and strong hands, and he seemed to fill the space between them with his presence. And despite his elegant clothes and the neatly trimmed beard that gave him an intellectual air, there was no mistaking his force of character. She was very aware of being alone in this room with a virile and perhaps dangerous man.

He shook out the match and threw it into the cold fireplace. He seemed to be enjoying her nervousness.

"I am a gentleman," he said with a smile. "And I treat a lady with all the respect she deserves. The question is how much respect you deserve at the moment, Miss Du Pre. *Abigail.*" He paused, enjoying the sound of her Christian name, then went on, "I made it quite clear to your father that any reticence on your part, any reluctance to do exactly as I wished would immediately abrogate our agreement, and in that case I would return you to his care. I would of course then hold him to his financial obligations to me, which would no doubt mean ruin. I imagine he would be most displeased."

Abigail's back stiffened and she fought to keep from blushing. "This is hardly legal, sir. May I remind you that this is the year of our Lord 1897. I am an adult woman and not a slave, and what you propose is against the law."

"Yes, you're quite right. This is strictly an extra-legal agreement — a gentleman's agreement. But I assure you that this does not excuse you from your obligation, and I intend to get my fair value out of it."

He drew on his cigar as he contemplated her, then said, "Your father informs me that you're a virgin, Abigail. Is that true?"

She felt the blood immediately rush to her face. She opened her mouth to speak but before she could give voice to her outrage, the Doctor silenced her with a gesture.

"Please. Let's not act like children, Miss Du Pre. We are both adults, are we not? You must have known what you were getting yourself into when you agreed to this arrangement."

"No sir, I did not," she said with all of the pride she could muster. It was a lie. She knew what would happen to her. She wasn't a child. She had just chosen not to think about it. "I do not think in those terms. As I say, I was under the impression that you were a gentleman."

He smiled at her.

"Oh I am, I am," he said expansively. "But a gentleman of some particular taste. You're a very beautiful woman, Abigail. Far too beautiful to be wasting your life taking care of your father's estate out in the middle of nowhere."

He stood up and flicked the cigar into the fireplace. He approached her and took her face in his hands. His hands were surprisingly hard, not like the hands of the boys she'd met at the occasional dance or ball. Hard but warm, and his touch was gentle. Again, she felt herself blushing as she looked into his dark eyes.

"You must be tired after your journey, Abigail. Tired, and it's late. I'd hoped to show you the house, but it's too late for that now. I think it's best that we both go to bed."

He pulled the bell rope at the end of the fireplace.

"I'll have Hannah show you to a bath where you can refresh yourself. You'll find the closets supplied with clothes I had sent up. I believe they should fit. I have a good eye for the female figure. You may wear what you like for bed."

"And where shall I sleep?" Abigail's eyes barely met his.

He looked at her with amusement. "Why, with me, of course. You'll be sleeping with me, Abigail."

He'd been skeptical of this arrangement at first. When he'd finally called Colonel Du Pre to account for the absurd sum of money he owed, the Colonel had proposed sending Abigail to work for him solely as manager of his house and estate, a duty she fulfilled in her own household. But the Doctor already had servants and plenty of money to hire more if he needed them. He handled his own affairs, so what did he need with Abigail Du Pre? Her father had told him that she was a fine young lady, smart as a whip, capable of running a household and balancing his books as easily as kissing her hand. He still hadn't been interested. The money the Colonel owed him was considerable.

But then, he had caught sight of her fair figure coming down the stairs to be presented to him. Her fine carriage, her grace and pride, and her wonderful womanly shape made him reconsider. And when Colonel Du Pre had lowered his voice and whispered to the Doctor that Abigail had never had a beau, the Doctor's interest had perked up.

He might not need another housekeeper, but there were other duties he had in mind that a woman like Abigail could fulfill quite nicely, duties that did not lend themselves to open discussion in polite company. For the Doctor was a gentleman of particular tastes, as he had said, and these tastes ran to certain types of sexual gratification that could not be satisfied through the usual avenues of social intercourse. Instead, they required visits to the demimonde of the professional sex worker — visits that were perilous, expensive, and often less than satisfying.

With a woman like Abigail, however, and with the total control of her person he had in mind, he would have the opportunity to mold her sexually, to shape her into just the kind of woman he desired. He would create the type of lover he dreamed of, make her into his own sexual Pygmalion creation and teach her to love the chain and shackle, the sharp kiss of the whip, those arcane and exotic pleasures he enjoyed himself.

She was everything he desired — comely, intelligent, and unsullied by public foolishness about sexual propriety and perversion that had warped most young women of his acquaintance. Plus, as she descended the staircase that day, he saw that she had the pride, that spark of fire that told of deep currents of untapped passion that not even she was aware of. She was like a wildflower waiting to be cultivated, waiting to be nurtured and trained in such a way as to bring out her latent beauty. She was a rose, waiting to be plucked.

He had agreed to the Colonel's proposal on the spot.

Abigail followed the elderly servant up the carpeted stairs and down the hall to a large bathroom where a hot bath had been drawn, the water fragrant with perfume. Hannah's efficiency and her own strange feeling of numbness did away any thoughts of modesty she might have had, and she let herself be undressed, then climbed gratefully into the steamy water, eager to wash away the dust of her journey and the haunting ghost of the Doctor's touch. The day had been a veritable hell, and she was tense and aching. She lowered herself into the water with a deep sigh. The feel of the hot water was wonderfully soothing to her skin.

Although she was a virgin, she was no child, and she knew what lay ahead for her. She knew too that it was senseless to fight against it. She was no longer a girl and was of an age where she had all but given up on the idea of ever marrying, yet the desire to love and be loved was strong within her. To her own considerable embarrassment, her body longed to know the feel of a man's caress, and even as she lay in the bath wrapped in her own sense of hurt and outrage, her body was growing excited with a delicious apprehension of what was to come. Did he really mean to take her tonight? Would this be the night she became a woman?

By the time Hannah helped her from the bath, she was almost trembling with nervousness. The older woman seemed to sense this, and was kind and solicitous and spoke to her in soft, motherly tones. She dried her, powdered her, and showed her to the closet. Hannah must surely know what was to occur. When Abigail paused before the selection of gowns and sleepwear, Hannah suggested a simple nightdress of white silk, innocent yet elegant.

"He's a good man," Hannah said as she brushed out Abigail's long auburn hair and arranged it about her shoulders. "He has a passionate nature, but don't let that scare you any. He can be fierce, but he's tender. He'd never hurt a fly."

"Then you know? I suppose all the servants know."

Hannah smiled gently. "He's the master of the house. It would be strange if we didn't know. And we know that he needs you, Miss. We've all waited so long for him to find someone, and he cares for you, that's easy to see. I know you'll be fine."

Hannah led her into the Doctor's bedroom, where Abigail tried to ignore the big canopy bed with the covers turned down. That was where she would sleep, and she didn't want to think about that right now. Kerosene lanterns burned on the night tables, and the big French doors were open to the sounds of the night.

"I'll tell him you're ready," Hannah said softly, and left the room.

Abigail stood looking out at the moon, as strange and alien as the feelings that swirled within her. Below her, the gardens were dark in shadow, and Spanish moss barely moved in the languid breeze. She thought of her father, now miles away, and of the Doctor, and of how her life was about to change, and in her reverie, she heard him enter the room and heard his soft intake of breath as he saw her standing by the window. She didn't move. She closed her eyes and waited.

A touch on her shoulders sent chills through her body. She felt weak, dizzy. She wanted him to stop and yet she silently begged that he wouldn't. Then his strong hands gripped her arms and she felt him press her back against his body. His hand came around and caressed one breast, and she had to fight down the impulse to resist him, to make him stop.

He swept her hair to one side, exposing her neck, and his lips were warm and gentle on her shoulder as he kissed her slowly, tasting his way up to her ear, savoring her sweetness. With his hand on her breast, he could feel her chest heaving as her breathing accelerated. He could feel her warmth through the gown, and her nipple grew stiff and eager against the palm of his hand.

His other hand came up and cupped her other breast, and her gown rustled softly as he pulled her back against him, his hands closing on her, feeling her, exploring her. She closed her eyes tight and bit her lip to keep from moaning.

Wherever he touched her, she felt the heat of his hands through the silkiness of her gown as it slid against her skin. He tightened his grip on her, letting his hands slide along her breasts until he found her nipples, which he touched lightly before taking them between his thumb and forefinger and squeezing, filling her with the most intense pangs of longing. She felt his cock, thick and hard, pressing against her buttocks and she was dimly aware of the fact that she should be alarmed or insulted, but in fact, she was filled with a kind of languorous excitement. Her blood felt like warm honey in her veins and her body seemed to rise to meet his touch with a mind of its own, pressing back against him, thrilling at the heat and hardness of his cock. It was for her, she realized—he was hard because he wanted her.

He had barely touched her and already he had taken her further than any other man had ever taken her. No one had ever taken command of her body so quickly and so thoroughly, and instead of being upset and embarrassed by his caresses, she found herself wanting more, wanting his hands all over her.

"Abigail," he whispered. "Abigail…"

He turned her to face him and she complied like a sleepwalker, afraid to open her eyes lest it all prove a dream. He took her face in his hands and brought her mouth to his, and she let herself be kissed, not knowing what else to do. He kissed her tenderly, in a way she had never been kissed before in all her life, as if she were something delicate and precious, telling her how much he cherished her, and yet taking possession of her as well. He showed her how gentle he could be, yet at the same time making it clear that she was his and that he would do with her what he desired.

He let her go and she opened her eyes to see him staring at her, his eyes burning with a fire that sapped her will and made her suddenly weak. No one had ever looked at her like that, with such an intensity of passion, and she knew now if she hadn't known before that this would be her last night as a virgin. That this man, this stranger, was going to take her as his own this night, was going to do to her that thing that she'd never even allowed herself to think about.

His fingers were working at the buttons on her gown, slowly undoing them, one by one, exposing her body to him.

"I want you to know this about sex, Abigail. That despite what you hear from others, despite what you may hear in church or Sunday school, that it is a rare and beautiful thing, just as you are, and it is meant to be enjoyed, again, just as you are. I'm going to show you some of that beauty tonight, my dear, because I'm going to make love to you. I'm going to show you how sweet it can be. Do you understand?"

His words set of an unexpected gush of wetness between her legs. She nodded her head quickly, like a child, reluctant to break the spell he was weaving about her.

His fingers finished with the buttons on the bodice of her gown, and now he brought her to him and kissed her again. She surrendered herself to his kiss gladly, marveling at the things he could do with his lips upon hers, the things he could make her feel. His hands came up and parted the fabric of her nightdress, and for the first time in her life she felt a man's hands on her naked body.

How well he knew her already. He found her breasts again, and he caressed them, his desire for her obvious in the way he touched her. When he lowered his head and kissed her naked breasts, she let her head fall back with a moan, her embarrassment burned away by the rising flames of pure desire.

No one had ever done this to her before. No one had made her feel what pleasure lay within her breasts, the way they seemed to swell and ache at the touch of his lips. When his tongue came out, she thought she might faint, and she dug her nails into his shoulders to hold herself erect. He sucked at her nipples and she felt it immediately between her legs. She felt as if she was dissolving into his mouth and she had no desire to stop. Whatever shame she had, whatever last vestiges of resistance, melted beneath his mouth's caress, and she knew that she was lost.

With a mild flick of his hands, the robe slid from her shoulders and spilled from her body, leaving her totally naked before him. Now, as he kissed and sucked her breasts, another hand traced lower over her belly, her hip, coming to rest on her most private part.

Abigail gasped as he touched her. Her body was on fire for him now and she wished he would hurry. She knew what she needed, and he did too. Why wouldn't he just give it to her now, before this magical feeling ended? Surely it couldn't last. It was too sweet, too arousing to last.

He bent over, then suddenly picked her up bodily and held her in his arms, amazingly strong. She hadn't been held like this since she'd been a child. He took a few steps to the bed and laid her down on top of it. He stood back and took off his robe, undid his trousers and let them fall, and Abigail found herself looking at his cock, proud and erect, thrusting out from his dark pubic hair, impossibly long and hard. His balls seemed to be unusually large as well, and all in all, he radiated a sense of virile potency that excited her terribly.

She had grown up around animals and knew the ways of a male with a female, but still she had never seen a man erect before, and certainly not for her. The idea that this was somehow her doing left her dizzy and trembling, and for the first time since he'd kissed her, she was afraid. He would never fit. She would have to stop him before he tried. He would never fit.

But then he was in bed with her, his naked body pressed to hers and there was no time to speak. There was his mouth to attend to, the way he kissed her, passionately now, his tongue exploring her own mouth, taking possession of it. Abigail put her hand up against his chest and felt the power in his body, the muscles hard and defined. Despite her fear, her body pushed back up against him, seeking contact with his strength, his hardness. She felt dizzy with need. She felt herself opening like a flower to him, needing him inside.

Suddenly her virginity seemed like such a nuisance. She knew what he was going to do to her, shove his cock up into her body and fuck her, push into her, fill her with his male hardness, fuck her until he shot his semen inside her, but now instead of being afraid, she was desperate for it. If she didn't get him inside her, she felt like she'd just die of longing. She needed him, she needed him now.

She moaned hotly as one of his hands boldly spread her legs apart and delved into the sodden wetness of her sex. She should be embarrassed, outraged, but instead, she spread her thighs and let her knees fall open, and her hips began to pump tentatively against his hand with a mind of their own, seeking the hardness of his touch. She tightened her grip around his neck, holding his mouth a prisoner to hers, and now her own tongue came out and engaged his in a delicious battle as she urged him on, invited him to take her, to fuck her, to make her his.

He growled in his throat, his own impatience now matching hers. He rolled over and in a second was between her knees and she felt his stiff, hot prick searching for her. She spread her legs even wider and moved her own hips searching for him as well. All thoughts of shame and modesty were gone, as if they'd never existed. She needed his cock inside her, needed his weight lying on top of hers, thrusting into her, pushing his way into her.

She sobbed and arched her back when the head of his cock suddenly found her. Like a common whore, she threw one leg around him and tried to pull him into her, beside herself with need.

He found her hands, lifted them above her head and held them hard against the bed and she looked up to see his eyes glowing down at her. She held his gaze with her own as she felt him sink into her, opening her for the first time, taking her, fucking her.

She winced and cried out as he pierced her barrier, tearing her and thrusting it aside. There was a moment of pain, a brief stab of heat that separated before from after, and then he pushed into her. She moaned, afraid to move, and she felt her virginal blood begin to seep out around him, staining him forever with her mark. She sobbed once, not knowing whether it was in fear or desire, and then her own animal instincts asserted themselves and she lifted herself, still trembling, onto his ravaging cock.

She'd assumed he would just take her and finish quickly and be done with it, but as he lay on top of her with his cock sunk in her belly, she began to respond to him, tentatively at first, but then with growing enthusiasm, her hips rising up to meet and enclose him.

Now it was his turn to groan, and the sound of his voice thrilled her and gave her a delicious sense of power, knowing that he found pleasure in her as well. Her pride returned, and she decided that she might not have any say in her deflowering at this man's hands, but that she would do everything she could to make damned sure that he remembered her and remembered this night. Sexual pleasure seemed to be a language she understood instinctively, she'd only been waiting for a chance to speak it.

She could not keep still, her body would not let her. Although she herself might be confused and frightened, her body knew exactly what it wanted and she was not afraid to give her body its lead and trust to her instincts. In any case, she seemed powerless to keep still or control the lewd rolling of her hips or the stream of sighs and moans that spilled from her parted lips.

He held her wrists over her head, pressing them down into the bed and leaving her body defenseless. He stared down at her beautiful face, innocent yet suffused with lust. Holding her like that brought her breasts into prominence, and as he began to move against her, her stiff nipples brushed his chest, increasing his lust that much more.

"My God!" he moaned down at her. "Where did you learn to fuck like this? I've never had anyone like you!"

His words made her blush and she turned her head to the side and bit her lip to hide her smile of shame and pride, but the shame was nothing compared to the wild sexual heat that burned through her body. Yes, it hurt. He was the first man she'd ever had, and he stretched her cruelly, filled her completely, but the pain hardly mattered against the deep fulfilling pleasure she felt, a pleasure she responded to with every fiber of her being.

The Doctor couldn't resist her any longer. She was too good, too thrilling. The way her hips moved was too deliciously obscene, too insistent. She was a virgin, yet she moved beneath him as if it were her destiny to fuck and be fucked. She did it naturally, expertly, and exquisitely, moaning and gasping with pleasure as she stirred him around inside her tight sheath, wanting to feel him everywhere, wanting his big cock to find a home in her body. She drew him into her with her woman's strength, and she conquered him with her total surrender.

He began to move on top of her, drawing his hips back and thrusting into her, driving her ass down into the mattress and taking complete control of her.

Despite her inexperience, Abigail knew she was in the presence of a master, and she opened her legs wide and let him have his way with her, content now to just lie back and feel what it was like to be fucked by a man. His hands on her wrists excited her terribly. It was as if he were forcing her to do this, as if she had no choice, no say in what he did to her, and she was free to just experience his lust and desire.

He bent down and captured a nipple between his lips, lashed at it with his tongue and she felt a new thrill join the others in the pit of her stomach. She wanted him to suck her breasts, to squeeze and bite them, to take her roughly, with all the force of his need for her. She would take anything he wanted to do to her. She would take it all gladly.

He began to fuck her with deep, sure strokes, his cock entering her and then retreating, entering her again, to the very hilt, pumping himself relentlessly into her soft body. The strength in his arms and his loins was terrifying as he fucked her. He was like an animal, a machine, undeniable and implacable. She opened herself to him, she had no choice. She wanted more, always more.

He started beating into her fast, pummeling her cunt with his cock, and Abigail felt the thrill of what he was doing radiating throughout her body. She managed to lift her head far enough off the pillow to look down between her jouncing breasts and see his big, thick shaft spearing into her, pink with her virginal blood, spreading her little pussy apart, stretching her, filling her again and again.

"Oh God!" she moaned as she felt sheet lightning flicker through her body. She had never expected it to be like this. She had heard that it could be good, that some women even enjoyed it, but she never expected that she would be one of them. Those were bad woman, whores and white trash. A proper lady might endure her wifely duty, but never enjoy it. It was too animalistic, too crude and obscene.

But she couldn't deny the pleasure that surged through her now. There was no denying this exquisite mix of joy and pain he was causing her as his hard cock pistoned in and out of her body. There was no denying this new feeling, this sensation of a giant wall of sensation gathering over her head, like a giant, dark, tidal wave about to crash down on her and carry her off to she knew not where.

The wave gathered, she felt herself lifted up into it. She felt him hammering away at her pussy, then felt him freeze, go rigid inside her, every muscle in his body flexed rock-hard. She heard him groan, heard him call her name. His big hands closed on the cheeks of her ass and pulled her against him hard.

Abigail gasped, threw her head back and surrendered to the tidal wave of sensation, felt it come crashing down on top of her just as she felt his deep-buried cock throb savagely, shooting his essence into her in great burning gouts of molten semen. That was the last thing she noticed before she screamed and fell into her own shattering orgasm.

She had never known, never imagined. From far away she felt every twitch of his cock as he flooded her with his cum. Far away and yet she felt as though she were right there, watching it erupt into her thirsting body, filling her with it.

She rode that wave with a feeling of triumph and fulfillment like she had never known before, felt her animal soul join to something divine and angelic, felt the raw currents of life pulse through her body. She strained up for it, as if she were rising to a great bright light, and then she fell, shattering into a million pieces of pure physical pleasure too intense to be borne.

The next thing she was aware of was lying there sobbing as he held her close, his hands stroking her hair and wiping the tears of joy from her cheeks. She ached, she hurt, she felt wonderful as she never had before in her life. She put her arms around him and squeezed him with trembling arms, squeezed him like she would never let him go.

She didn't know what had happened to her—had no idea. But she would not let go of this man until she found out.

Chapter Two

Abigail slept unconscionably late, and by the time she woke up, the sunlight was already filtering through the Spanish moss that covered the ancient live oak outside, filling the bedroom with a strange, underwater light. She was alone in the bed, in his bed, and the memory of what had happened last night came flooding back to her with all its confused welter of emotions. One fact, though, was very clear to her—she had made love to a man and she had pleased him, and that knowledge filled her heart with a strange excitement.

As to what he had done to her last night, and worse, what she had done back to him, she wasn't ready to think about that yet. She wasn't the same person she'd been when she came into his house—the soreness between her legs was reminder enough of that—but she wasn't yet ready to meet the new woman she'd become. She lay in bed and looked around the room, seeing his things, his possessions, and she wondered where she now fit into this scheme.

She had no sooner sat up in bed than Hannah entered the room, carrying a tray with a pot of coffee in one hand and a pile of fresh linens in the other. She poured Abigail a cup of the thick brew while she went about opening the bedroom curtains, then she cheerfully teased Abigail out of bed and into the bathroom where a bath had already been drawn for her, the water hot and crowned with bubbles and fragrant with lilac. Abigail couldn't resist. She let herself slide into the water with a deep sigh.

It was obvious that Hannah knew, and as she scrubbed Abigail's back, she whispered, "You should have seen him this morning, Miss. Never seen the Doctor looking so happy of a morning. Whatever you did, you made that man happy."

All the confusion of emotions she felt seemed to evaporate under the heat of that one fact—she had made him happy.

Hannah hummed as she helped Abigail in the tub. "The Doctor's away on business, lady, and won't be home until this evening. In the meantime, he said I should see that you rest and have whatever you need. Now when you get out of this bath, you just slip into a dressing gown and there's a nice breakfast laid out for you in the back parlor. The Doctor should be back around eight o'clock and he'll want you to look fine and beautiful for dinner."

Abigail didn't argue. The Doctor was her employer, nominally at least, even if in reality he was something more, and if he ordered her to rest, then she would carry out his wishes. She was, in fact, more tired and weary than she'd supposed, the emotional strain of the previous day and the physical exhaustion of last night only showing up now as the day wore on.

Hannah showed her about the old gothic mansion, a maze of hallways and rooms whose layout bewildered Abigail. The house was ancient and had had many owners, each of whom had added on to it in strange and quirky ways, so that she despaired of ever understanding all the hallways and staircases. The kitchen, dining room and parlor were easy enough to find, but when she ventured into the numerous wings and additions, she grew lost and disoriented.

Hannah was wonderful to her though. Abigail had worried that she might have trouble with the Doctor's household. As part of the agreement between her father and the Doctor, she was supposed to be their new overseer, but Hannah treated her with the deference due to the Mistress of the house, a Mistress for whom she felt a special affection.

The only time she was less than gracious to Abigail was when they passed the door to one room, a room that was locked and definitely off-limits. Then she just hustled Abigail away from it, saying no more than it was "private", or "the Doctor's special room". Abigail thought that odd, but didn't press her on the subject.

There was lunch, a walk around the garden and grounds, and then Hannah insisted that she lie down. She was very solicitous to Abigail, asking her several times how she felt, about her strength, and Abigail had the feeling that Hannah knew more about what happened last night than she let on. It soon became apparent that Hannah knew more about what would happen tonight than she was telling as well.

In the evening, as the sun was going down and purple twilight gathering, Hannah drew Abigail another bath. After a long soak, she took her out and wrapped her in a fine silk robe. She led her into another bedroom where she sat behind Abigail, combing out her mistress' rich hair and arranging it upon her head.

"The Doctor's very pleased with you so far, Lady," Hannah told her, obviously pleased herself. "Very much pleased. He was even whistling when he left the house this morning, which is something that these ears have never heard before."

Despite herself, Abigail smiled. Did she really take such pride in pleasing him? Obviously she did, though she wouldn't dare admit it to herself, because if she had pleased him, it had been through the use of her body, a subject that still sent nervous thrills through her.

Still, the velvet twilight outside, the warm light of the kerosene lanterns, the smells from the kitchen downstairs, and the hypnotic feel of Hannah's capable hands in her hair soon built up an air of excitement and anticipation in her breasts. She was anxious to get to the task of picking out the gown and jewelry she would wear for dinner tonight.

But she was still in her dressing gown when she heard the commotion out front that signaled the Doctor's return. She was afraid she'd never be ready in time, but Hannah hushed her.

"First, he'll have his bath, then he'll dress, then he'll have his brandy, Lady," she told Abigail. "The Doctor likes things just so, and so you have plenty of time."

She led Abigail to the walk-in closet, which was filled with clothes and shoes of all types. But before they went in, Hannah took her arm.

"Remember what I said, Lady," Hannah told her. "He might have his peculiarities, but at heart he is a good man. You just be patient with him and let him have his way, and you'll do fine. He won't ever hurt you, not really. It's just his way."

Abigail looked at her curiously, the fingers of a chill dragging down her spine, but Hannah said no more, and concerned herself with getting Abigail dressed. She had laid out a dress of emerald green with a daring décolletage and she held the gown for Abigail to step into.

"But Hannah, what about a slip, my underthings? Am I just to wear this gown only?"

Hannah held the gown and barely nodded, and for the first time, Abigail saw a glint of steel in Hannah's eyes. The look told her not to argue, and she stepped naked into the dress, but as Hannah fastened the buttons, Abigail began to get nervous. Why should the Doctor wish for her to be naked beneath her dress? What sort of woman went around with no underthings?

All day she had floated on the euphoria of her first sexual experience, but now a lifetime of conditioning reasserted itself. She remembered how shamefully she had behaved last night. How she had writhed beneath him, wallowing in carnal pleasure. How she had spread her legs to his cruel invasion and let herself go in an explosion of lewd sexual pleasure. It seemed obvious to her now that the Doctor considered her little more than a common whore, a trollop, and she blushed furiously with shame and anger. She fought back tears as Hannah fastened a cameo around her neck, and when it was time to go downstairs, she found her hands were shaking.

By the time she descended the stairs, she had herself under control. The Doctor stood in the dining room watching her come down the stairs, and even from that distance, she could see the gleam in his eye as he took her in. She felt a flutter in her stomach that she tried to dismiss as being part of her recent upset, but she knew better. The feel of his eyes on her excited her, and she cursed herself for it. She was determined not to play the whore for this man again.

Dinner would have been delightful had she been able to allow herself to enjoy it. The food was excellent and the Doctor was perfectly polite and attentive, asking her about her day and her opinions of the estate. She found she had little appetite however, and she found even conversation awkward. She was acutely aware of her nakedness beneath her gown, and of the Doctor's own threatening masculinity so close to her. Her shame over her behavior last night hung like a pall around her.

At last the meal was over and as the dishes were cleared away, the Doctor sat back in his chair with a satisfied smile.

"Have you thought about last night, my dear?" he asked. "I know it must have been a bit unnerving for you. I wondered if you had any questions for me, or needed to express any concerns?" he asked her.

Abigail sat frozen to the spot, uncertain what to say, or whether she should even say anything. Perhaps he was just trying to embarrass her, daring her to admit what had happened last night. She felt herself blush and hated herself for it.

The Doctor laughed. "Come, now. You needn't be so shy with me, Abigail. I'm a medical man. Besides, we both know what happened last night."

"You needn't tease me," she said evenly, keeping her eyes on her plate. "I'm ashamed enough over what occurred, and I assure you it won't happen again."

Barrows, the old half-Cherokee butler, was attending them — Hannah did not serve unless there was a lavish party. Barrows was dark, ageless, and as quiet as a shadow as he moved about the table. He made her uneasy. He set down a silver tray with the after-dinner drinks, brandy and port, along with some fruit and dessert cheeses, then he quietly withdrew.

"I'm sorry to hear you say that," the Doctor said. "Because it's my intention to make it happen over and over again. You were exquisite last night, Abigail. I never imagined anyone could be so overtly sexual, especially a virgin."

Abigail threw down her napkin and stood up. "Excuse me, Doctor, but I'm not feeling well. I think I'll…"

"Sit down," he said quietly, but with such natural authority that Abigail immediately resumed her seat, eyes down, back erect. "What happened last night was that you had an orgasm. Your first, no doubt."

Abigail blushed furiously. Really, this was too much. Everyone knew that there was no such thing as a female orgasm. The most prominent medical men of the day had stated that women didn't even enjoy sex, they simply didn't have the capacity.

As if reading her mind, he said, "Yes, women orgasm. Not like men do, but in their own way, equally pleasurable, if not more so. I myself have seen it happen many times. It is, in fact, the area of medicine that most fascinates me, and one in which I have done a great deal of work. But never have I seen a woman climax as you did last night, totally, unashamed, with her whole body and spirit, like a sexual goddess!"

Abigail turned her head to the side and squeezed her eyes closed against the tears of humiliation she felt gathering there. And yet at the same time, she felt a nagging excitement stir in her body, remembering what she had felt last night as he had fucked her with his big, hard cock, sliding into her, opening her up.

She tried with all her might to deny the memory, to make it lie still.

His touch on her arm jarred her back to reality. He had seized her thin wrist in his hand and pulled her arm across the table.

"Don't you understand? You have a gift, a talent. You, among all the women I have known, are sexually receptive, sexually alive. You feel what all the others deny. You are real, a true woman. All the others are just charades."

His words fell like blows on her bowed head, so harsh, so lewd and degrading. She knew she wasn't like that. She wasn't a whore. He had done something to her, perhaps drugged her. That's the only way she could account for her shameful behavior. He must have drugged her.

The Doctor rose suddenly and pulled her to her feet. With a word, he told Barrows to dismiss the servants and see that they weren't disturbed for any reason, then he dragged Abigail down the hallway by her wrist, pulling her into his study and slamming the door after him. Before she could catch her breath he had both her wrists in his hands and he pushed her up against the closed door, holding her there with the weight of his body.

"This is how it is, Abigail. Just the sight of you brings out these feelings in me, this passion. And I want you to feel it too, Abigail. I need you to feel it too! It's the only way this can work!"

His sudden violence frightened her and she fought him, but she may as well have been fighting off the day of doom for all the good it did. His strength was incredible. He held her as easily as if she'd been a child, and as he held her and she tried to free herself, he talked to her, saying things she could hardly understand in her distress.

"There's no use trying to fight it, Abigail. It is a gift, a treasure, and I own it now, just as I own you, my dear. You will be mine!"

She struggled against him, fighting against his words. Her hair came undone and fell across her face as she felt his lips search for hers. She wouldn't. She couldn't. But he was so strong, it was like he was made of steel.

When she finally stopped struggling, she realized that he was still holding her, but that the bodice of her gown had opened. Her breasts were naked in the light of the kerosene lamp and as she sobbed for breath, she felt his mouth on her nipple, licking at her, sucking her.

It was too much. She couldn't fight him. She had no strength and she had no defense against what he was doing to her, what he was making her feel. Her sex was aching for him again, and her breasts felt swollen and full, burning for the feel of his lips upon them. His strength and desire overwhelmed her and she collapsed weakly against the door, letting him do as he would with her.

The next thing she knew, he had lifted her away from the door and sat her on the edge of his desk, her feet still touching the floor. She was naked beneath her gown, the hem of which was pushed up around her waist in a tangle of clothes. The Doctor was stripping his trousers down his legs and again she found herself captivated by the sight of his rampant manhood, thick and engorged and colored an angry red.

She just had time to gasp in surprise and grab onto the edge of the desk as he lifted her thighs around him. She bit her lip hard, but that did nothing to stifle the long moan of salacious pleasure that issued from her open mouth as his cock sunk into her willing flesh.

Just as he'd suspected, the mere touch of his hard cock against her made Abigail melt with desire, and all pretenses of prudishness or shame vanished as he pushed into her eager body again, his hard cock forging a passage through her hot and swollen vagina.

She clung to him at first, fighting not to give in, fighting for her dignity, but as his hips began to move, he saw her lose control. Tears streamed down her face as she realized how helpless she was to control the fires of lust and illicit desire that coursed through her body. She was a slave to her animal passions, a slave to this man's virile cock.

A few more thrusts and she surrendered completely, not even trying to fight him anymore. She fell back on her elbows, her head thrown back, and she raised and spread her knees, hooking the heels of her boots on the edge of the desk so she could use the strength of her thighs to fuck herself back on his rampaging cock. If she had been sore before, she wasn't sore now. Each time he thrust forward and filled her was sheer heaven. She'd never imagined anything could be this good.

The Doctor looked down at this woman he was fucking. Her hair had completely fallen out of her French twist and strands were in her face. He combed her hair back from her face and looked at her, her eyes closed in angelic rapture, her nostrils flared, her teeth trying to still her quivering lips.

"Tell...me...it's...good!" he gasped, his words punctuated by the thrusts of his hips. "Tell...me...you...love it! Tell me!"

Abigail tried to ignore him, but it was impossible. His terrible need for her, the power he put forth in taking his pleasure in her body made her weak and intoxicated. She had never felt such desire from a man, had never even dreamed such passion existed. She grabbed onto his arms to steady herself against his bruising thrusts and felt his arms like steel through his sweat-soaked shirt. Her nails couldn't even make a mark. What chance did she have against such desire?

"Yes..." she said. "Yes...do it to me! Oh, do it to me!"

The Doctor grinned, baring his teeth. He would soon encourage her to voice other words in which to express her needs, but for now it was a start.

Abigail's big breasts were quivering with every thrust, her skin shiny with perspiration. On impulse, he reached out, took a nipple between his fingers and pinched.

"Oh God!" she cried out. Her brows furrowed in pain but her hips suddenly thrust up at him, taking on a life of their own. "Don't, please! It hurts!"

Never breaking rhythm, the Doctor leered down at her.

"Yes, it hurts!" he sneered. "It hurts but you love it, don't you? You love it!"

He squeezed her nipple again and Abigail groaned, but at the same time, her hips began to fuck at him feverishly and her chest began to heave like a runner's at the end of a race, fast and shallow.

"Oh God! Oh God!" she wailed. "It's happening again! It's happening to me again!"

The Doctor smiled and redoubled his efforts, sending his big hard cock plunging into her cunt at a breakneck pace. Abigail's angelic face alternated between a look of profound agony and one of desperate sexual impatience as he brought her closer and closer to the release she sought.

"You're going to come, aren't you, Abigail? You're going to come!" he hissed.

"Oh yes! Oh yes! I'm going to come! Hurt me again! Oh, please!"

She pushed herself up to him, no longer in conscious control of her own body, and through his fog of lust, he took her nipple and slowly applied pressure until her body went rigid on the desk below him, rigid and quivering like a bow string.

"Oh God, yes!" she quailed. "Oh God, make me come! Make me come!"

This time, her orgasm hit her hard and sharp, a blow to the center of her body. Her head fell back and her mouth opened just as she felt the Doctor push hard, throb, and then burst within her, splattering her with his hot ejaculate. She felt the feverish way he grabbed at her in his excitement as she glided on a cloud of sensual fulfillment, leaving her body far behind.

What a marvelous thing it is to be a woman, she thought. How wonderful it is to feel a man's strength when he desires you, and his weakness when he satisfies himself in you!

She felt him ebb inside her, his cock softening as he gasped for breath. She put her arms around him and held him close, feeling his heart thudding against her chest.

Chapter Three

Abigail's hands were still trembling as she brushed her long hair at the dressing table. Behind her in the soft glow of the kerosene lamps, the covers on the big canopy bed were turned back, showing an expanse of clean white sheets, the pillows fluffed and perfect. Only a day ago, Abigail might have looked at the bed and seen nothing but a place to sleep, but now, the sight of the bed made her think of other things, of the illicit pleasures of sexual love, the delicious descent into passion and fulfillment.

She put the hairbrush down and sat waiting. He'd just had her not an hour ago and yet she wanted him again. It was insane but she wanted him to take her again. It was as if a dam had burst inside her and all this desire, so long repressed, now came flooding out. She could hardly control her need for him.

He had sent her up and told her to prepare for bed but not for sleep, as their evening was not yet over. He had something more to show her, he'd said, and she looked forward to whatever it was with avid excitement. She was no longer a prude. She would no longer pretend to be other than what she was, a woman eager for her lover's touch. He had begun to show her that incredible pleasure lived in her body, that she had gifts and secrets unknown even to her, and she was greedy to learn more.

The Doctor came in wearing his dressing gown. In his hand, he held a collection of rope, leather straps, perhaps some sort of riding tackle or harness work. He stood behind Abigail so his crotch was at a level just below her face. The way his robe tented out before him showed Abigail that he was erect again and she knew she was going to have her wish fulfilled—he was going to fuck her again.

Abigail had chosen a black negligee to wear to bed, imported from France, as sheer as a shadow. She could see her own breasts rising and falling beneath it as she looked in the mirror, see the Doctor standing right behind her as he selected some objects from among the things he carried and let the others fall to the floor—leather straps, studded with rings and buckles. She felt a thrill of fear and excitement.

"Give me your hand," he said, and she lifted her right hand, trying to still its trembling.

She watched fascinated as he buckled the cuff around her right wrist, then offered her left to him and he buckled a cuff on that one too. She wanted to ask him why he was doing this, but she couldn't bring herself to speak. Besides, she already knew. Instinctively, she knew. The sight of the black leather and silver rings against her pale skin was unexpectedly exciting. She felt her nipples begin to harden, her breathing quicken.

He held both of her wrists in his hand, right in front of her face where she could see, and then he attached a silver clip through the rings in the cuffs, binding her hands together. Abigail was transfixed. She knew he was making her his prisoner and she wondered why she wasn't more frightened. Instead, the feel of the leather cuffs made her feel safer, more secure.

The Doctor bent down and affixed two more cuffs to her ankles, the feel of his fingers on her skin as he buckled them in place causing a flood of wetness between her legs. The soft grip of the leather against her skin felt wildly wicked and erotic, as if he were caressing her there.

She knew now what he was doing, and her shock was not nearly as great as her arousal. She had heard vague stories of men doing this kind of thing to women, and even of women doing this to men, but she had never imagined that the victim would feel thrills as profound as she did now. She was ready to be taken just as she was.

The Doctor took her by her bound wrists and she followed him to the bed without a word, as if she were sleepwalking. He bade her lie down on her back and put her hands over her head, then he sat down on the bed next to her. He caressed her face with his hand, slid it down over her throat to her aching breast, letting his fingers linger over the stiff bud of her nipple, teasing her.

"There is one more thing we must do. One more test you must pass. But don't be frightened. I won't hurt you."

Abigail tried to say something, but her voice wouldn't work. Instead, she just nodded. She didn't know what he was going to do, but she wasn't really afraid of being hurt.

The Doctor bent down and picked up a piece of rope. He let her see it, then he took the soft, frayed end and ran it over her face, down her body and over her breasts. He tickled her nipple with the soft end and Abigail moaned, instinctively pressing herself against the source of her pleasure. The Doctor smiled at her and she felt as though a swarm of butterflies had been let loose in her stomach.

Quickly and efficiently, he tied her bound wrists to the headboard. He tied each ankle to the bedposts at the foot of the bed, pulling the ropes tight, spreading her legs apart, immobilizing her. Her sex was exposed, covered only by the gossamer fabric of her gown, and she would have been painfully embarrassed had she not been so terribly excited. The cuffs and anklets held her secure to the bed, exposing her, but somehow protecting her as well.

"This is necessary," he said, "Because I need you to be patient. I'm going to teach you about yourself, and I can't have you interfering. Do you understand, my darling?"

He called her his darling! Something in her rose eagerly to his words.

"Yes," she whispered eagerly. "Yes, I understand. Show me, teach me, Doctor. I want to learn!"

"Don't you think it's about time you called me Lucien?" He leaned forward and kissed her mouth—the softest, most tender kiss, worshipful, yet hot with desire, and as he kissed her, his hand parted the front of her gown, exposing her breasts, her belly, her aching pussy, hungry for his touch.

He took a nipple in his mouth, his touch featherlike, and as he teased her with his tongue, his hand traced down her naked body, almost to her sex, but stopping short. His lips left her breast and kissed softly down her body, over her ribs and her stomach, stopping only at the soft bowl of her hips, where his kisses grew more ardent and impassioned. At the same time, he reached down to the inside of her knee and ran his fingertips up the tender inside of her leg, almost reaching her crotch, but stopping short. First one leg, and then the other.

The effect on Abigail was electric—the feel of his lips on her lower belly, the feel of his fingertips on the insides of her thighs, tormented her and yet the cuffs and ropes held her securely against the bed so that she could not protect herself, could not respond. All she could do was writhe on the bed and try to somehow urge his hands to make contact with her where she needed him most.

"Please, Doctor, please! Touch me!" she gasped. "Touch me, darling, please!"

The more his lips and his hands worked at her, the more desperately aroused she became. She pulled hard at her bonds, making the ropes and the old canopy bed creak under the strain of her excitement. The air in the room seemed thick with her arousal and need and she moaned and gasped shamelessly, begging him to touch her aching sex.

So excited was she, that by the time the Doctor pushed himself down between her legs and stopped there, his face above her mound, his intentions obvious in the hungry gleam in his eyes, that she didn't even think to be horrified. Instead, she cocked her hips up toward him, offering her sopping pussy to his mouth, and she begged him, "Please! Do it! Kiss me there! Oh God, do it!"

She watched, fascinated, as his face hovered above her pussy. He teased her pubic hair with his fingers, then she saw his tongue come out and he dipped his head.

She couldn't believe it. On one level, it was revolting, disgusting, something that animals might do, and yet her body told her it was heaven, or as close as she could ever hope to get, the way he kissed her, licked her, pushed his tongue inside her where a tongue was never meant to go. She burned with shame and embarrassment at the same time that she begged and pleaded with him not to stop what he was doing, not to stop for anything.

But he had no intention of stopping. He held her open with one hand while he sucked at her sex with his lips and tongue and pushed one finger into her with his other hand, giving her the presence inside her that she needed so badly. Abigail writhed on the bed. She turned her face to the side and in her excitement licked at her own arm, simulating his kiss. The thought that she still bore the seed from his last ejaculation inside her only fired her already feverish brain. She realized he must be sucking his own semen from her body, tasting himself in her, their fluids commingled.

"Oh God! Ohhh!" she moaned, trying to close her legs around his head, to capture and hold him there against her until she died from pleasure. But the ropes were unyielding. She could move so far and no farther, no matter how she struggled.

"Abigail, darling." He lifted his face from his feast, his lips smeared with her secretions. His finger still pumped steadily in and out of her. "Give yourself to me. The ropes are there to hold you, to keep you safe for me. As for the rest, give everything to me! Let me drink you up! All of you, you delicious thing!"

She moaned. She didn't know how to do what he said, she didn't understand. But then his mouth was on her again, licking and sucking, his tongue swiping at her little bud of pleasure. His hands came up and found her breasts and he toyed with them, taking great handfuls of her flesh and squeezing, pushing them about on her chest. His fingers found her nipples, the source of that maddening pleasure-pain, and as he squeezed them, she again felt those sharp spears of longing stabbing into her very being. That seemed to be the perfect sensation she needed to bring the pleasure in her pussy into sharp focus and make it rush like wildfire through her body. She was going to come.

"Lucien! Oh God! I'm coming again! Oh darling!"

Her hips started to buck and he held onto her, using her breasts to hold her against himself as he captured her clitoris between his lips and sucked gently on it, coaxing her, easing her up over the very edge of ultimate pleasure to where she began to fall down into that great sea of ecstasy.

She screamed. She felt herself spasm on his tongue. Despite the ropes, her hips came up off the bed and she hung there bridged on her neck and ankles, her loins shivering under the strain as powerful waves of release tore through her body, making her jerk like a rag doll in a hurricane.

"Oh God! Oh God! Oh God!" she chanted as she collapsed weakly back onto the bed.

But no sooner had she fallen back than the Doctor was between her thighs, his cock thick, hard and angry red. Without giving her even a moment to recuperate, he thrust himself into her, eager to taste the orgasmic contractions that still racked her insides.

He groaned deeply, raised himself up on his hands and looked at her impassioned face. He could feel her cunt still quivering with orgasmic aftershocks and he knew he wouldn't be able to hold out much longer.

"Abigail," he said to her, his voice hoarse with need, "Abigail, I can't last. Look at me! Look into my eyes when I come inside you! Look at me!"

The nearly hysterical girl forced her eyes open, forced herself to look into her master's eyes. She saw them staring at her like hot coals, but as she watched, they suddenly lost focus, glazed over, went sightless although he was looking straight at her. She felt his cock swelling in her pussy and then he groaned and pushed himself deep into her.

Abigail had to look away. His lust, his vulnerability, it was too much, too intensely erotic. She sobbed as she felt him throb inside her, once again filling her with his semen, and, as she felt him throb, she was carried up yet again into another orgasmic maelstrom, not as intense as the first but sweeter, more intimate, because her lover was coming with her.

Later the ropes were gone, the cuffs removed. The Doctor reclined against the headboard with Abigail nestled in the crook of his arm, feeling too wonderfully relaxed and satisfied even to sleep.

He sighed. "I must leave early tomorrow, but I want you to be ready for my return. There's something I want to give you tomorrow. A collar, a symbolic gift that binds you to me."

His words were so serious, they almost alarmed her. She looked up at him, this man who made her feel such amazing and wondrous things. "Whatever you want me to do, I will do, darling."

"You will become my slave," he said. "Not that kind of slave. I would not have you serve me like that. But you will submit yourself to me sexually from now on, and the collar will be the symbol of that submission. But you must decide yourself that you want to wear it. It has to be your own free will."

She said nothing, but his words thrilled her in a strange, unexpected way.

"I was going to wait, but there's no need to wait now. You are everything I've ever wanted and more, Abigail. You're everything I'd even given up hope of ever finding, and I want you with me always, darling. Abigail, I love you."

Chapter Four

His confession of love for her lifted Abigail's heart into her throat. It was a word she didn't take lightly, and she'd known him only such a short time. How could he be sure? How could he say that? But when she tried to answer him, when she tried to protest, he stopped her, going so far as to put his fingers over her lips when she tried to speak.

"I don't want you to say anything right now, Abigail," he'd said. "I want you to think about the collar, and I want you to decide if you will agree to wear it. I know things have been happening very quickly, and that you must be confused. But I also know that you are capable of choosing or I wouldn't have asked you. For now, let's just sleep. You have tomorrow to think about it, and you can tell me what you've decided tomorrow night."

He was right—things had been happening very rapidly and she was confused. She was a welter of jumbled thoughts and emotions, and it didn't help matters that at a time when she needed to be objective and clearheaded, she felt giddy and intoxicated and not like herself at all. Whenever she thought of the Doctor, what he had done to her and what he had made her feel, she felt a most delicious anguish, a wonderful longing as unfamiliar as it was unmistakable.

As she bathed, she recalled the old upright piano that had stood in the parlor of her father's house, totally neglected—no one played. She had grown up with it and taken it for granted until one day while she was still a child, an aunt had come by and, to Abigail's astonishment, had sat down at the piano, lifted up the cover, and brought forth the most wonderful music. Up until then, Abigail had looked at the piano as a curious piece of furniture that made sounds when you touched the keys, but she had never dreamed that it hid such beauty inside, that it just needed someone who knew how to play it.

She felt like that piano now. She had lived a perfectly normal life in a perfectly normal world, never dreaming that she was capable of such feelings as the Doctor brought forth from her. She realized now how gray and sullen her previous life had been, how drab and shallow. When he touched her, when he kissed her, when he tied her to the bed and took her, it was like the scales fell from her eyes and she rose to the light of a new sun where she burst into bloom, just for him.

She stepped out of the tub and wrapped a robe around herself. Even her body was different now, as she saw it through his eyes. She couldn't look at her breasts without feeling his lips there, and she couldn't look at her body without seeing that look of hot desire in his eyes. That was most wondrous to her, that he saw her as beautiful and desirable. Her body had been of little interest to her before—something to be fed and washed and attended to. Something that was no more than a shell for her soul on earth. He changed all that. He was teaching her, step by step, just what that body was for and what kind of music it held inside. He had redeemed her and made her new, made her an object of pride and fascination to herself.

Was that love? She was sure and she wasn't sure. She realized now that all she had felt in the past was suspect, all her certainties and the things she had taken for granted, all that had changed. Still, she was aware of infatuation and how it worked, how it came and presented itself as love, only to quickly disappear, leaving shame and embarrassment in its wake. She had been here so brief a time and yet so much had happened. How could she tell?

And could she even trust him? She had trusted him with her body, but a body was a sturdy thing, it could be bent and broken and would heal. But this new part of her, this part that now reached for him like a flower for the sun, she knew instinctively that this was something fragile—something that needed to be guarded and protected. She didn't know if she were ready.

She was truly exquisite that night. She might not be certain of her own feelings, but to Hannah and the other servants who saw her, there was no doubt that Abigail was in the full flush of new love. She had a radiance and an eagerness about her that made everyone who came in contact with her smile. They all knew, even if she didn't.

The Doctor felt it too, and as they dipped into their lobster bisque, he reflected on how much she had changed in a few short days. It was more than her growing accustomed to her surroundings. She had a new confidence, a presence, a womanliness she hadn't had before. There was a grace to her motions. She no longer seemed so hunted, so meek.

The meal passed in a blur, excellent though it no doubt was, both of them too excited to pay much attention to the food. Though there had been no mention of the collar or of what he'd spoken of last night, they both were aware of it. It was like a third person sharing their table demanding their attention, and when Barrows brought in dessert, the Doctor could ignore it no longer. He politely thanked the old butler but dismissed him before he had even served. They were no longer hungry, not that way, and no sooner had the door closed behind the old man than the Doctor stood and helped Abigail from her chair.

Immediately he took her in his arms, pressing her body to his, finding her lips, warm and still tasting of wine. His kiss was dizzying. They stood embracing in the candlelit dining room, the only sound the crickets outside and the soft rustle of her gown as he sought out her body beneath her clothes. They seemed to sink into one another, dissolve in one another, a fusion that went beyond anything sexual, and yet the result of that kiss was to leave them both in a state of high, almost unbearable arousal.

"And now, I have to show you something, my darling," he said softly. "It is the last thing you have to know about me. My final secret. After this, there will be no secrets, no surprises."

He led Abigail down the darkened hall to the one room on the first floor that was always kept locked, tucked away in back, adjacent to his library. She followed nervously, her heart in her mouth, not knowing what to expect, intoxicated with excitement and fear.

She stood close to him as he opened the locks on the thick, oaken door and pushed it open. He led her inside.

At first she saw nothing. Just another room. But then, the Doctor went and lit the lamp on the wall and the darkness retreated before the warm glow of the gaslight. Abigail looked around the room and raised her hand to her mouth in alarm.

The room was a dungeon of some sort, equipped with strange furnishings of wood and metal that looked like nothing so much as instruments of medieval torture—racks, pillories, strangely shaped chairs and tables covered in leather, decked with silver chains and rings. Against one wall stood an armoire, open to show a collection of harnesses and whips, floggers and devices whose use she couldn't begin to imagine. Abigail felt a cold thrill run down her spine. Was this her beloved? A sadist? A torturer?

He was right behind her, his hands on her arms, fully aware of her reaction and anticipating it.

"I can't begin to explain my own proclivities, Abigail," he said softly, but the excitement in his voice was unmistakable. "I can only say that what satisfies other men is not sufficient for me. The pleasures that others find in sex seem somehow pallid and pale compared to what I seek to experience, what I need to experience."

Abigail looked about nervously.

"But, these are instruments of torture, Lucien. It's something out of the Inquisition!"

"No." Going over to the wall, he took hold of some chains that hung from hooks in the ceiling. "It looks that way, I confess. But pain is not my objective. Hurting anyone, hurting you is not the goal at all. Rather it is an expression of my need to possess you, to have you to myself, utterly and without question."

He stopped and looked at her, gauging her reaction. He knew this wouldn't be easy, but it had to be done. He had to show her.

Her shock hadn't abated, and the Doctor sighed and lowered his eyes.

"I express myself badly, my darling," he said. "But it is the best I can do."

"But the whips…" she began.

"Yes, I know. They look cruel and wicked, and, yes, that is part of the magic. There is fear involved, I know that much. Some fear is essential. But there is always fear when we love, isn't there? There's always fear when we put our hearts in someone else's keeping. When we made love, there was fear there too, wasn't there? And wasn't it fear that made it so exciting, so meaningful?"

She tore her eyes away from the evil equipment and sought out his own.

"Lucien, I don't know what to say, what to think. What do you want of me?"

He came toward her and took her hands, her wrists, in his hands. "I want your trust. I want your surrender. I want you to be mine."

She turned away from him in confusion. This was so unlike what she had expected, so cruel and ugly where she had expected something sweet and loving from him. She could not reconcile what she saw with what she knew of him. Yet at the same time, there was a strange and eerie thrill in the pit of her stomach. To think of him binding her in chains, of him taking her like that, of him punishing her, holding her helpless for his own pleasure…

She closed her eyes, feeling faint.

Immediately he was behind her, his lips against her neck. The feel of him, his strength, the commanding way he held her, almost made her swoon. One of his hands came across her chest and found her breast, the other went boldly between her legs, not to arouse her, but as if he sought to take possession of those parts of her that were most feminine. He pulled her back against him so that she felt his cock, already rock-hard, pushing against her buttocks.

"Abigail, trust me, I beg of you, trust me. No woman has ever made me feel the things that you do. Now that I've known you, I can't live without you. I must have you like this. Tell me that you agree, that you'll be mine."

Tears overwhelmed her. His words, the feel of his breath on her neck, the urgency of his hands on her body, it was all more than she could stand. "Oh Lucien, darling! Of course I'm yours! But this…"

"Remember last night," he whispered in her ear between impassioned kisses. "Remember how you felt when I tied you to the bed? How the ropes set you free? How you rose to your pleasure, how you gave yourself to me? That's all I ask of you now. Only that you be like that for me again, be like that for me always, that you be mine, mine in a way that goes beyond what most people will ever know."

As he said this, his hands on her body became more ardent, more demanding. She felt his need, his desire, and it brought forth her own need as well. She stood there, torn between fear and desire as his hand took possession of her breast and he pressed her against him.

She bent her head down and pressed her lips against the hand that held her breast, even as she felt his fingers tighten on her and felt the honey-sweet pain that always left her helpless. She arched against his body as he tightened his grip, feeling that she might swoon right then and there just from the fear and desire that consumed her.

She knew then that she already belonged to him, that no one else would ever make her feel this way. He had made a woman out of her, he had shown her things she never knew existed. How could she abandon him now?

"Yes," she whispered. "Yes. Whatever you want me to do, whatever you want to do to me, yes. Yes, darling, yes."

His grip tightened on her body and he buried his face in her neck. She felt the emotion in his embrace and he gripped her so tightly she gasped in surprise. Such passion in a man! How he must ache with it, how he must suffer! If she could do anything to ease his pain, she would do it gladly. She would bear it for him.

He released her and turned her to face him, and when she looked into his face, she found his features composed but intense, his eyes glowing like coals as they sought out her own. "Then you will do it? You will wear the collar?"

She found that her voice refused to obey her. She nodded once.

He stepped away from her, and quickly lit the other lamps along the walls. Abigail stood in the center of the room where he'd left her, her eyes on the floor, not knowing what was expected of her.

"Your gown. You must remove it."

Numbly she unbuttoned her dress and let it slide from her body so that she stood in her shoes, stockings and black satin corset. A few days ago it would have been unthinkable that she would disrobe in front of any man with so little compunction, but he was her lover now and he was already her master. She had no secrets from him, and no modesty where he was concerned. She stood tall, apprehensive but not ashamed. She realized that she did trust him. She trusted him completely.

She had heard stories of this kind of thing, of men and women who sought out certain brothels where whips and chains were used, but she had dismissed it as of no account to her. It was not part of her world, nothing more than another example of men and women's depravity when it came to matters of sex. She had never imagined that one day, she might be in the presence of someone who practiced such perversions, let alone be in love with him. Yet as she watched him fetch some leather bracelets from his cupboard, she realized that this world had come and found her now, that she was a part of it.

"Are you going to beat me?" she asked as he buckled one of the black leather bracelets around her wrist.

"No. It's not like that. You will see. If you want me to stop, you only have to say the word, Abigail. Do you understand?"

"Yes." She already knew that she would never tell him to stop. Not as long as he wanted it. She would do whatever he desired.

He brought her to the center of the floor where silvered chains hung from hooks in the ceiling, and he attached her wrists to the chain so that her arms were stretched out cruciform. He bent down and attached cuffs around her ankles, and clipped these to rings hidden in the floor, leaving her feet comfortably yet immovably apart.

Abigail began to tremble. As a girl, she had heard stories of how men used to beat their slaves, how they would chain them up and lash them with a whip. How the men would cry out and twist in the chains, trying to escape the lash. How the women would often come down and watch, fascinated. And now it was to be her turn.

She gasped and stiffened suddenly as she felt something touch her between her legs. Without looking, she could tell it was some kind of a switch or crop, ending in a small square of soft leather. It dragged up the inside of her thigh and she closed her eyes, waiting.

He seemed intent on teasing her first. The crop touched her on her shoulder, traced down the underside of her arm and down over her waist. She opened her eyes to see him standing in front of her. He had removed his coat and shirt, and his well-muscled body was already filmed with a thin sheen of perspiration. It was very warm in the room, stuffy, but the heat was nothing compared to the incandescence she saw in his eyes as he looked at her, helpless in the chains.

"Do you know how much I want you? Do you know how I ache for you, Abigail? Ever since you came to this house I've had no peace. Not a minute goes by that I don't long for you, not a minute. Did you know that?"

His gaze was riveting, but as he said this, he walked around behind her, and Abigail found her voice.

"Lucien, I never meant…"

"It's not your fault, Abigail," he said, cutting her off. "Not intentionally. But still, you have to pay for it. You have to pay for my desire."

Abigail closed her eyes against the tears she felt welling in her eyes. She was trembling in the chains, trembling before this man's implacable passion. She could feel his anguish, his longing for her, but all she could do was hang her head and wait. She knew now why he had to do this. In some remote part of her mind, she understood.

She jumped in surprise when the first blow landed on her bottom, sharp and sudden, the sound like a pistol shot in the room. It wasn't the force of the blow, it was the shock that made her cry out—the shock of being whipped by the man she loved, of being whipped not for something she'd done, but for something she was.

Whap!! The second blow landed, harder, and she jerked in the chains. She felt the sting of the crop on her ass followed by a spreading warmth that suffused through her buttocks. She reminded herself that she could stop this whenever she wanted. She reminded herself that she was in control. She reminded herself, but she didn't believe it.

The blows started falling regularly now, the ringing heat of one punctuated by the sting of the next as she arched reflexively in the chains to escape the crop, clenching her eyes tight against the pain, biting her lip to keep from crying out. There was a growing heat in her loins, a tickling warmth, as if she were beginning to glow there. Each blow made her buttocks jiggle slightly, and she felt the vibration between her legs. She was getting excited, sexually excited, and her nipples grew stiff on her trembling breasts and thrust eagerly into the air.

Slap! Smack!

She heard him breathing hard behind her now, starting to pant from the exertion. He sounded like he did when he fucked her, the same hoarse excitement, and Abigail groaned with lust, thinking about him fucking her. It was almost like that. The whip on her naked ass, her pussy shaking from the blows, her wetness beginning to seep from between her lips. The shame and overwhelming excitement.

She understood it now. She understood why he had to whip her. It was necessary. It was what she needed, like a man dying of thirst needed water, only she never before even knew that she thirsted for anything like this. But now she needed it— his lust, his anger, his desire, all coming to her from the whip in his hand. It took her out of herself and set her free. Even the pain pushed her up and away, closer to him. It was his pain too, and she wanted it.

Abigail cried out. She grabbed tight to the chains as a minor orgasm racked her body, making her flex every muscle and hang there quivering as the crop continued to fall. She was paralyzed with pleasure. She couldn't move as the glow became a fire and flames licked at her flesh. She shook as if she were freezing, and then it exploded over her in great racking sobs that forced her body to jerk like a rag doll in the unyielding chains. She was coming—coming, climaxing from being whipped. It was too much—the shame, the humiliation, the complete ecstasy.

At once the Doctor was with her, unclipping her wrists, caressing her, kissing her face as she quivered helplessly in his arms. He freed her ankles and picked her up, carried her away from the chains and laid her down on a daybed tucked against the wall. He embraced her, ran his hands over her, kissing her eyes and her cheeks and her trembling lips.

She finally stopped shaking enough to look at him and meet his eyes. He was looking right into her soul.

"So now you know," he said simply.

"Oh God!" Abigail flung herself into his arms and pulled him down on top of her, not knowing what to do, whether to be horrified or ashamed or grateful.

What was she? What had she become? How could she respond like that to the disgrace of the whip, and what was he doing to her? How did he know that she'd respond like that?

But those were questions for another time. Now his lips were on hers, demanding, hungry, knowing. She felt his shaft pressing hard against her and realized that he hadn't had his pleasure yet, but there was little time for rational thought because his body was demanding hers and as unready as she was, she couldn't resist.

"Tell me," she whispered hotly into his ear as he feverishly kissed her breasts. "Tell me what to do, darling. What can I do to give you pleasure?"

He stopped and laid her back against the cushions, then got up, and Abigail watched him walk to where his coat was hanging. He took a box from the pocket and turned to her.

"Come here, darling."

She didn't know if she could walk, but she put her feet on the floor and carefully stood up. She was shaking, her thighs trembling, but she went to him, one cautious step after another. She saw he had taken a black leather collar from the box.

"Kneel, Abigail."

He took her hand and helped her kneel. She put her head down, her hands on her thighs. Her bottom still smarted from the whipping, but it felt right somehow. He tilted her face up to him and asked the question with his eyes. She didn't hesitate.

"Yes," she said. "I don't know what you're doing to me, but yes. I'll never belong to anyone else now. I'm already yours."

He moved her hair from her neck and buckled the collar in place. The leather felt cold at first but it quickly warmed to her skin. She fingered it nervously. It felt strange, perhaps degrading, but if it was his, if it came from him, she would wear it.

She looked up at him and saw that look in his eyes again, that look of passion, and she watched as he slowly unbuckled his trousers and opened his fly. She knew what was coming, but she was beyond shock now. She was beyond terms of right and wrong and should and shouldn't. She watched eagerly as he freed his hard cock from his pants, and with no more than a nod of his head, Abigail knew what he wanted. She leaned forward and took him into her mouth.

She'd never done this before. Up until yesterday she'd had no idea that people actually did this kind of thing at all, took each other's genitals into their mouths, sucking and licking at them like animals. The very idea was just so obscene that her nipples stiffened in excitement as she worked to get the Doctor's immense shaft in her mouth, holding it in her hands, licking and sucking at it with unbridled lust. Her poor whipped ass hurt where her heels dug into it as she knelt before him, and that and the collar reminded her that she was his now; she belonged to him, an instrument of his pleasure, and that no doubt there would be other, even more perverted and shameful acts he would require of her.

The thought gave her chills, for she knew that she would do whatever he asked of her. Even now, the knowledge that she belonged to him was incredibly liberating, as if she were no longer responsible for what she did. He was making her do this, he would take responsibility. All she had to do was obey.

She licked feverishly at his big cock, and the feel of his smooth, hard prick in her hand and against her tongue made her groan loudly. When she opened her mouth, the Doctor took her head in his hands and pushed his cock deep into her face, so far that she had to fight the urge to gag, and tears came to her eyes but she wouldn't stop. Let him fuck her mouth until his cock filled her belly, she wouldn't stop.

The Doctor looked down at his slave, at the way her lips stretched around his big meat, her eyes closed in bliss as saliva ran from the corners of her mouth. She twisted her head this way and that, trying to feel him in every part of her mouth. She knew that he was secreting something because she could taste its pungent bitterness, feel it seeping down her throat. She didn't care. If it came from his body, if it was of him, she would drink it.

She knew what she must look like on her knees before him in her dark stockings, her breasts spilling over the top of her confining corset, her nipples almost as hard as his cock in her mouth. The lewdness of her mental image made her already soaked pussy ooze with wetness. She ached for him, but she couldn't stop sucking him.

"Oh yes, Abigail!" he hissed. "Ahhhh, my beautiful little slut! You don't know how good that is, darling. You don't know how good that feels."

His words shocked and inflamed her and made her redouble her efforts. Pleasing him was all that mattered now. Anything he wanted, she would give. She had no pride, no honor. She was his to command, and her surrender gave her a delicious freedom to be as uninhibitedly carnal as she wanted. She was his whore, and she loved it.

As if reading her mind, he said, "Show me how you love me, darling. Touch yourself. Show me how wicked you can be. Play with yourself. Do it!"

With a groan of shame, Abigail slid one hand down to her aching sex. She had never even touched herself like this before, but now she would not hesitate. It was wrong, evil and depraved, but if that's what he wanted, then she would do it. Her shame was nothing now, it didn't matter at all. If this was what he told her to do, then she would do it.

Her fingers found their way into her damp slit and for the first time she tasted the sin of self-pleasure. The touch of her wet, hot pussy on her fingers was terribly arousing. Is this what she felt like to him when he touched her? All soft and needy, weeping with desire? She found her hot little clitoris and slid her fingers against it. Sensation flooded her, pleasure so intense she opened her mouth around his big shaft and cried out in excitement.

"Yes, my beautiful bitch! Good little whore!" he whispered hotly. "Your hand is in your cunt now, isn't it, darling? Touching your own hot pussy. Pretend it's me, Abigail. Pretend it's my tongue licking you, entering you, devouring you."

Again she moaned. She had never heard language like this from a gentleman's mouth, and she was both excited and repelled. But the feel of him on her tongue, filling her mouth, stuffing her face with his thick flesh, was exquisite. His cock felt hard and virile, dominating, throbbing with hot male potency as it seeped onto her tongue.

She found her clit, forked her first and middle finger around it and rubbed, letting it slide against her fingers, giving her chills.

"Yes, darling, I'm going to come," he gasped. "I want you to see. I want you to see it come out of me. I want you to watch, watch me as I come! Ah! Ahhh!!"

He grunted and grabbed her hair in one hand, pulled her head off him and held her, inches from the quivering tip of his cock. Abigail's eyes were wide, her mouth still open in awe as she saw his cock twitch, saw his thighs quiver, the muscles standing out like steel cords.

"Oh Fuck! Yes! Yes, darling! Catch it in your mouth! Catch it! Here it comes!"

She mewled with excitement, opened her mouth wider and stuck her tongue out in encouragement, giving him a target, and as she watched, she saw his cock expand, jerk, and spit a thick wad of pearly white semen that hit her cheek with such force that she cried out in shocked delight.

Again and again his prick reared back like a cobra and then spit a big rope of cum onto her waiting face. It was so hot, so thick, and the force of his ejaculation so hard that Abigail felt another thrill shoot through her body, as if in sympathy with what he was feeling. She shoved two fingers into her pussy, pretending it was his cock spearing into her. She closed her eyes and gave herself up to her pleasure, her tongue licking at the seed dripping on her face, getting her first taste of her lover's semen, her own man's seed.

"My God, my God," she whispered as she trembled in her release.

The Doctor was hunched above her, still twitching as the last of his ejaculate seeped from the end of his cock and ran over her knuckles. He looked suddenly so weak and so vulnerable that her heart went out to him. How strange that she could reduce such a powerful man to a weakling by the magic of her sex.

"May I stand now?" she asked, still on her knees.

Slowly, he regained his breath. He stood over her, still weak, but his voice remained strong. "No, you may not."

Instead, he fell to his knees in front of her. He took her head in his hands and turned her face up to look at him. The hot flush of sexual arousal was still on her, her pupils dilated, her lips swollen and shiny with her saliva and her face spattered with his ejaculate. Her chest too was dotted with pearls of semen, and was heaving from the powerful and contradictory emotions she'd just experienced.

"You have no idea how beautiful you are at this moment." He fingered the silver rings on her collar, rings now warm with the heat from her body.

He pulled her to him and bent her head back for his kiss, tender, loving, tasting his own seed in her mouth. "Give me your hand."

He took her wrist and guided her hand to his manhood, now flaccid and shrunken. "Keep it there. I want to show you something."

She did as he said while he continued to hold her head in his hands and kiss her, licking at her lips, catching them in tender lover's bites, slow, sensual. He used his thumb to wipe the semen from her face and feed it into her mouth, where she sucked it down. He lowered one hand to her breast, found her nipple and teased her by running his finger lightly in circles around it, making her shudder.

Abigail felt him stir in her hand. As if with a mind of its own, his cock began to stir, raising its head, growing longer, thicker.

"Oh!" Abigail exclaimed. "Lucien! Your...your..."

He smiled as he kissed her.

"I know," he said. "It's for you. You do that to me, Abigail. Just the sight of you like this. The feel of your lips, your body. Knowing now that you're mine."

"But so quickly! Do all men recover so quickly? I mean..."

He nodded. "There are herbs I know..."

She melted into his kiss. She held him lightly in one hand, the other on his bare chest. His cock continued to grow in her hand from its sad, withered state to the powerful and vital weapon she knew as the mysterious envoy of pleasure. He was throbbing with life, he felt almost angry in her hand, aggressive.

"Does it hurt when you get like this?" she asked him. "It's so very hard. It feels like it might burst."

"Hurt?" he laughed at her innocence as he continued to kiss her face, her cheeks, her eyes. "Not when I'm with you. Not when you hold me like that, Abigail, not when I'm inside you, so close to you.

"Come," he said.

He helped her stand and walked her to the door. There was a robe hanging there and he put it on, then tossed a velvet cape over her nakedness. His arm around her, he led her out of the terrible room and slowly up the stairs to his—their—bedroom.

She laid her head on his shoulder as they walked through the darkened house.

"Lucien," she said tentatively as they mounted the stairs. "What you said to me there...those names you called me. Is that how you think of me? Is that what I am to you?"

"Hush. Of course not. Those are words of passion, darling, no more. You mustn't worry about that. I said them just to encourage your own passion. If they didn't do that, pay them no mind. I won't use them again."

He stopped on the stairs and looked at her gravely. "Surely you don't think I would think that of you. You are my lover, my darling. The woman I esteem over all others. I would never have said such things had I known you would take them to heart."

"I'm sorry, darling. It's just that this is all so new to me, so strange. I don't know what to think. You made me touch myself..."

She couldn't hold the tears back any longer, and he stopped and took her into his arms, pulling her tight against his chest.

"I'm not like that, Lucien," she said, weeping. "You seem to want me to be a whore like that but I can't. I can't demean myself for you, no matter how much I love you. I can't do that, and now I feel so ashamed. If you love me, why do you make me do those horrid things?"

He turned and continued with her up the stairs without comment, mulling over his reply. He let them into the bedroom and even though they were alone in the house, he locked the door.

He sat her on the bed and took the cape off her shoulders, then squatted down so that his eyes were level with hers.

"I make you do them because they are not horrid, and because I have to prove that to you. How can touching yourself be degrading? How can taking pleasure in each other's bodies be demeaning?

"You are a woman, Abigail, and all that I am showing you is your lot as a woman. As for the whipping, should you care to do that to me, I would submit myself gladly. Would you like that? We can do that right here, right now."

She shook her head no. There was so much she didn't understand.

"I am trying to give you back to yourself," he said to her, suddenly stern. "All the things you think you can't do, all the things that are below you, or above you, the things that frighten you, the things that bore you, we are going to do them all. I am going to take you through them and together we will find just who you are, Abigail. We will find out what is in your heart and what is in your soul."

He pushed her down in bed, taking her hands again and automatically raising them over her head and pressing them to the mattress. Then he realized what he was doing and he smiled. He released her hands. He stroked her face, her body. He pushed her legs apart gently and he touched her there and Abigail felt herself falling under her body's spell again, her limbs filling with sweet honey, her hips beginning to move of their own volition.

He kissed her, and with his lips still on hers he got between her legs. She felt his cock touch her, seeking her out, and she couldn't refuse. She moved beneath him, and when she felt him come into her, she sighed deeply. She may not know what was happening to her, but she knew that she wanted him here. She was made for him.

He got up on his hands and knees, unmoving, letting her work her body against him as she saw fit, use him as she would for her own pleasure and she couldn't resist. Her body seemed to open to him like a flower for the sun, and slowly she began to fuck him.

Chapter Five

She awoke to an empty bed again, but this time she wasn't confused, wasn't disoriented. This time she had the memories of his arms around her in the night, his kisses on her face and her hair, his warm hands traveling over her body, tracing her curves, rousing her from her sleep with his lips and his soft words. She had turned to him and taken his lips on her throat, on her breasts, his hand softly caressing her sex, gently arousing her.

She had risen to him from the warm, languorous haze of half-sleep, turned her face shyly into his chest as she felt him play her body like a master, bringing her to life. When his fingers worked their way to the tops of her thighs and found her wet and wanting, she had encouraged his tenderness with kisses of her own, planted amidst the tickling hairs of his chest. She had opened her legs to him yet again, unable to resist, and even through the haze of her sleep, she knew she could no longer blame only him for her almost constant state of arousal; she wanted it too. She was becoming just what she'd always been afraid of becoming—a woman who loved sex, who lived for her lover's caress, for the pleasure of him inside her.

But in her half-sleepy state, the nagging voice of conscience could hardly be heard amidst her body's urgent cries for the pleasures of his touch. Her carnal desires for him ran deeper than her fears about her reputation or her concerns about preserving her own self-image. As his hands continued stroking her and she felt her heart begin to quicken with the knowledge that he wanted her again, she gave up all pretense of resistance. She turned her face to him and with only a little whimper of protest, she surrendered gladly to his desire.

He had told her that now that she wore his collar, he would be her conscience, and he would be the only one whose opinion mattered. Strong words, easier to hear than to comply with. But now with him so close to her and his hands and mouth on her naked body, she understood what he meant. At one time, not so very long ago, the idea of being awakened in the night to serve a man's sexual needs would have filled her with revulsion, but now her heart beat quicker in her breast and she silently urged him to hurry. In the absence of her normal waking reservations and silly reluctance, her need for him was very strong, and when he rolled between her legs, she felt her whole body reach up for him with eager openness.

He came into her slowly and tenderly, concerned for her well-being, but he need not have been so cautious. She had learned to welcome that initial pain, that discomfort she felt when he filled her. It was the feeling of being made complete again, of having him where he belonged. She turned her lips to his ear and, only half aware, she urged him on using words she never would have used had she been fully conscious.

"Oh, Lucien! Your cock feels so good in me. Fuck me, darling! Fuck me. Hard. I want to feel you!"

He found her breasts, held them both in his hands and went from one to another, kissing and sucking as his hips moved with a sweet, slow rhythm like the surf washing up on a moonlit beach. Her toes curled at the exquisite feeling of him inside her and she drew her knees up, seeking to feel him grinding against her little bud of pleasure as he filled her again and again.

She realized now what he meant by the ropes setting her free, for she missed them now. She hardly knew what to do with her hands. Her urge was to lie there and just let him love her, just concentrate on everything he was doing to her. But without the discipline of the ropes, she had to do something, and she stroked his back, his head, finally slipping her hands down boldly to hold his buttocks and feel his muscles flexing as he assailed her with all the strength of his male desire. He was so strong, and she thrilled to feel his strength when he fucked her, the way he focused and concentrated all the power in his body on the single-minded task of driving his cock into her, of holding her close, not letting her get away.

"Oh God, my darling!" she cried out as the first shuddering orgasm washed over her body.

How could she tell him what he made her feel? If she couldn't do it when she was wide-awake and lucid, how much less could she do it now with the fog of sleep still upon her? What could she give to him in return except what pleasure he could find in her? That he could find such satisfaction in a body she took so much for granted never ceased to amaze her. His love made her new, made her something remarkable to herself.

He stirred suddenly, as if reading her thoughts.

"Turn over, darling," he said, lifting himself from her. She didn't know what he had in mind but she rolled over onto her stomach, her legs spread slightly. She felt him move over her, felt the delicious weight of his body upon hers, crushing her into the mattress. She felt his cock probe at her and she realized that he meant to take her from behind. She felt a thrill at the lewdness of his desire, but she automatically cocked her hips for him, and she groaned with pleasure as she felt his big prick find her and enter.

"Yes, yes!" she moaned.

He got to his knees and pulled her hips up against him so that she rested on her knees and elbows, and he began to fuck her hard, swinging his body from his knees. His hard cock sluiced in and out of her with thrilling speed and power, and Abigail could do nothing but hold onto her pillow with all her might, crushing it and biting it to stifle her moans of pleasure. It was so lewd, so obscene with him taking her as if she were a dog, less than human, a bitch in heat.

Suddenly he slapped her ass and she cried out in shock and alarm. She was still sore from her whipping and the pain in her ass was like a stab of flame. He slapped her again and this time, she screamed into her pillow for the blow not only hurt, but it excited her terribly. She needed this. She needed to be punished for loving it so much, his thick, hard cock plundering her pussy. She needed to be punished.

He reached up and grabbed her hair. He pulled her head back, holding her hair like it was a horse's reins, and she reached out and braced her hands against the headboard to keep from being driven across the mattress by his powerful thrusts. She loved him when he was like this, brutal in his desire for her. He was so rough now, so passionate and savage, but it was just what she wanted. It was his desire, his need for her, as primal as a force of nature.

"Oh God!" she cried out as she felt him punch into her hard, pushing her down, riding up on his toes and pushing deep. She felt him throb inside her, and as if his seed awakened some sleeping force from within her, a great bubble of pleasure rose up from inside her, enveloped her and brought her bursting into her orgasm as she cried out his name.

There was a key lying upon her breakfast plate, and a note beneath it.

My Dearest Abigail,

You know that if I could, I would spend all my time with you, darling, but regrettably that can't be, and I have business to attend to. Still, I will hurry with my work and should be back with you no later than midafternoon.

Here is your key to the room downstairs, the private room we used last night. You will go downstairs and let yourself into the room, where you will find a black trunk. There are various pieces of apparel inside. You will dress yourself out of what you find there, and you will make yourself beautiful for me. Hannah will, of course, assist you, if you need help. You may trust her completely — she is the very soul of discretion.

When you are so prepared, you will tell Hannah, and she will dismiss the servants and retire herself, so that we shall be alone in the house when I return.

You will then cover yourself with the red velvet robe that hangs in the closet of that room, and you will wait for me in the dining room.

You will, of course, remember to wear your collar.

With all my love,

Lucien

Abigail picked up the key and turned it over in her hand, feeling a thrill. She hurried through breakfast, scarcely noticing what she was eating, and as soon as she was through, she flew to the room, found the trunk, and opened it excitedly. What she found made her gasp.

There were parcels and packages from vendors and milliners in New Orleans and St. Louis, and even Paris. Some she had heard of, many she had not, and inside these parcels were all sorts of lingerie and intimate wear—black silk stockings, long black gloves, silken corsets and French brassieres and garter belts. There was a kind of very tight leather corset with cutouts for her breasts and a crotch piece that could be snapped off that would leave her bare from the base of her spine all the way to just above her privates. There was a kind of harness made entirely of leather straps and silver chain—in fact, there was a whole collection of leather wear, from the softest of kidskin panties to sturdy leather harnesses. There were masks of lace and leather, with sequins, metal studs, feathers...

She felt the blood run to her cheeks as she looked at these things, and despite herself, she felt scandalized. She couldn't wear things like this! They were obscene, whorish.

She picked up a yellow satin corset with black lacing and garters. The top was cut so that her breasts would be supported but uncovered. There was a full-length mirror in the corner and she stood in front of it holding the corset in front of her. She saw herself blush as she looked at her image in the mirror, and then she saw the excited gleam in her eyes as well.

These were the clothes of a whore. Was that was she'd become? Someone whose only value was as a sexual plaything? She reminded herself that she wore his collar now, and if he wanted her to wear these things, she would have to do it. Besides, a whore would dress like this for anyone. She did it only for him, because he wanted it.

She went to the door and made sure the triple locks were all thrown, then she came back to the trunk, removing her dress as she walked.

Chapter Six

The house was quiet, the late afternoon sun made dappled patterns through the stained glass windows as it filtered through the leaves outside. The servants were gone, the house empty, and Abigail sat alone in the dining room with the candelabra burning beside her despite the fading daylight, waiting for her master to come home. The candles, the late afternoon light and gathering shadows gave the room an almost churchlike feel, but what sort of church had such a parishioner?

She was wearing a black leather corset laced as tight as she could manage on her own, so that it cinched her waist in sharply and caused her breasts to bubble up, almost threatening to spill over the demi-cups of the garment. Her panties were leather too, but of kidskin, treated so that they were as soft as silk. The crotch piece came up through her legs and attached in front to a small silver buckle, and she had drawn this tight too, so that it bit into her sex, so she could feel it. She liked feeling the tight embrace of the corset and the leather crotch piece pressing between her legs. She was wearing the collar he'd given her, and over all, concealing her outfit, was the red velvet cape.

She'd been aroused all day, ever since she first opened the trunk, and she needed to feel contained, held in and stimulated. She wore black silk stockings, and her shoes were French with wickedly high heels, so that when she walked, the roll of her hips was exaggerated, causing the strap between her legs to chafe against her in the most delicious way.

She heard his horse, the familiar gait coming up the cobbled drive. There was a moment of silence when she knew the Doctor was handing his mount off to the elderly groom, and then she heard his boots on the veranda. The front door opened and her hands tightened on the arms of the chair. Her heart beat faster.

She had never dressed herself like this for anyone. She had certainly never sat waiting for a man who was going to have sex with her. She had never even thought of dressing to emphasize her sexuality, and she was terrified that he would find her ridiculous in some way. The robe she wore was warm, and she was very much aware of the feel of her clothes on her body, the tightness across her stomach as she breathed, the way the corset embraced her breasts, the cups cutting across her hardening nipples, the pressure of the leather between her legs. She was aware of everything.

She heard him climb the stairs and then she lost him as he went into his room, presumably to change. She licked her dry lips, then took a sip of water. Surely he wouldn't forget that she was waiting for him downstairs. She would die if he forgot. She dared not leave the chair however. She had her instructions and she would carry them out to the letter.

Then she heard his boots again. This time there could be no doubt. This time he would be coming into the dining room. She tried to compose herself, tried to sit up straight and yet look relaxed, yet her heart was hammering in her chest and she was wet with excitement.

This was silly. He loved her and she him, why should she be so nervous?

His footsteps were back, crossing the upstairs hall and descending the stairs. She heard his steps as he crossed the carpet, and then he was there in the doorway, looking at her and her heart was in her mouth.

He wore his black riding boots, tight black pants, and a white shirt, unbuttoned almost to the waist. The sight of his powerful body excited her as if she were seeing it for the first time.

He stood and looked at her as well, where she sat in the chair. The elaborate feather mask she wore gave her a surprising feeling of protection. Of course he knew who she was, but still, the charade of wearing a mask gave her a feeling of freedom, as if she might not really be herself.

"Open your robe," he said after a long moment. "Let me see what you're wearing."

The robe was actually a cape that fastened around her neck, and she only had to put her hands through the front and shrug it back over her shoulders to reveal the leather corset, the stockings and briefs. She was terribly conscious of her body now and of his eyes on it. She felt her nipples begin to peak with excitement and her heart leaped in her chest when she saw the look of lust and pleasure on his face as he drank her in.

"You're beautiful," he said thickly. "Exquisite, my love. Just exquisite!"

Abigail felt her spirit leap toward him. Such a weight off her heart—she'd wanted so much to please him, and now the fire and hunger in his eyes told her that she had succeeded. She could have laughed with joy had she not been so aroused. The bulge in his trousers was large and very apparent.

He went to her, took her hand, commanding her to stand. She did so and again she felt his eyes devour her.

"Turn around."

No sooner had she turned her back on him, than he put one arm around her, taking her breast in his hand and immediately finding the nipple. His other hand went quickly down within her briefs, his fingers sliding down to her wetness. How easily he took command of her body! Without so much as a by-your-leave, his finger slid inside her and his hands tightened on her. His lips found the side of her neck, just below the collar. The huge bulge of his cock pressed into her buttocks—her wetness told him all he needed to know.

"Oh, Lucien!" she moaned softly. "I was afraid…"

"My lord," he corrected her. "When we are like this you shall call me 'My lord'. Do you understand?"

"Yes… My lord."

He led her down the hallway, the sharp rap of her French heels muffled by the thick carpet, and opened the door to the room. He led her to a spot near the far wall, removed her cape and threw it aside.

There was a black velvet sash hanging from the ceiling that Abigail had not noticed before, hidden as it was behind a welter of chains and rope. The Doctor seized it now and gave it a tug, and with a clatter of chain, something fell from the ceiling and dangled before her eyes — something made of leather. She didn't know what to make of it.

The Doctor guided her to stand against the chain, and he fastened her ankles to the bottom, her wrists above her head. There were thick leather straps that buckled around her thighs too, and these also hooked onto more chains.

"My lord, what is this?" She looked about her. The chains seemed to run up to a series of pulleys and bars suspended from the ceiling, forming some sort of bizarre apparatus whose use she couldn't fathom.

The Doctor didn't answer her. He checked to see that she was securely fastened, and then he came around in front of her.

With her arms over her head, she was defenseless, but she was becoming accustomed to that now, and she let the chains take her weight as the Doctor embraced her, running his hands over her body, like a man who had never seen a woman before, as if his desire made him blind. He slid his hand up the smooth column of her thigh until he found her sex, and then he began to stroke her, summoning up the sexual demons from the depths of her soul like a conjurer.

Abigail had been aroused all day and by now her need for him was a deep ache in her loins and in her breasts, as if her body was so ripe it threatened to burst. She wanted him now and she saw no need to hide the fact. She stood before him entirely at his mercy, her body his to use as he desired, her legs aching to feel his body between them. Having her face hidden by the mask made her unusually bold, and as he touched her, she hissed and gasped without inhibition, like a cat in heat. He kissed her and she snapped at him, trying to bite his lip. He stood back and smiled wickedly at her, enjoying her distress.

She realized again that the chains were indeed her safety harness. Had she been free there's no telling what she might have done. She felt her sexual need as a strength now, no longer a weakness. She was prepared to go after what she wanted. He stuck his finger inside her again and she moaned, pressing her teeth against his shoulder, showing him a wilder side of herself than she had ever seen.

The Doctor stepped back. He seemed satisfied with her level of arousal.

He stepped back to the wall where there was a large iron wheel and several smaller ones. Abigail had seen them before, but amidst the bizarreness of the room, she had not thought to ask what they did. The Doctor put his hands on the big wheel now.

"Don't be afraid. This won't hurt you."

She trusted him, but still, as he turned the wheel and the chains began to lift her off the ground, she gave a little scream of surprise. The apparatus clanked, ratchets clicked, and Abigail began to rise in the air. Her feet came off the floor and she fell back, her bottom falling into a small leather seat. Her arms rose, and then her legs as the chains pulled her thighs up and apart.

"Oh my God!" she exclaimed as she realized what was happening to her. She stared around her in astonishment as she fell back against the leather sling, her arms above her head, her legs spread. Still she rose until she stopped with her hips at just the right height for his cock.

The Doctor came over to her and placed her feet in some stirrups. She was recumbent as if in a hammock, albeit a hammock that stopped just where her buttocks met her thighs. Her thighs were each held in a broad and secure leather strap, which was in turn attached to a separate chain, allowing her legs to be spread and held that way.

"Stay here," he said, though it was hardly necessary. There was absolutely no way she could free herself. She was hanging in the chains like a piece of meat.

He left the room and returned carrying a towel-covered tray that he sat down on a small table. He removed the towel, and Abigail saw it contained a shaving mug and soap, a pitcher of water and a straight razor. Her eyes went wide with fear.

The Doctor took the mug and splashed some water into it and set about directly working up some lather in the mug. She knew what was coming, but she couldn't quite believe it. As she watched him, he unbuckled the crotch band from her panties and pushed the flimsy garment up her hips. She was arranged so that her bottom hung on the very edge of the leather seat, leaving her pussy entirely exposed.

She gasped when the warm lather touched her skin, but he only smiled and went on with his work. When she was entirely lathered, he picked up the straight razor and looked at her.

"I would suggest that you stay quite still," he warned.

Abigail only nodded.

He worked dexterously, efficiently, but very cautiously. Abigail watched with apprehension, all of her sexual desire gone now in her fear for her own safety. She hardly dared breathe as she watched him shave her naked, doing a thorough job, stopping only to clean the razor on a towel he kept over his shoulder. She bit her lips and clenched her eyes shut as he shaved the lips of her sex, but his hands were sure and his care exquisite.

He was sitting on a small stool, his face right on a level with her privates, and Abigail was terribly embarrassed at the way he looked at her—so clinically. She might as well have been at her medical doctor's. But after he had finished, he fetched another basin of water, warm this time, dipped a clean cloth into it and laid it over her freshly shaved mound.

As he gently wiped the last of the cream from her body, he said, "You will have to learn to do this yourself. I want your body to be totally hairless and smooth. I like to see you, all of you, and besides, shaving makes the skin wonderfully sensitive."

As if to prove his point, he removed the cloth from her mons and lowered his face. He breathed on her and she was startled to feel his breath against her shaved skin. Then he kissed her lightly where the razor had just been and she jumped. She was indeed sensitive, exquisitely sensitive, but when his kisses turned into long, tender licks, she began to relax again—or rather, she began to feel a more familiar kind of tension.

He was obviously quite pleased with his results. He laid his cheek against her, he blew his breath upon her, he kissed her as tenderly as ever he'd kissed her mouth, and Abigail could scarcely control the little moans of encouragement that welled up in her throat. She was helpless in the leather hammock and could neither escape nor respond, so all she could do was lie there and watch as he aroused her.

His mouth barely touched her, but she was so sensitive that she could all but feel the very expressions on his face. She moaned, turning her face to the side, giving herself over to the pleasure of his kisses on the insides of her thighs and across the top of her bare mound.

When she was once again aroused and swelling with eagerness, he stood up and opened his pants. His cock sprang free, angry at having been confined so long. He was hard and already seeping with lubricant, and he was at just the right height. He laid his cock on her newly shaved mound and let it rest there like a serpent on a hot rock.

Abigail gasped. She looked down and could see his cock lying there, claiming her. Her thighs were held apart by the chains, her wrists held over her head, bound to the chains that ran from behind her shoulders to the framework above. There was nothing she could do but watch as the Doctor moved up against her and placed his hard cock against the cleft between her legs.

With a slight shove on the chains, he set the hammock to swinging in a small arc, no more than an inch or two back and forth, and he stood there, hips thrust forward as Abigail's exposed pussy slid back and forth against the length of his cock.

She groaned deeply and closed her eyes behind the mask. This was terribly lewd. She hung in the hammock like a piece of beef, unable to move, while the laws of physics sent the knobby underside of his shaft rumbling against her turgid little clit.

"Oh God, darling," she breathed. "Please…"

The Doctor ignored her plea. Standing above her, he had the appearance of a Greek god, dominating her, threatening her by his very presence. She'd never felt so exposed and helpless, and the feeling was deeply thrilling.

She could look down and see the crown of his cock emerging over the shaved mound of her pussy as she swung forward, then disappear like the setting sun as she swung away, and all the while, those lewd intoxicating thrills were shooting through her limbs as his shaft massaged her lips and her hard little clit.

Finally he tired of this game. As she swung away, he used his thumb to press the head of his shaft down, and the next time she swung toward him, he slid into her soaking pussy like a warm knife into butter.

"Ahhh!" Abigail arched her back in the hammock. His entry was so clean, so relentless. He shoved his hips forward, stopping the swing of the hammock and Abigail was impaled on his cock like a butterfly on a pin.

Standing as he was at right angles to her, the reach of his cock was increased. Her whole body was exposed to him and he ran his hands up to her face, then down her throat, over her breasts, down over her belly and her hips, savoring every inch of her. He peeled down the cups of her corset, took her nipples between his fingers and squeezed gently, and Abigail arched in pleasure. She tugged reflexively at the chains of the hammock, which set it vibrating and made his cock twitch inside her.

She was helpless, but she found that by using her arms and legs, she could somewhat control the hammock, and thereby control how he moved inside her. Her clit was being squashed against his pubic bone, her labia spread wide by the broad base of his cock. She could feel every twitch and jerk of the hammock in her pussy.

The Doctor watched her for a while, seeming to enjoy her struggles, then he pushed against her, sending her swinging away an inch or two, and stood there as she swung back, her pussy engulfing him again. He set up a subtle rhythm by pulling on the chains, sending her up and back, up and back, each time his hard cock pierced her to the root, then pulled out. All this time, his hips never moved. Gravity and physics did the work.

Abigail was beside herself. She was used to him fucking her with the force of his hips and the strength of his body, but this, to swing back and forth like a pendulum with his cock waiting for her at every oscillation, was unlike anything she had ever known. It seemed so terribly mechanical, so implacable. It was almost inhuman.

And yet, there was the feel of his cock inside her, hot and hard, and the rhythmic pressure on her pussy as she swung against him. It was relentless, irresistible. It was not the rhythm she wanted, it was not her rhythm—it was too slow. She needed it faster, harder, but there was no changing it. Physics—pendulums always swing at the same speed, and that's what she was, a human pendulum, a pendulum to his pleasure, each swing slicing her with desire.

"Faster, darling! Please, faster!" she begged, flexing her legs in the leather straps, trying to get up to the speed she wanted.

"No." His eyes bored into her. "Just like this. Just like this. Not quite fast enough. Not enough to make us come. Keeping us on the edge."

Now she understood. The hammock did indeed act like a pendulum, and the physics of pendulums was that no matter how far they swung, the time it took for one swing remained the same, and as long as he kept her in this little arc, she would have to endure this maddening pleasure. It was fast enough to titillate, but not fast enough to satisfy. She was poised on the brink of orgasm, unable to reach the summit.

"Oh God, Lucien! Please!" she groaned. "This is torture!"

He closed his eyes. Sweat was rolling down his body. This was agony for him too, but delicious agony, teetering on the brink of orgasm but never reaching it. Never fast enough, never hard enough.

Abigail felt deep thrills running through her nerves, her body on edge, hanging on the brink as she swung up and back, inexorably up and back, his big cock entering and withdrawing, entering and withdrawing. She ached. Her arms and legs felt shot full of needles and her breasts hurt, felt swollen and hot. Her entire body throbbed with the beat of her clit being rubbed by his cock as he plunged in and out, in and out.

She whined. She writhed in the hammock, her body on fire. She pitted her frail strength against the chains, against the unyielding rhythm, but to no avail. She felt she must faint or pass out. Too much pleasure was torture—there was no relief.

"Please! Please!"

"How much can you stand, my darling? How much pleasure can you bear?"

"Not this!" she wailed, "Not like this!"

He growled suddenly, gripped the chains and pushed his hips forward and now at last he began to fuck her, shoving his hips at her as she swung back in the hammock, pushing so hard that their flesh slapped together with loud, dull thuds.

Immediately Abigail felt her orgasm gather within her. This time, there was no question of controlling it, of refusing it. It didn't ask her permission, it didn't wait until she was ready. It came boiling out of her loins like lava from a volcano, carrying her with it. She had time to catch one look at his straining face, and then all the tension and buildup just welled up in her body and exploded upon her in a maelstrom of release.

She knew he was throbbing inside her, that he was pouring his seed into her in his own orgasmic ejaculations, but it was hardly a concern to her. Her own climax was so overdue and so intense that it almost tore her loose from her senses and for a moment, she swung over the dark chasm of unconsciousness, her senses overloaded. But soon she was back, groaning with pleasure and relief as her lover poured his cum into her trembling belly, joining them as one, fused together by their helpless pleasure.

Chapter Seven

"How did it feel?" he asked her after they had both caught their breath.

Abigail was still bound in the hammock, her stomach trembling with orgasmic aftershocks.

"It was terrible," she said. "I mean, to just have to lie there like that, unable to do anything…"

"It's something you will have to get used to. Being used like that. Your body used as a repository of pleasure, as a sexual object."

"It's so dehumanizing!" she said.

He raised one eyebrow. "Dehumanizing? I don't think so. It's letting go of everything that isn't sexual, but I don't call that dehumanizing. Our sexuality is what makes us human. No other animal would go through this sort of thing. No other animal has this capacity for pleasure, and it's something you have to learn, darling. You have to learn to be entirely sexual on demand, to let go of your inhibitions and your fears, to give all for the sake of sensation."

Abigail looked at him through the mask she still wore. She didn't know if she'd ever be able to do that, nor if she wanted to. It had been deeply satisfying in the end, but it had also been strangely mechanical and absent of passion—sex without emotion.

She said nothing though. She was still learning.

She knew that they weren't through yet, that he had something else in mind for her, and as if he read her mind, he changed the subject.

"Now there is something else I want you to do, my darling. I want you to play with yourself while I watch," he said softly. "I want you to make me hard again by touching yourself. I'm going to unfasten your wrists."

It was something he'd always wanted from her, something he'd had her do when he first put the collar on her. He knew how difficult it was for her, for as far as she'd come in a few short days, her inhibitions about touching herself were still strong. If she would do this for him, it would prove that she put his own desires above even her own sense of decorum, her own sense of dignity.

He had made her touch herself before and seen her reluctance, her uneasiness. He knew that it offended her sensibilities, threatened her very idea of what kind of woman she was. But now, lying back in the sling, her eyes glazed with lust, still panting with excitement from her orgasm, she was a different woman. Without hesitating, she reached her hand down between her legs, eager to feel his seed as it seeped from inside her. She moaned as she explored the very place he had just been, the center of her soul.

He stood by her head and he unfastened her other wrist. The leather seat supported her comfortably. Her thighs were still held apart by the chains.

Abigail knew that she had changed. She would never be the woman she had been, not while she was with this man. He had made something new out of her, someone fascinated by her own sexuality and proud of her ability to give him pleasure. And knowing that she had changed, she ran her hand over her body, as if feeling it for the first time. She squeezed her breasts, imitating the way he touched her when he loved her, seeing if she could raise memories of his hands upon her and trying to imagine what he found so exciting when he touched her this way. With her other hand she stroked her sex and felt a rush of lewd pleasure at her very wantonness, her shameless behavior.

He'd been right. She was a sexual animal, and the feel of her own touch now excited her. Her breast felt wonderful in her hand, and her hand felt wonderful on her breast. She was so warm, so soft and firm, so very ripe. The feel of his semen trickling from her pussy made her groan with passion.

She looked up at the Doctor to see if he was enjoying the sight of her playing the whore for his benefit. His eyes were wide, his nostrils flared. She could not help but notice his cock was already erect and throbbing. He looked like he might explode with desire.

"Like this, darling... My lord?" she whispered, licking her lips salaciously. "Is this how you want me to touch myself? The way you touch me? The way you do when you make me mad with desire for you? Does it please you to see me excite myself?"

The heat in his gaze was almost comical. It seemed silly that such a simple thing could reduce him to such a state of wild arousal. She knew she was making a spectacle of herself, but it was a spectacle for his benefit, and it was driving him insane.

"Yes!" he hissed, unable to take his eyes away from her. "Yes, my love, yes!"

Abigail moaned. She had found her nipple and was pinching it rhythmically in time to the rubbing of her hand in her pussy. There was no shame now, no embarrassment, nothing but that delicious feeling in her body and the knowledge that she was driving him wild with desire. It was so easy, so simple, she might have laughed with joy had it not felt so good. Even so, there was a broad smile on her face, the smile of a woman who has discovered herself, who has claimed her own sexuality, who has rediscovered the joy of her own body.

Her joy was interrupted momentarily by the sudden clanking of the chains and she felt her head and shoulders slowly falling. A quick look showed her that the Doctor was turning a wheel and lowering her head, and when she realized why, her smile only got wider. He stepped up to her and his cock was now on a level with her mouth.

"Yes, my lord," she gasped. "Let me suck you. Let me suck you while I play with myself."

Breathing heavily, the Doctor pushed his hips forward and Abigail opened her mouth and took him inside with a groan of pleasure. His thickness, his virility on her tongue ignited her. She could actually feel his need for her in her mouth, and it made her drive her fingers even more vigorously against herself.

With a deep moan, Abigail realized that she was about to make herself orgasm like this, that she was close to coming again. She longed to tell him but she didn't want to let him out of her mouth. He must have known though, for suddenly he withdrew himself and then the entire swing was coming down, depositing her gently on her feet, her legs weak and shaking as the Doctor fumbled with the clips to free her.

"Oh no. Oh no you don't! You're about to come again, aren't you, my darling, my delicious slave. You're about to come from your own touch. No, not while I'm here. I want you in my mouth. I want you to come in my mouth."

He picked her up bodily as if she weighed nothing at all, and quickly deposited her on the bed in the corner. No sooner had her bottom touched the mattress than the Doctor had his head between her thighs and she felt his excited lips on her newly naked pussy, his tongue dipping inside her.

Was it really this simple? she wondered. Were men so easy to manipulate and control that the sight of a woman masturbating was enough to reduce them to such need?

Abigail pulled off her mask and threw it aside. She'd never felt him so excited, so trembling with eagerness. She spread her legs to him, giving herself to him entirely, without fear, without reservation, thinking of nothing but of his mouth on her and of his waiting cock, soon to be in her pussy again. She smiled and let her arms fall over her head in a gesture of absolute freedom, and as his tongue entered her, she threw herself into her orgasm, grinding up against him, coming with a sweetness and purity she'd never known before.

It was all so easy.

Chapter Eight

Abigail woke up to find herself nestled against Lucien's back in the small bed in the dungeon room. They were both naked, and she felt a sudden chill and pulled the sheet up to cover both of them. The room was still dark, and she realized they had spent the night there instead of retiring to his bedroom…their bedroom, she corrected herself, still amazed by it all.

Only a few days before, she had been an ignorant virgin, hardly aware of the opposite sex. She had never even looked at the most intimate parts of her own body, much less gazed upon a man's nakedness.

Yet this man had taken her and made her into a woman in every sense of the word. He had not asked, but simply stormed her gates with persistence and passion, and she had willingly let down the bridges to every part of her being.

What special, magical quality did this Doctor possess, to enchant her in this way? She knew not, but one thing she did know. She belonged to him, body and soul, and there was nothing she would withhold from him.

He had taught her to control her fears and open herself to new experiences, showered her with affection, explored her body in the most pleasurable manner imaginable. And she wanted more, more of everything he had to offer her.

She did not wish to wake him, but she sought his heat, and pulled a bit closer until her belly was nestled up tight against his lower back. She laid her head on his side, wrapped her arm around him, and found herself fondling his lower belly.

Lucien stirred, made a low sound like a moan, and turned a little toward her.

She gasped to find that he was already hard, enormously erect. She pulled her hand back as if she'd been burned, afraid of waking him, but it was too late. Somehow she could feel him smile though she couldn't see his face. He stirred and turned over to face her.

He didn't say anything, but she felt the warmth and love in the way he looked at her. She could feel his sense of pride in her and she blushed even as she felt her heart beat a little faster.

"Don't stop now, my love," he said. "There's no finer way to wake up."

"Oh, my lord, I didn't mean to wake you." She felt his hand tracing up the inside of her thigh. She had forgotten about her shaving until she felt his hands on her super-sensitive nakedness.

She gasped. "My lord, I haven't even washed yet."

"Why wash when you'll only need to wash again?" He took her hand and placed it on his cock as he slid his other hand up between her legs and began to stroke her.

She was shocked at how quickly and shamelessly her body responded to his touch, her hips rising to meet him, her fingers closing on his hardness with gentle longing. She was still full of sleep, but that just made his touch take on a wonderful dreamy aspect, as if she had one foot in the world of reality and one in the world of dreams, and for once, she couldn't tell which one was better.

He leaned over her, and as his fingers dallied idly between her legs, his lips found her shoulder. Aside from her collar, she was naked beneath the sheets, having taken off the corset from last night so she could feel him against her when they slept, and now his lips trailed down over her shoulder and slowly down to her breast, his beard tickled her. He suckled gently at her nipple, nuzzling her with his mouth, pretending to bite her, humming with sleepy pleasure.

"Have I told you today that I love you?" he asked her, bringing a sudden surge of happiness to her body.

"And I love you, my lord. So much."

He growled with happiness and pushed her over onto her side, and Abigail followed his lead, not knowing what he intended to do. He pushed her top leg up, as if she were climbing a ladder, and he rolled on top of her, straddling her lower thigh. He got to his knees, letting the sheet slip from his shoulders, took his cock in his hand and brushed the tip against her wetness.

"My lord, shouldn't we wait?" She was concerned that she had not washed her mouth, hadn't bathed yet to free her body of the excesses of last night, but she felt him start to enter her, so effortlessly, so easily, and all she could do was grab the pillow and moan.

He pushed inside her again, his hand massaging her breast and dipping down to feel her where he entered and tease her there. His touch had the desired effect and Abigail closed her eyes against the delicious feeling of having her man inside her again. Did he never stop? Never have enough? God, she hoped not, he felt so wonderful this way. Her spirit rushed up to meet him even as her body lolled drowsily in bed. His moans were low and soft as he fucked her tenderly, yet with that same thrilling urgency he seemed to convey whenever he took her, that sense that he was just barely holding onto his self-control, as if he might lose it at any minute and take her savagely.

Abigail hummed with pleasure as she closed her eyes and gave herself to him. He reached out and touched her lips and she opened her mouth. He slid two fingers into her mouth and she took them in her hand and sucked tenderly on them, ran her bared teeth over them in soft lover's bites. Her breath was coming fast, matching his own.

When he came, it was so soft and effortless, like part of a dream—save for the hard pulsing of his cock. She let herself go and joined her pleasure to his, her body thanking him for his gift.

Later, as they sat washed and dressed at the breakfast table, he behind his newspaper toying with his eggs, he told her, "Remember, darling. Tonight is the ball at the Mowbrys. It will be your social debut, and I want you to look beautiful."

Abigail hid behind her coffee cup. She hadn't forgotten, but she had chosen not to think about it, for she dreaded going. It was a casual affair, he'd told her, and there was to be no official presentation to society, but still, she would be there with him and there were bound to be questions about just who she was and about their relationship, and what would she say then? It was one thing to be here with the Doctor in his house where she was free to be his lover and slave, but the thought of being out in society made her very uneasy.

He lowered his paper and looked at her. "I know it's tedious, but the Mowbrys are my very close friends, and many more friends will no doubt be there. It is time you met them."

She kept her eyes down as she asked, "But what will they think of me. I mean, our relationship..."

"The Mowbrys already know about you, and that's why they're so eager to meet you. As to the rest, I don't really care what they think."

He folded his paper and leaned forward. "You won't be able to wear your collar of course, but I've purchased a little necklace for you that will be a symbol of our bond. A little secret between us."

The Doctor reached into his pocket and withdrew a blue velvet jewelry box. Abigail took it and opened it, and found a black velvet choker decorated with one perfect teardrop pearl, simple and elegant.

"Oh, my lord...it's beautiful!"

The Doctor watched her carefully for her reaction, but when she lifted her eyes to him, he quickly hid behind his paper, pretending it was nothing.

"As far as these people know, you are my ward and I, your guardian. They are not so naïve though as to believe the literal truth of that."

He saw Abigail's sudden look of dismay and added, "I don't want you to trouble yourself with what these people do or do not think of you, Abigail. This is not your father's plantation. New Orleans is a bit more sophisticated than that and the idea of a man having a paramour is not so outlandish or scandalous here. You might be surprised and delighted with some of the people who will be there."

"In any case," he continued. "I know you'll look as beautiful as you always do. Hannah will help you dress. You will, of course, wear nothing beneath your gown. You will be naked for me beneath your clothes."

Chapter Nine

The Mowbry house was only a few miles from town but had the air of a great country estate. While they were still some ways off, Abigail could hear the distant sound of music and an occasional laugh wending its way through the still summer darkness. She looked to the Doctor for reassurance but he seemed lost in his own thoughts. Finally, when they were close enough to see the Chinese lanterns glittering like fireflies in the trees and lighting the drive all the way up to the grand portico of the mansion, he turned to her. His eyes were shining in the dark, and his teeth looked especially white when he smiled. "You will like Claretta Mowbry. She and Alphonse are old friends, and she already knows much about you. She is very eager to meet you, and should you find yourself in any sort of awkward situation, she will help you out."

"Awkward situation?" she asked.

The Doctor looked at her in the darkness. She had chosen to wear a gown of pale blue that set off her fair complexion, a gown in the new style that didn't require all the elaborate architecture of petticoats but draped more naturally about her figure. The décolletage and the bare arms would keep her from growing too warm in the close atmosphere of the party.

"I don't know everyone who will be here tonight. Judge Mowbry and his wife are old and dear friends as I say, but they have a wide circle of acquaintances, and no doubt, there will be some people there who will wonder at our connection. I would expect them to behave themselves, but one never knows."

She wanted to ask him to elaborate, but already the lights from the mansion were sweeping the inside of the coach as they pulled up to the steps, and it was too late to explain any further.

Abigail let him help her from the coach with a feeling of trepidation.

Judge and Mrs. Mowbry met them at the door with effusive greetings and much fussing over Abigail. The Mowbrys were an older couple, the Judge tall and distinguished with long silver hair, Claretta a handsome woman, but with an easy and graceful manner that put Abigail at ease from the start. As the Doctor had promised, Claretta took an immediate liking to Abigail and quickly whisked her away from the gentlemen and into the ballroom for punch and introductions.

"I've heard so much about you," Claretta sang to her as she greeted her other guests with polite nods and smiles. "And I am so glad Lucien has finally found someone worthy of his affections. But, my dear, when they said you were beautiful, I never imagined…"

Abigail blushed. She noticed that Claretta also wore a velvet choker, hers of black with an ivory silhouette on a lapis cabochon that matched the blue of her eyes. That in itself was not unusual, a number of the women also wore similar chokers; they were quite in fashion, but there was something about the way Claretta wore hers that drew Abigail's attention.

"That is such a lovely stone, Mrs. Mowbry — Claretta. It's the very color of your eyes."

Mrs. Mowbry raised her hand to the silhouette and looked curiously at Abigail. "The blue is for faithfulness. I have belonged to the Judge for twenty years now." She nodded to indicate the pearl that Abigail wore around her neck. "And your pearl means that you are very special to him. A pearl means that you are his special one, because each pearl is unique."

Abigail smiled uncertainly at Claretta's words, and the older woman seemed suddenly confused by Abigail's lack of understanding as well. Then Claretta's face broke into a sudden smile of understanding.

"Oh, I see!" she said, and laughed. "Lucien never told you? No, he wouldn't. That man!"

She quickly pulled Abigail out of the mainstream of people and raised her fan to hide her lips as she whispered, "I belong to Alphonse just as you belong to Lucien. We're the same. Lucien never told you?"

Abigail colored with embarrassment, but Claretta smiled. "I thought not," she said and laughed. "Bless them all, but men can be so dense and thoughtless sometimes! And we are not the only ones who have this special relationship either. Mrs. DuPres, Mademoiselle Charles, Lady Espinosa... But you must not be embarrassed, child. You should be honored. Not all women are loved as much as we are. We indeed are the Queens of our Masters' hearts!"

As she had named these women, Claretta had pointed subtly with her fan, and Abigail noticed that most of them wore chokers.

"Does the choker always mean...that kind of relationship?" she asked.

"No, not always," Claretta said. "Mrs. Van Dyne for instance—over by the French doors, my dear. In the red? She wears a choker too, but she would no doubt be terribly shocked to know of its hidden meaning. But then, she's such an old harpy anyway."

The thought of any of these women engaging in the sort of things that she engaged in with the Doctor made Abigail slightly dizzy. The thought of Claretta especially, so regal and handsome, the apotheosis of feminine dignity and decorum, lashed in chains and being whipped, brought a nervous excitement to the pit of her stomach. For the first time in her life, Abigail saw the people around her as sexual beings, and it gave her a shocking, almost forbidden thrill.

She looked at Claretta and wished that she'd brought a fan to hide behind as well. She again realized how naïve she'd been and indeed, how naïve she still was. Of course, the entire world was a sexual place. There was much more to people than what they showed to polite society—and in the privacy of their homes and bedrooms, there was no telling what sort of things went on.

The same people who were gracefully moving about the room, sipping punch, laughing and talking so easily, might later tonight be bound in leather, pleading for the kiss of the whip, mouths open in the rapture of orgasm.

Why this thought should leave her so dizzy, she did not know, but when the Doctor strolled in with Judge Mowbry, both of them laughing and smoking cigars, she went to him and clung to him with a sudden urgency that surprised them both. It was not fear that made her grip him like this. It was excitement. The world seemed suddenly a different place to her.

"Are you all right, darling?" he asked her solicitously.

Lucien was wearing a white suit and a dark shirt that made him look very commanding and almost evil, and Abigail suddenly longed to throw herself at his feet, to feel the strength of his lust and the cruelty of his desire, to know that she belonged to him. She was his, she wanted so much to belong to him body and soul. She loved her choker, but she so longed for the feel of the collar around her neck.

"Yes, yes," she said quickly, feeling herself blush. "It's just the excitement."

There was no formal dinner, just hors d'oeuvres and finger sandwiches served by the help and a cold buffet set up in the other room for those desiring heartier fare—cold ham and roast beef, shrimp and shellfish, cheeses and smoked meats. There was punch and several varieties of wine and champagne—all imported, of course—and, for the gentlemen, bourbon, whiskey and brandy. A string orchestra was established in the ballroom overlooking the gardens, and as the evening wore on, their playing grew livelier as they supplemented their dinner music with tunes suitable for dancing.

The Doctor excused himself to take brandy and cigars in the Judge's billiard room, leaving Abigail in Claretta's charge. The older woman took her around, introducing her to some of the ladies and regaling her with stories and uninhibited gossip that at times made Abigail blush. Abigail grew more and more flushed and excited. Part of it was the wine and part of it was the natural high spirits of the ball, but also there was that revelatory idea she'd had about the sexual proclivities of the guests. The very air seemed charged with sex now, and as Claretta pointed out this one or that to her, Abigail couldn't help but wonder if these women knew the same pleasures she did—if they took their husbands in their mouths or if they knew the feel of shackles on their wrists, the whip on their naked bottoms.

She grew giddier and more excited, and it didn't help that she was totally naked beneath her gown, a fact she was conscious of every time she moved. The candles were lit in the ballroom and reflected from the mirrored walls in a thousand flames of light that illuminated the colors of the women's dresses, the sparkle of the jewelry. It was all too heady, too intoxicating and when she saw the Doctor standing on the terrace overlooking the garden talking to a group of men, she excused herself and went to him, pressing her body against him as if to keep herself from floating away.

He laughed, surprised by her ardor, and excused himself from the other men. He took her arm and walked her out along the patio. "You seem flushed, Abigail. Are you enjoying yourself?"

"Oh yes, darling! But what do they know of us? What did you tell them?" she begged.

He looked confused for a moment, but then replied seriously, "The Judge and Claretta know me. The Judge and I are old friends, and I know that Claretta is his just as you are mine. She wears his collar. But that is all they know."

He smiled and touched the choker around her neck, the one perfect pearl.

"And, of course, those who know see you wearing this. They know what it means, that you are mine in that special way. You are my slave."

His voice was low but his words still thrilled her. To hear him say that in a public place was as if he had stripped her naked there before their eyes. Abigail took his arm and pulled him suddenly back against the wall of the house, into a dark alcove in the ivy. She couldn't bear not touching him. The excitement, the lasciviousness, the wine; she was on fire.

She took his hand and kissed it feverishly, then pressed it to her breast, naked beneath her dress, so that he could feel how hard her nipple was for him. "Lucien…my lord…my darling! I need you so much. Please, just touch me now. Just once. I need you!"

He laughed and looked at her to see if she was serious. Her lips were slightly parted, her eyes glazed with desire. One look into her eyes and he saw her need and like a brushfire, it ignited his own desire. The smile disappeared from his face.

"Come with me," he said.

He led her down the steps and across the formal garden, across the moonlit lawn, past marble benches and a ghostly gazebo, making for a tall hedge at the very end of the garden. When they reached it, he plunged boldly inside, finding an entrance she hadn't even seen. Abigail realized that it was a maze constructed of hedges, and the Doctor seemed to know his way as he led her this way and that through the dim, moonlit corridors of shadowy green. The noise and music from the party faded away 'til there was no sound but the soft stirrings of the night crickets and the soft rustle of her gown as she stumbled after him.

They came to a clearing in the maze where there was another marble bench, and here he stopped. He took her shoulders so that he could look at her and she stood there breathless, waiting for him to do something to her, anything. She needed his touch, he could see it in her face.

"Abigail…" He took her in his arms and kissed her and she threw herself against him with all her strength, drunk with desire. The feel of his lips on hers, the strength of his arms around her made her legs weak.

As if reading her mind, he made her sit on the bench, white in the moonlight. She was already panting and her hands were trembling. He stood beside her and looked down at her, trying to understand what she was feeling. She met his gaze and he saw the pleading in her eyes, begging for something she couldn't bring herself to ask for. Without a word, he unfastened his trousers and opened his fly.

"Oh God, yes!" Abigail breathed in relief. She felt feverish and her sudden greed surprised her as she opened her mouth and sucked him inside, one hand immediately reaching around his cock to hold him in place, the other going inside his pants to cup his heavy balls.

He groaned as he felt her wet mouth envelop him, and the sound of his pleasure raised goose bumps on the back of her neck. Without looking, she could tell he had thrown his head back and gritted his teeth against the sudden rush of excruciating pleasure.

"Mmm! Ahhh!" Abigail groaned around his shaft as she felt him harden in her mouth, felt his pulsing weight on her tongue. She was almost delirious with need for him and one part of her mind told her that she was out of control, she was shaming herself, but the other part listened only to his gasps of helpless pleasure as she sucked his stiffening cock. She felt a thrill of power over him, a thrill that was all the more lewd and illicit for knowing that she was supposed to be his slave, and yet here she was, all but attacking him, a slut to her own desires.

She couldn't help herself. She pulled her dress up and fell to her knees on the cool grass, the moonlight shining on her gown and pale skin, her hands on his hips as she impaled herself on his shaft, trying to force it down her throat, trying to make herself gag with it to show him how much she wanted him. She knew they weren't safe. The maze was neither large enough nor sufficiently complicated to offer them real protection from prying eyes. Another couple might easily stroll by and hear the obscene sounds of her sucking mouth or her animal-like groans of salacious desire and perhaps decide to investigate, and then they would be discovered. Then everyone would know her secret, what a whore she was for this man.

Abigail sucked at him shamelessly, turning her head to work him around inside her mouth, making no attempt to contain the saliva that dripped over her lower lip and down her chin. She pumped at his hardness with one hand, fondled his cum-laden balls with the other, oblivious to the world outside or her own moans of servile pleasure as she bobbed her head in the moonlight.

He was enormous now, fully hard, and his stomach worked like a bellows with his excited breathing. He began to move his hips and Abigail moaned submissively as he slid his cock in and out of her mouth. She wanted nothing more than to be used for his pleasure, the blessing of his cum in her mouth, on her face, to hear the sounds of his bliss as he ejaculated on her. She needed it. She knew she was out of control, she was making a spectacle of herself, but she didn't care. It was thrilling to let herself go like this, to surrender to all her animal urges without shame or scruple, to be entirely a creature of sexual desire, burned clean by her overwhelming passion.

She could tell by the way he fucked her mouth that he was close. She heard the little shuddery catch in his breath that told her he was reaching the limit of his endurance and she tightened her lips on him and swirled her tongue wildly in the velvety head of his shaft. She wanted his seed in her mouth, in her belly.

But no. He pulled out of her, gasping, lifted her up and made her lie down on the moonlit bench. The marble was cool on her back as he brought his cock to her lips again.

"Like this, like this. Open your legs, Abigail. Pull your dress up. Let me see you."

She moaned in heat and arousal, lifted her bottom from the bench and pulled her skirt up to her waist. Beneath, she wore nothing but stockings and garters, as he had ordered her. Her shaved mound was totally naked and wet with the nectar of her arousal. She sucked him hungrily into her mouth and she felt him slide a finger into her.

The effect was electric. It was not just that she needed his touch, it was the very lewdness of her situation, naked in the garden with his cock in her mouth, her dress pulled up to reveal her naked pussy which the Doctor now fucked with an insistent finger. Abigail was on fire. She tried to concentrate on the hard cock in her mouth, but it was impossible to ignore what his finger was doing to her, and her hips began to grind up at him. She grabbed his wrist and pulled his hand tighter against her crotch as she worked herself shamelessly against his fingers.

"My beautiful slut! My beloved whore!" he breathed as he watched her writhe and groan beneath him. They were horrible words and they thrilled her deeply because she knew they were true. That's what she wanted to be now and she wanted him to know it. His slut, his whore.

Even before she heard that savage groan that told her he was coming, she had lost herself in her own dark world of pleasure, spearing herself at both ends with his cock and his finger. He gasped and grabbed her hair, pulling her tightly against his loins as his other hand drove deeply into her soft and weeping pussy. She humped against him, crushing her clit against his thumb. She felt him harden in her mouth and then spurt the hot milk of his release onto her tongue.

Gasping, moaning, she didn't know if she was coming or not, but it hardly mattered. She was in total bliss, swallowing his seed as quickly as it pumped into her mouth, and wallowing in the pleasure of his hand as it forced her open and demanded she yield her pleasure. She let go of his cock and gasped out her orgasm through semen-coated lips, holding his wrist against her with one hand, her other crushing her breasts together as he would do.

She felt him deflating in her mouth, felt the weakness in her legs, and she dreaded the return to normalcy—what he would think of her now. But before the spasms had even stopped in her trembling belly, he had pulled her upright and enclosed her in an embrace that all but squeezed the air from her. He pressed her head against his chest and held her, rocking her as if she were a child.

"Oh my God!" he breathed. "Abigail! My love, my love!"

She was horrified at what she had done, what she had become. As he held her and rocked, she felt her shame and bewilderment at her own behavior gather in her throat and burn in her face. She couldn't hold it in and she began to sob, overcome with emotion.

He held her to him. Somehow he knew. He hushed her and whispered endearments, but he never once asked her what was wrong. He knew. When he went to kiss her lips and she turned her head aside in shame, he took her face in his hands and forced her mouth to his. He wouldn't let her hide, wouldn't let her escape. He would force her to face it. He loved her for it.

Chapter Ten

It took her some time to calm down and the Doctor held her all the while until she knew that it was all right. Then he said, "We should get back."

Abigail nodded. She sniffed back the last of her tears, straightened herself up as best she could, then took his hand as he led them out of the maze and back out onto the broad lawn where now some couples strolled arm in arm. He stopped for her on the patio so she could look at her reflection in a darkened window and try to arrange her hair. Her storm of tears had come and gone so quickly that her eyes still looked clear, if a bit moist, but she sorely wanted to freshen her face.

His eyes were dark and glittering with that same look of love and desire as he watched her fix her hair, but she still couldn't meet his gaze.

"It doesn't matter," he said. "They'll know. Even if they don't know what we've been up to, they'll notice your glow. You are glowing, Abigail, did you know that?"

"Please, darling. If we go around to the front I can slip into the powder room…"

He smiled at her in the darkness. "You've never looked more radiant, Abigail. I want you to look just as you do. Watch the reactions of the guests as you pass by."

She was too weak to argue, and she let him lead her through the French doors and back into the ballroom. No one seemed to pay them any special notice, but perhaps there was something to what he had said, for the men suddenly seemed to notice her now, and they made way as the Doctor followed her through the crowd, insisting that she precede him. The men's eyes opened in pleasure as they acknowledged her, and even the women seemed to pay her a grudging respect, as if she somehow wore the mark of her Master's love on her sleeve and they envied her for it. Slowly, Abigail calmed down.

There was a group of older women standing by the punch bowl, however, who turned and raised their noses in the air as she passed, and the Doctor reached out and took her arm and steered her to the punch.

"Excuse me, ladies," he said sweetly as he gently but firmly moved them out of the way, "but Mademoiselle desires some refreshment."

The women gathered themselves together and left their post like a gaggle of unhappy geese as the Doctor filled a cup for Abigail and one for himself. He made her stand there and drink it until the women had retreated to the other side of the room, then he took her cup from her and placed it on the table.

The orchestra struck up a tune and the Doctor bowed to her, then said in a voice loud enough to be heard by those around them, "My most beloved, would you do me the honor of this dance?"

Abigail felt the tears begin to well up again as he led her to the dance floor, and then, after the briefest moment of trepidation, he put one hand around her waist, took her hand in his, and they began to dance. They had never danced together before, had never even shown any sign of affection in public and Abigail wasn't even sure of the steps, but he took such command of her that it was as if he carried her in his arms and all she had to do was follow. For one so serious and given to such dark moods, he was a wonderful dancer, as good as he was a lover, if that were possible, and in much the same way. He led her without forcing her, his delight obvious in the way he held her.

The music throbbed and the lights spun, and Abigail felt that all eyes were on them as they danced. He was showing her off. She knew this, and she would have been terribly self-conscious had she been with anyone else, but as it was, he soon commanded all her attention and she forgot where they were, forgot the eyes, forgot her shame over what she'd just done in the garden. Whatever she might think of herself, she knew that his opinion of her had not changed. He was proud of her and he was showing her off.

The music ended and the world came flooding back in. The applause of the other couples seemed directed toward them, and Abigail blushed. The lingering taste of his semen was still on her tongue, and she wondered suddenly whether anyone had seen them in the garden, whether they were mocking her with their applause. But no, it seemed genuine enough. The crowd was responding to the sight of a handsome couple, and if Abigail's glow seemed more apparent than those of the other women present, she gave no hint of its origin.

Lucien didn't give her too much time to grow embarrassed, however. He led her quickly from the floor, stopping only to make hasty introductions to the men and women who now seemed so anxious to meet her. It seemed that suddenly, everyone wanted to make her acquaintance, the men lingering over their kiss of her hand, the women politely restraining their envy long enough to make civil and polite greetings.

She realized that the Doctor was now saying their goodbyes and that they were leaving, and yet, she was now almost reluctant to go. The Judge beamed at her and Claretta kissed her cheek and whispered in her ear, "Do you enjoy his love, darling? Do you enjoy what he is teaching you? Tell me yes or no!"

Now Abigail could not keep from coloring or containing her smile as she looked at the older woman and said, "Oh yes! Oh my, yes!"

Claretta laughed with delight and embraced her with real warmth, and Abigail knew she had made a friend.

She was still bubbling with high spirits as they drove away, asking the Doctor about this one and that one, telling him what Claretta had said, wanting to know about everyone who was there. He answered her with smiles, delighting in her own excitement at having been received so graciously.

By now they were out on the highway, old Barrows asleep over the reins, the horses following their familiar way home. Moonlight filtered down through the trees that arched over their heads, making the road into a kind of passageway, secluded and quiet, the only sound being the chirp of crickets in the grass and the sleepy beat of the horses' hoofs on the road.

Abigail ceased her chatter. Words seemed suddenly out of place and she looked out at the night, how mysterious, how romantic. Then, rising up like a wave unbidden, she suddenly remembered how she had acted in the garden, how she had lost all decorum, all sense of dignity and become a shameless slut, doing things that made her wince with embarrassment even now.

She felt the Doctor's hand caress her cheek and she turned and looked into his eyes, dark in the coach, but filled with desire.

She couldn't bear his look. The wave of remorse suddenly engulfed her with shame, and when he leaned over her, she sank back in the soft leather seat, afraid of what she would feel in his kiss, but his feelings for her were as intense and passionate as ever. Nothing had changed. If anything, his lips sought hers with a new urgency, and she opened her mouth to him eagerly when his lips found hers. The soft kiss grew wild from his own need. His fingers found her nipple through the dress and he pinched her, and she rose eagerly to the pain, once again shedding her ladylike manners as she did so. She sucked his tongue into her mouth and groaned as he slipped his hand under her dress, and the way she spread her legs for him and began to move against his hand was anything but ladylike. By the time they broke the kiss, she was flushed with excitement and panting.

He opened his pants and freed his cock, hard and pale white in the moonlight and Abigail ran her tongue over her lips, remembering the taste of his seed and the feel of him in her mouth.

"Lift up your dress and mount me," he whispered.

She gathered the gown up around her waist, showing the tops of her stockings against the bare white of her thighs, the nakedness of her sex. Then she climbed onto the seat over him, trembling with anticipation, one knee on either side of him. She reached behind her to guide him but he was already holding himself up with one hand, the other on her naked ass, guiding her. She felt him move into the right spot and, holding her breath to keep from moaning too loudly, she sank down on his wonderful cock.

She threw her head back and despite her best efforts, a deep gasp of pleasure issued from her lips. Her dress spilled over his lap and hid the view of him entering her, but that only fueled her passion as she locked her hands behind his neck and began to ride his hard pole, lifting herself up and falling down on it, letting the gentle rocking of the coach set the tempo—slow, languorous.

The Doctor made a sound somewhere between a sigh and a growl and reached for the bodice of her gown. He pulled it down until her breasts spilled free, then he took one in his mouth and the other in his hand and Abigail arched her back, pressing herself against him. She felt it again, that current of wild intoxicating sluttiness, but this time, she worked to keep it in check. The Doctor was content to sit in the coach and feel her around him, groaning occasionally, enjoying the way she worked to bring herself off on him, but whenever she got too wild, too insistent, he would put his hands on her hips to still her. He had no intention of coming again. He was just trying to keep her at a fever pitch. He succeeded wonderfully.

Barrows didn't wake up until the coach finally stopped in the Doctor's own courtyard, but that was fine with the two lovers. By that time, they had untangled and managed to arrange themselves so that they could enter the house without the servants being aware of what had happened, though Abigail's agitation and high arousal was so pronounced that she could hardly walk straight and had to rely on the Doctor to guide her. She ached inside and the muscles in her legs wouldn't stop trembling.

Hannah met them at the kitchen door. She knew the Doctor and his habits and had already adapted to the changes that Abigail's coming had brought to the household, so she only needed one look at their flushed faces to guess what was happening. She immediately rushed the other servants out of the house and sent them to their quarters, then nodded discretely to the Doctor and let herself out, locking the door behind her and leaving them alone in the mansion.

They went upstairs together, but on the landing, he stopped and embraced her. "There is a leather corset in the top drawer of your room. I want you to wear it. I want you to take your hair down, and don't forget your collar."

Although she slept in his bed, Abigail had been given her own bedroom, spacious enough for another bed of her own, the dressing table and the armoires that held all her clothes and the exotic apparel he had purchased for her. She went there now, and after lighting the lantern, she took off her party dress and quickly washed, found the garment he'd mentioned and put it on. It was no more than a cincher that laced tightly in front but left her breasts exposed and covered nothing below her waist. She left her stockings on, took her hair down and brushed it out, then put the collar on. Buckling the collar around her neck always left her trembling with excitement. She threw a sheer dressing gown over her nakedness and went to his room.

The doctor was wearing a red satin robe. He led Abigail into the bedroom and stood behind her as he slid the gown from her shoulders, kissing her neck as the garment slipped from her body. She raised her hands at his command and he buckled leather cuffs around her wrists, then fastened them to the footposts of the big bed so that she stood facing the room. He then buckled cuffs around her ankles as well, and fastened her feet to the legs on the bed so that she stood spread-eagled again.

He kissed her neck again and ran his hands over the naked perfection of her ass and around to her hairless mons.

Abigail watched as he went to the bureau where he kept his toys and took out a crop, then a curious flogger. This was a collection of many soft velvet thongs, perhaps twenty or thirty in all, all attached to a wooden handle. He laid the thongs on her shoulder so she could feel them on her skin, and they were soft and benign, and hardly seemed capable of inflicting any pain.

She closed her eyes and waited, eager this time. She wanted him, and she knew instinctively that the way to him now was through the whip. More than that, she was still feeling remorse from her shameful performance in the garden, and deep inside, she ached for the chastisement of the flogger. She had been out of control, and now she had to pay. She wanted to pay—she deserved this.

She was about to tell him that when he raised his hand and the whip came down directly across her naked breasts, the soft lashes landing like a thousand little tongues on her flesh. She gasped from the intense stimulation. Even though the thongs were gentle, there was still the initial sting, and there was the fact that she was still being whipped, with all the indignity that implied. She looked at him and he was watching her face.

"You need this, Abigail, don't you?"

"Yes," she answered, her voice hardly belying the emotions she felt. "Yes, I need this."

"Open your mouth."

He had been holding the crop in one hand, and now when she opened her mouth, he placed it between her teeth like the bit of a horse's bridle. She closed her teeth on it, tasting the leather.

He raised his hand and she closed her eyes, biting the crop so she wouldn't cry out. He whipped her again and her nipples stiffened from the wicked caress of the whip. The thongs kissed her skin with just enough bite to sting, then the lingering drag as he pulled the whip back made her feel as if she were being licked by butterfly's tongues, soothing and tickling her nipples and making her eager for more.

On the third blow, she groaned and actually thrust her chest out, seeking more of this maddening pleasure, wanting it harder and more intense. Her wrists pulled at the sturdy leather cuffs as if she wanted to get free, but that was the last thing she wanted. She wanted to feel captive, a prisoner of his desire, helpless before him. She ached for him, ached to feel his strength and his need. The symbolic violence of the whip was like his lust for her, and she needed the pain to redeem her, to burn away the lingering taste of her shame.

He lashed her again, the blows coming rhythmically now, first on the downstroke, then on the return, in a figure eight. Her nipples were hard and exquisitely sensitive, and she felt the bite of the supple thongs followed by that delicious drag throughout her body now, especially between her legs, as if her breasts and her sex were intimately connected.

The blows continued to fall and she felt sparks of wild sensation in her arms and in her legs, running up the insides of her thighs to her sex. Her breasts felt swollen and heavy, as if filled with warm, thick honey, and her whole body felt hot and overripe, bursting with some viscous sexual nectar. She felt wetness seeping from her pussy and leaking down the insides of her thighs. She bit the crop between her teeth and groaned, wanting more.

He stopped for a moment, breaking his rhythm and she looked at him, only to see his eyes burning into her with sexual hunger. He'd taken off his robe and stood there naked, his cock painfully erect, jutting from his body in its rampant glory. He was filmed with sweat and he was breathing fast as he hefted the flogger, feeling its weight, judging where to land the next blow. Abigail couldn't take her eyes off the whip. It was the bond that held them together now, and the sight of it excited her even more than the sight of his engorged cock.

She closed her eyes again and bit down on the crop as he brought his hand back. This time, the blow landed unexpectedly across the tops of her naked thighs, the strands slapping against the bare flesh above her stockings. She cried out in surprise and looked down at her naked and vulnerable sex, then up at his eyes. Surely he wouldn't…

The next blow came up between her legs and the velvet thongs landed against her pussy, curling against her flesh, her labia, the tender skin on the inside of her thighs. Abigail cried out in alarm. The whip was soft and his control exquisite but even so, this was her most delicate and sensitive spot. Should he lose control…

Swattt! He whipped her again between her legs and this time, the jolt of fire that ran through her body was tinged with a terrible kind of pleasure. Yes, she deserved it there between her legs, on her sex. It was her pussy that made her so wicked, so lustful, that turned her into such a whore at his touch. It was the center of her desire, and it was where she wanted him, right there, fucking her, shoving his big cock inside her cunt. That was what made her act so shamelessly. The brief sting, the warm caress of the lashes—they were good, they were wonderful, they were just what she wanted.

He whipped her again and the thongs came up from below and landed in the wet cleft of her pussy, some of the strands reaching up to sting the cheeks of her ass. The thought of being whipped like this was too obscene, too exciting. She tried to close her knees but couldn't. She sobbed around the crop she still held between her teeth.

He whipped her until her pussy was throbbing, her clit erect and emergent, stupidly seeking the punishment of the whip, looking for that brutal sensation. She felt faint, on fire with lust.

That's when he dropped the flogger and took the crop from her mouth. He grabbed her hair to hold her head up and he tapped the crop against her exposed clit, spanking her pussy as though it were a naughty child—not hard, but with a tense and relentless rhythm, each blow driving her higher and higher.

"Ahhh!" One more stroke and she was suddenly up and over the edge, her muscles clenched tight, her body shattering into shards of burning pleasure. She stood shivering with the intensity of her terrible release, the exquisite surrender of it. She was a slave to him, a slave to his whip, and all she could give him was this agony of pleasure.

The Doctor threw down the crop and unclipped her from the bedposts with fingers that fumbled in their urgent eagerness. Abigail couldn't move. She was rigid, paralyzed in a rictus of intense and sustained orgasm, her entire body clenched and trembling. He pushed her roughly back onto the bed and climbed on after her.

No, he wouldn't! She was still coming, still in the throes of this massive and sustained orgasm. She was like one giant, exposed nerve—she couldn't stand any more stimulation...

He levered her legs apart and threw her knees over his shoulders, gripped his dripping cock in one hand and speared into her tight, quivering pussy.

"Oh God!" she wailed, arching her body off the bed, trying to retreat from his rending thrust, from the force of his desire.

Her pussy was clenched tight but he pushed into her with all his strength, forcing her to yield, to open to him, but she was too sensitive—his cock was more than she could stand.

"No! Oh my lord, wait! Wait!" she cried, pushing her shaking hands against his shoulders, but she couldn't stop him, couldn't budge him. The man was made of iron and his lust was irresistible. He was tearing her, filling her, his pubic bone pressing hard against her throbbing clit.

She couldn't hold out. Her strength left her like water pouring from a shattered vessel and all she could do was try and hold onto the sheets to keep herself from being slammed into the headboard by his brutal thrusts.

"Please! Darling, please!" she wailed.

She begged him to go slow, to show her some mercy, but he took no heed. His thrusts were inexorable, driving her ass into the mattress. He grabbed her wrists and lifted her hands over her head, pinning her down against the mattress and fucked her so hard that her breasts hurt from the jostling on her chest.

"You're mine, Abigail! All mine! All of you, all of you!"

She wanted to tell him to stop, to slow down, that she was his, that he owned her entirely, but his strength and the power of his attack left her breathless — she had no wind to talk. No sooner had the pangs of her last orgasm left her body, then she felt herself rising to another one. She didn't think she could stand it. It was too much. She would pass out, faint, but still the pressure grew in her and she felt her body respond, digging her heels into the mattress and lifting herself to him, offering herself to his terrible desire.

"Oh God! Abigail! Abigail!"

He sobbed into her neck, shoved his hips hard against her and she closed her eyes in mute acceptance as her orgasm lifted her up and away, her lover's cock spurting and throbbing inside her, pouring its load of hot seed into her depths.

He groaned with every spasm, and with every spasm she felt him grow weaker. He let go of her wrists and Abigail wrapped her arms around him, holding him close as he emptied himself into her. She gazed up at the ceiling of the room, at the shadows cast by the soft glow of the kerosene lanterns, and she felt that if she wanted, she could just let go of herself completely and somehow flow into him, fuse with him, get inside him and in some way ease his terrible anguish, his wild passion.

With a long and soulful moan, he stilled and slowly grew quiet, though she could feel their hearts thudding together like distant thunder after the storm has passed. He got his hands beneath him and rolled off her and lay on his back, one arm thrown over his eyes as he gasped for breath.

"My God," he said between breaths. "What you do to me, Abigail. How you make me feel! I'm sorry, darling. I don't mean to be so rough."

Tentatively, Abigail tried her muscles and found that they worked, albeit grudgingly. She had still not returned to normal, but she was able to roll over so that she lay by his side and she nestled against him.

"You shouldn't apologize, my lord," she said softly. "You should never apologize for feeling like that or for what you do to me. And truly, I feel as though I needed it. I was terrible tonight."

Now it was his turn to look at her. "What do you mean?"

"The way I acted tonight in the garden. It was inexcusable. I'm so ashamed."

"Don't say that, Abigail. Don't be foolish. Do you have any idea of how exciting you were tonight?" He stopped and looked at her. "Do you think that's why I used the whip on you?"

By his question alone, he told her that her behavior wasn't the cause for the whipping.

"If it wasn't my behavior, what was it?"

He sat up and ran his hands over his face. "I don't know. I don't know why I have to do that to you. I only know that I get to a point where I want you so much, where my need is so great, that I have to. All I can think of is the whip. It's the only way I can express what I feel."

"But you." He leaned over her and held her face in his hand. "You mustn't feel ashamed of what you gave me in the garden. That was all you. That is what I've been trying to bring out of you."

"But it frightens me to feel like that. I feel out of control, almost like an animal."

She was so lovely now, her hair down, her face placid with sexual satisfaction. He felt himself stir again as he remembered her on her knees in the hedge maze, her mouth searching for him, beside herself with desire.

"Don't ever worry about being out of control." He stared into her eyes. "I'll see that no harm comes to you. The ropes and chains will protect you. That passion is you, Abigail, it's your nature. You must learn to let it out, let it possess you. It's why I love you so much."

"It is?" She couldn't accept that.

How could he love the very part of her that she found so humiliating and shameful?

"Yes," he said. "Not just for that, but for everything you are, and that animal passion is part of you. It is who you are, and that's what I want from you—everything you are."

She didn't understand, and she didn't want to think about it right now. She snuggled against his chest, pressing her body against him, and felt his cock against her thigh, throbbing with new life.

"Lucien! My God! Do you want more, my darling?" She was still inexperienced with men and did not yet know their habits and capabilities, but she knew almost by instinct that this man's appetite was unusual, almost uncanny.

He laughed and pulled her to him. "Sometimes when I'm that aroused, it takes me several times. But you? It's been hard on you."

She was sore and had hardly caught her breath but she could not refuse him. She lay back down and he rolled easily between her legs, and she was shocked anew to find that he was again fully erect. It hurt when he entered her but it felt wonderful too, for despite her soreness, his recent roughness with her, she was not that different from him and she was ready for more. She groaned with pleasure as he took her once again.

"Forgive me, Abigail, but I just want you so much!" he breathed. "You're like a madness, a disease. Ah! Oh my precious, you don't know how wonderful it feels to be inside you!"

Abigail could have bathed in his words. She could have taken them and crushed them to her breasts and been satisfied. Just to have her lord on top of her, to be safe in his strong arms, his cock in her keeping, made her flush with joy. His lips found her nipple, red from the lash and he sucked on it gently as his cock began to work its magic once more between her legs. She arched her back with pleasure, pressing her breasts up for him to kiss and suck. She wrapped her legs and arms around him and held him tight. She could feel his exhaustion, his weakness, but that just made her want him more, knowing that he was expending the last ounce of his strength to make love to her.

If he was weak, she would be strong for him.

"Rest, beloved," she whispered, hearing him gasp on top of her. "Let me do it. Let me please you. That's all I want."

He had little choice—he was almost totally spent. He didn't answer but he rested his weight against her, his lips at her throat, and Abigail began to move beneath him, move with that feminine grace that always aroused him so. She lifted her hips to him, squeezed him inside herself and then let herself fall back, drawing on him. He trembled on top of her and groaned, and Abigail smiled.

"Hush, my darling," she whispered. "Let me…let me…"

His hands were on her bottom, and he could feel her strong yet supple muscles work at him, drawing her woman's pleasure from him. Her body undulated like the surface of the sea, and he was like a ship upon it, tossed on the gentle yet powerful swell. He kissed her with kisses feeble yet passionate. He moaned in her ear.

"Abigail, I love you. I love you so very much!"

"Yes, my darling, oh yes! And I love you! More than life itself! Hold me, Lucien! Hold me close! I'm going to come… you're going to make me come…"

Chapter Eleven

Her days were never routine, though they did settle into a more or less predictable pattern. At her insistence, the Doctor turned more and more of the tasks of running the household over to Abigail, and she eagerly rose to meet the challenge, welcoming the opportunity to prove to herself and to him that she was more than a mere sexual toy, that she had real capabilities. With Hannah as her lieutenant, Abigail now saw to the running of the house, dealt with the provisioners and vendors who kept the estate running smoothly, leaving the Doctor free to concentrate on his business dealing in herbs and medicinal plants.

Her sexual explorations with the Doctor had a paradoxical effect on her views of herself and her dealings with the outside world. Her sexual submissiveness to his desires, rather than making her meek and passive, strengthened her and made her more assertive, more formidable in dealing with people. It was partly her new sexual confidence—she knew now that men found her beautiful, and she wasn't above using her desirability as a tool in order to get what she wanted.

Then too, her sessions with the Doctor gave her an unexpected advantage over the people she had to deal with. She knew that she had sexual experiences beyond what most people would ever know, and it gave her a kind of immoral authority in her dealings with them. She was beginning to lay claim to the sexual being she was inside and she found it to be a potent source of personal power and presence. As the Doctor had said, he was giving her back to herself.

And yet, when the Doctor came home to her in the evening, when he beckoned to her after dinner, she eagerly set aside her new persona and was again his to command and use. There was power in the act of sexual submission, a power she'd never imagined, that came of trust and sacrifice and manifested itself in terms of strength and forbearance. Yet what she felt was not really that complicated, and the excitement and anticipation he was able to evoke in her with just a gesture or a look never lessened. That nervous exhilaration still consumed her whenever she heard his step on the stairs or the familiar gait of his horse coming up the drive.

* * * * *

On a sultry August night with the servants all gone, he had taken her down to the room and bound her again standing in the chains as he so often did when she was to be whipped for his pleasure. She had been wearing nothing but a diaphanous blue gown which she had let slip from her shoulders at his command. Aside from her collar and the blindfold around her eyes, she was naked, and she stood with her hands stretched out to the sides, her feet held apart by a spreader bar attached to the cuffs on her ankles.

She waited for him to tell her why she was to be whipped — for being too desirable, for having invaded his thoughts during the day, for some minor lapse of judgment — it didn't matter. She knew that these reasons were no more than pretext for him to worship her through the medium of the whip. She waited for him to retrieve tonight's implement from his collection of crops, floggers, scourges, and paddles, but she heard nothing.

Instead, he stood in front of her and ran his hands up her body to cup her breasts, to hold them to his mouth and kiss them, sucking gently on her already erect nipples. His hand dipped down to fondle her between her legs as his kisses continued up the side of her face, looking for her ear.

"So beautiful," he murmured, gently biting her earlobe. "Abigail, you simply grow more beautiful every day."

She flushed with excitement, and yet she knew it was true. Something had happened to her since she'd been with him. Her body had become more womanly, less that of a girl's. She had blossomed like a flower under his careful nurturing—her hips had become more substantial, more welcoming; her breasts had grown fuller from his constant attentions—her entire body firmer and stronger from the exercises he insisted she take, exercises that made her more able to meet his demands in bed. She was in the very bloom of her sexuality and womanhood, ripe and eager for the taking.

He moved around her, trailing his hands over her body as if afraid to lose contact with her. He stood behind her as he so often did, hovering over her shoulder like an alter ego, an evil spirit prepared to take her to places unimaginable as his hands slid over her breasts and belly with hungry appreciation. She could feel his hot breath on her ear as he pressed his body against hers and his hands went to her hips, then down and slowly around to her sex. Abigail gasped as he touched her shaved and naked mound and dipped lower still. It always thrilled her when he touched her like this, when the chains held her helpless to resist, when he claimed her body as his own private possession.

There was a large mirror in front of her, though her blindfold made that of no use to her. Still, as he spread her apart, she knew he could see her most sensitive flesh and she knew what his eyes looked like as he watched himself touch her in the mirror. Despite the fact that she had been with him for some time now, she still felt that initial pang of embarrassment when he viewed her so intimately like this, the result of her stubborn female modesty, and yet she had come to realize that these uneasy feelings were always a prelude to her own arousal. It was as if she erected these natural barriers of shame only so that he could have the pleasure of smashing them down.

Tonight though, there was something tentative in his touch, a sort of curiosity, as if he were letting his hands confirm something his mind already knew.

"I have decided to take you with me to St. Louis," he said.

His statement was completely unexpected. Abigail gave a sharp gasp of surprise and delight, but she said nothing.

"You will contact the agent tomorrow and book us a cabin on the riverboat *Morningstar*, and you will see to all the other arrangements, the packing, the running of the house while we are gone. Does that please you, my love?"

Abigail was confused, standing there still naked and blindfolded. It was hardly the time to discuss travel arrangements, but she answered, "Oh yes, my lord! Very much! Thank you, my lord! Thank you!"

This trip to St. Louis was business for the Doctor, to purchase some herbs that had been sent back from his agents in the far Northwest, and Abigail had been dreading his leaving her alone. She knew she would miss him terribly.

"My lord, your pardon, but may I ask what has changed your mind?" she asked cautiously.

She received no answer. Instead, she felt the exquisite touch of a peacock feather against her exposed flesh. This was something new to him, the use of feathers and furs with which to stimulate her, bringing her to a point of near sexual hysteria by the wonderful maddening touch of these objects. Only a few days ago, he had caused her such an intense orgasm through use of the peacock feather that she had come near to passing out.

He touched her now, running the soft edge of the feather down between her labia as he held her open. Chills ran down her spine and she felt the hardness of his cock pressing against her from behind.

"What has changed my mind?" He kissed the side of her neck. "Because I think it's time you saw something of the world, Abigail, and I think the trip would do you good. There's more to life than this house, my dear, and more to experience than what we have here."

At the moment, she no longer cared. She responded to the maddening touch of the feather by testing her strength against the chains, pulling luxuriantly against their strength, reveling in her own feelings of helplessness.

"Besides," he said, kissing her neck again, adding more chills to the ones she already had. "I've come to doubt that I can live without you for that long, my precious."

Joy coursed through her body. His words were just like the feather, touching her in the center of her being. She rose up on her toes and thrust her hips forward, looking for his hand, but he was gone.

She heard him dragging something across the floor toward her, some sort of stand perhaps, or small table. Then she felt the tip of the feather again tickling against her sex, aimed directly at the level of her clit, but this time, the feather didn't move. Abigail gasped at the lewd sensation. He must have attached the feather to the stand in some way so that it projected out and touched her.

The Doctor walked behind her again and put his hand on her bottom, pushing her hips forward, forcing her against the feather. The sensation was exquisite yet maddening.

"Can you bring yourself off on this feather, Abigail?" he asked her with clinical detachment.

"I don't know, my lord. It's so soft. I need more pressure. It tickles."

"It is one type of sensation. Something like how what we do here is one type of activity. It feels good, doesn't it? It arouses you, but it's not enough. Not by itself. Even so, Abigail, try. Show me how you can pleasure yourself."

She felt her face redden. "My lord, I don't think I can. Not like this, not just standing here…"

He was firm. "Try."

She recognized a command when she heard one. With her ankles attached to the bar, all she could do was swing her hips out and back to make the edge of the feather slide along her crease. It was wonderfully erotic in a teasing kind of way, but it didn't satisfy. As she had said, she needed something firmer, harder, something capable of more pressure.

Still, it felt very good, and Abigail began to slowly work her sex against the soft feather, her stomach tight and trembling from the strain of controlling her hips. The edge of the feather was firmer than the tip, and she worked herself around until she had the edge sawing into her crease, the fibers flicking against her clit and tickling the entrance to her body.

She knew he was watching her and she was thankful for the blindfold, which gave her a paradoxical feeling of privacy. She knew it was silly, but the fact that she couldn't see him made her less concerned about hiding her own feelings, and her brows furrowed and she bit her lips, her face a mask of erotic concentration as she worked against the feather.

She heard him step away from her and then back, but didn't pay much attention until she heard the scourge hiss through the air and felt it land sharply on her bottom, giving her a wicked sting.

"Oww!" she cried out in surprise and shock, instinctively pushing her hips away from the sting and onto the edge of the feather. She clamped her lips shut in order to stifle any further outbursts. He hadn't given her permission to cry out.

He whipped her again and again she swung instinctively away from the lash. This whip was rawhide, and the thongs raised stinging welts on her skin. The pain was sharp and left her bottom red with heat, forcing her to clench her buttocks hard and shove against the gently yielding feather, making it saw against her flesh.

The Doctor found his rhythm, a stinging overhand, then a softer backhand to recover, a sort of timing stroke to give her hips a chance to retreat from their forward push. Each blow sent her against the feather, and then back as she was unable to hold that position. He was setting the tempo for her thrusts, setting the timing for her lewd masturbation against the feather, the edge of which was now wet with her juices.

By now, the peacock plume was not so inconsequential. The burning in her behind had spread to her loins, to her vagina, so that she was all afire down there, and the alternation of the sharp sting of the lash and the sweet, almost cloying tease of the feather was having its effect. Abigail was panting, her legs tingling with a pleasure she couldn't control.

She sobbed and grabbed hard at her chains as her thighs turned weak and watery. The whip was hitting lower on her buttocks now, in that sensitive area where her thighs met her ass. Stray thongs landed wetly in the crease of her sex, stinging her there and forcing her onto the maddening caress of the plume.

He was so cruel to her, so wonderfully cruel, adamant in his insistence that she surrender to orgasm, that she lose herself in sensation. The entire lower part of her body was on fire from the whip, glowing, incandescent, and yet, through the numbing burn of sensation, the soft kiss of the feather now stood out as a sharp spear of agonizing pleasure that consumed her entire mind.

She tried to hold out. For some reason, she always tried to hold out, even though she knew he wouldn't stop until she yielded. The refusal always made it that much sweeter when she finally gave up, when she finally surrendered, when her overloaded nerves could finally take no more and she felt herself rush upwards as if in the grip of a titanic wave. She rode this wave now, and at the very crest, she threw her head back and cried out, telling him without words that he had won again, acknowledging his mastery. She closed her eyes and gave herself over to the pleasure she had earned, the pleasure he had forced her to accept, dimly marveling at her body's capacity for sexual ecstasy before she found it impossible to think of anything at all.

"Oh my lord!" she gasped as her spasms released their hold on her. She wanted to tell him what she was feeling, but as always, he seemed to know.

He dropped the scourge and came around in front of her where he took her in his arms, holding her up as she tried to get her legs to support her.

"You see?" he asked her gently, breathing hard from his exertions. "This is how it is. The pain makes the pleasure sweeter, doesn't it? The hard and the soft, the dark and the light. This is how it always is."

She didn't understand him, and she was too spent to try. She let him take her down from the chains, knowing that he was still erect and unsatisfied and knowing that he would still have to take his own relief in her body before they were through. She was already eager for him to do so.

* * * * *

The *Morningstar* was a big side-wheeler steamboat, the huge paddle wheels placed near the stern, as white and as clean and ornate as the frosting on a wedding cake. The dock was a seething hornet's nest of activity when they arrived — cargo and luggage being loaded aboard and coal being shoveled into the bins beneath the mammoth boilers by sweating colliers. Stevedores and crewmen bustled about while passengers milled around in confusion looking for their cabins, followed by strings of porters carrying their things.

Their cabin was on the second deck and toward the front of the vessel. The Doctor had insisted on a suite, which was grander in name than in reality, comprising a bedroom, a sitting room and a private lavatory, all small, but sumptuously furnished. The flat-bottomed Mississippi riverboats were much like floating hotels, and their rooms had full-sized windows through which they could watch the loading going on below.

The Doctor was just tipping the porters when he looked up and saw someone approaching them along the deck. He immediately dropped the bags he was carrying and rushed forward excitedly.

"Well, Darcy, you old devil!" he cried, grabbing the man's hand in both of his, "Don't tell me you'll be on this trip too? You never told me! But then, I should have known, shouldn't I?"

The Doctor let go of the man's hand long enough to bring Abigail forward.

"Abigail, may I introduce to you the infamous Monsieur Darcy deLongville?" He turned back to the man. "I will be damned! I had no idea you'd be on this boat!"

The Doctor had told her of Darcy before. In fact, Darcy was one of his best and oldest friends and he had made a point of trying to arrange a meeting between them, but the plans had always been scotched by deLongville's haphazard schedule.

"And Darcy, this is Miss Abigail Du Pre at last. I believe I've told you of her as well." The Doctor presented her with unmistakable pride.

DeLongville's eyebrows went up over a pair of uncommonly blue eyes. He bowed and kissed her hand. "Miss Du Pre, this is indeed a pleasure. I see now how it is you have so captured Lucien's heart. His description hardly does you justice, if I may be so bold. But I do hope you have taken what he's told you of me with a most liberal dose of salt."

He was a very handsome man, dressed all in white save for his black tie, and was of the same age as Lucien, but where the Doctor was dark and intense and powerfully built, Mr. deLongville was fair and blond with a rakish air about him. He was clean-shaven save for a neatly trimmed mustache that Abigail thought he'd probably grown to help himself look older—he had that kind of youthful-looking face. He was quite handsome in a conventional sort of way, and there was a knowing look in his blue eyes that gave him a kind of dangerous and devilish charm.

The Doctor had indeed told her of Darcy, and of the scandal that caused the young man to leave his family's plantation near Baton Rouge so many years ago. The Doctor and Darcy had gone to school together and had been quite close at one time, a couple of young hell-raisers. But then, the Doctor had sobered up and became serious about his medical studies while Darcy chose to quit school and pursue a life of gambling and leisure in the French Quarter and on the boats that plied the river from New Orleans all the way up to St. Paul. She knew that the Doctor still saw him on occasion, though not frequently. Darcy's family was wealthy and well-connected. Abigail saw him immediately as a man it would be dangerous for a lady to be alone with.

She was aware of Darcy's eyes on her as he and the Doctor talked, but men's stares no longer concerned her as once they had. She had come to appreciate how great a part sex played in normal social intercourse and had come to accept herself as a sexual creature, and one of some considerable attraction to men. She was not above playing with men's affections to a certain extent, especially now, when she was safe under the Doctor's protection. She was aware too that the Doctor noticed her flirting, frivolous as it was.

They made plans to meet at dinner, but it was not to be, and the Doctor didn't seem especially surprised when Darcy sent his most sincere regrets and proposed meeting later. The Doctor and Abigail thus were seated at the Captain's table amidst the convivial conversation of the other first-class passengers. The food was sumptuous, the dining room glittering with crystal and silk, and the women all dressed in their finest. Abigail, wearing a new gown that left her shoulders bare and showed a daring bit of décolletage, positively lit up the table, to the Doctor's great pride and satisfaction. She wore her velvet choker. He never tired of seeing her in it.

Following dinner, they toured the boat, arm in arm. They came across Darcy in the card salon and the Doctor smiled knowingly, but they didn't go in. The Doctor said it was best to leave him to his work and besides, they were quite satisfied with each other's company. They found a position on the upper deck in the bow of the boat, from which they could watch the twilight descend on the river, fading to indigo in the east. The air was warm and silky, and she hardly needed the shawl she had fetched from her cabin.

"Darcy seemed quite taken with you." The Doctor leaned on the rail and lit a cigar. He seemed quite pleased with the fact himself.

"Did he?" Abigail asked, trying to sound casual. "I hadn't noticed."

The Doctor looked at her and smiled but said nothing. He knew very well that she was aware of her effect on men and women too. He'd taught her to be aware. And he'd seen her preening for Darcy when they'd first met.

He twirled his cigar in his mouth and asked, "How would you like to go to bed with another man?"

Abigail's blood went cold in her veins and she felt her face flush.

"Doctor! What are you saying?"

His face was difficult to see in the lowering twilight, so she could not tell if he was teasing her, but she knew he rarely teased. Still, she saw his teeth flash in a smile, wicked in the darkness, and she couldn't be sure.

"Are you so shocked, my love? That I'd ask you to share yourself?"

"Yes, I'm shocked." She stared at him and drew herself upright. "I'm shocked and I must say I'm hurt."

"And a little bit excited, I'd wager," he said.

Abigail opened her mouth and, finding nothing to say, shut it again. She wasn't excited. Not in the least. She stood up and pulled her shawl around her, as if she were chilled.

"You're horrified. You're wondering how I could even suggest such a thing. You find the very idea sordid and disgusting, don't you, my darling? You think it means I don't care for you or that I hold you in low regard."

"Frankly, yes," she said coldly. "And I'm very upset that you would even joke about such a thing. I thought you had more respect for me than that."

The Doctor was silent for some moments, and Abigail wondered if she had overstepped her bounds. Not that she would have taken back anything she'd just said, but his silence unnerved her. She gazed at the dark water, the still reflection of the emerging stars torn asunder by the riverboat's wake. She was afraid to look at him, afraid of what she might see, but she felt his eyes on her.

"I have nothing but respect for you, Abigail." His voice was soft. "Nothing but respect and love. You are my heart and my life, the source of my deepest joy and satisfaction, and I would rather part with my right arm than lose you or your affection, and yet there are still some things that I will require of you, and this might be one of them."

She felt a stirring in the pit of her stomach at his words and she knew then that his mind was already made up, that to refuse his request would be to refuse him. She felt numb.

"Lucien," she said, carefully choosing her words. "You know that all I have is yours. If you command me to do something, then I will do it, though I don't understand what would drive you to such a despicable and humiliating act."

He sighed. "It is hard enough to know one's heart's desire without seeking to know why. But for this, I might say that it has to do with showing you what strength you have within yourself, what you are capable of."

She turned from him, her lips set grimly together.

"Oh, Lucien. This is bad enough. But please don't pretend that you're doing this for my benefit. That is just unconscionable."

He stood up, drew once on his cigar and flicked it tumbling into the darkness of the river. When he reached for her, she resisted, the feel of his hands on her suddenly making her flesh crawl, but he grabbed her arms and pulled her forcibly into the shadow of the wheelhouse where he pushed her back against the wall.

He stared into her eyes and for once, Abigail refused to look away. Even when his lips came down on hers, she refused his kiss. He held her there, and she welcomed the feel of his strength against her as it gave her something to fight against, for fight she did. It was as if he were suddenly someone else, as if his asking her to share herself had already made him a stranger to her.

Not since their first night together had he made her feel like such a whore, and even then, she had known that she would still have her self-respect. But now, what did she have? She had given everything to him and still it wasn't enough. Now he wanted her to play the slut for other men. She was filled with anger and hurt, and to feel her body respond unbidden to his hot sexual advances only made her angrier yet. Whore of a body! What chance did she have?

He felt her resistance. Of course he felt it.

"Stop it, Abigail." He held her wrists in his hands. "Do you think I would feel this way for you if I thought any less of you? Have I even asked you to do anything yet?"

For all their play, all the whippings and punishments, she had yet to feel his real anger, yet she knew that she had pushed him to the edge of it now, and it frightened her, not for fear of her safety, but because she had so disappointed him.

He pulled her close and she abandoned all resistance. Suddenly, she wanted him with a wildness she hadn't felt in weeks, for she suddenly felt she might be somehow losing him.

He took possession of her as he always did, and she made no attempt to even try and resist him anymore. She pressed herself against him, opened her mouth and sucked his tongue inside. He was her master in every sense of the word, and she let herself fall once again into the sweet strength of his arms, letting his own desire wash over her like the waves of the ocean, taking her fears with it. Her anguish made her desperate for him and for all he meant to her. Her entire body stiffened against him, preparing to yield.

If it was a surrender, then he apparently accepted it without condition. He played with her lips, biting her, tasting her, fitting her to him, as the ship hummed with the steady throb of the big paddle wheel and the noise and laughter drifted up from below. When he released her from the kiss at last, her chest was heaving and she had to lean against him for balance. When next she looked, all was dark, but the stars were out and reflected in the smooth but moving waters of the Mississippi, and she felt like she couldn't tell up from down, the sky from the river. She was dizzy with need.

He kissed her again and now there was no disguising the passion he felt for her. His cock was hard against her, his hands pulled at her greedily, his tongue searched for hers in her mouth, and he groaned softly when she answered him, her body melting into his.

He broke the kiss and gazed into her eyes and again she refused to look away. In sex, she might be his submissive, but in all else, she would stand her ground.

He looked away first, then grabbed her wrist and led her inside as she stumbled after him. She'd never felt him hold her so tightly. She knew his anger was up, but strangely, she wasn't afraid.

The *Morningstar* was a broad and generous boat, and the rooms had the same sense of indolent luxury. Their room had its own veranda overlooking the river, but could only be entered through the central passageway. The door was louvered, providing little in the way of privacy, and as the Doctor led Abigail down the carpeted passageway, they could hear an occasional snore coming from the cabins they passed.

Inside, he made her disrobe, and she undressed quickly, as if eager to get on with it, pulling her gown up over her head and presenting herself in only her stockings and cincher, her breasts exposed. He tied her arms roughly behind her, drawing her elbows together to enhance the thrust of her breasts, and he tied a spreader bar to her knees to keep her legs apart.

"Open your mouth," he said as he fixed a ball gag between her teeth and buckled it around her head. "I'm afraid this is necessary. We don't want to disturb our neighbors."

Abigail was trembling with nervousness as he pushed her back until her elbows struck the wall of the cabin. He reached into his bag of sexual paraphernalia and withdrew a silver chain with small clamps on either end. She had never seen this before, but she didn't have to be told what it was for. She tried to keep her breathing still as he attached the clamps to her nipples.

They hurt, and she wanted them to hurt. She didn't know why but she was consumed by a masochistic need for pain tonight, as if that would wash away the sin he'd asked her to commit. Or perhaps it was her disobedience that she wanted to be rid of. She felt the clamps in her sex as well, a pain sharp and acute, and every time she moved, the chain swung and she felt the tug on her nipples.

The Doctor stripped off his shirt. His face was dark and dreadful and now, naked and trussed and ready for the whip, Abigail couldn't meet his gaze. He was displeased with her for the first time that she could remember, and she was glad of it. She wanted to feel his displeasure, his anger with her. She wanted to be whipped until it hurt.

The Doctor picked up a scourge, the rawhide one, the one that had hurt her bottom so exquisitely just the day before. She'd known then what it was capable of, but now knowing that he was going to wield it in anger made her knees weak, at the same time she felt herself grow wet with a kind of sick and trembling excitement.

Oh God, what was wrong with her?

He walked over to her, twitching the scourge in his hand, limbering up the cruel thongs. He stared at her for a moment, looking for her eyes but she kept them away. He reached for her and ran his thumb across her lower lip, wet with saliva from the ball gag, and Abigail's cry was muffled as he took the thin silver chain that draped between her nipples, lifted it and draped it over a wall sconce, pulling her breasts up and distorting her nipples painfully. She clenched her eyes shut against the pain and readied herself. She heard him try the lash, whipping it against his trouser leg.

And then he stopped.

Abigail's heart was thudding in her ears in time to the throbbing in her nipples.

"No," he said, dropping the flogger. "Not like this."

He reached up, unbuckled the gag and pulled it from between her lips, then turned his attention to the nipple clamps. But before he could loosen the clamps, Abigail ran her tongue over her lips and looked at him, breathing hard.

"Please, my lord. Please."

He stared at her, and the need and silent pleading he saw in her eyes gave him an unexpected chill of an excitement that went beyond the mere sexual. She wanted it.

"Very well." he said. "But not in anger. God strike me dead if I ever hit you in anger."

He quickly replaced the ball in her mouth and buckled the gag around her head. The clamps still tugged at her sensitive nipples, but the pain had blended into the hot longing she now felt for the whip, and no sooner had she got the gag secure in her mouth, then she heard the lash hiss through the air and felt it tear into her naked ass.

She gasped and bit down on the gag, giving herself over to the exquisite pain. She was still sore from yesterday, but each stroke was like a kiss of fire that made her gush with humiliating wetness. Although he had denied his anger, she could feel it in his strokes. He hit her not to arouse her but to punish her, and it was just what she wanted. She closed her eyes and wallowed in the pain, groveled in it, letting it wipe her clean of all thoughts.

At some point, he dropped the whip again and took her down from the sconce, his hands trembling with his urgent need. He bent her over the footboard of the bed, and Abigail was beyond resisting. He was her master, and he could do as he wished with her. She was feverish with illicit excitement and the pain in her breasts and in her ass seemed to pulse in time with the steady throbbing of the riverboat's engines. The image of the big pistons working steadily to turn the massive paddle wheels, churning the dark river to white foam came unbidden to her mind as he turned her facedown on the soft bed and tore at his trousers.

He entered her hard, one hand on her hips, the other pressing on the back of her neck, and he began to fuck her brutally, his belly slapping against her red and beaten buttocks with a sound loud enough to be heard above the thrum of the riverboat. Abigail didn't care, she was weeping behind the gag, tears of joy at his violent passion, his savage possession of her. She moaned as she climaxed and felt herself squeeze down on his implacable cock. She felt him tighten and shudder, then felt him gush into her, all his anger and lust transformed into this simple, incredible gift.

Chapter Twelve

It was as if a storm had passed, and the next day they spent in pure leisure, lingering over breakfast in the salon, the Doctor reading the papers and Abigail a novel. He had treated the welts on her backside last night before retiring as he always did, and then again this morning. If anything, he was even more solicitous and concerned than usual. Abigail heard his sharp intake of breath as he examined the damage he had wrought in his passion, and such was his remorse that he kissed each bruise before applying the salve he had made especially for her. It gave Abigail a feeling of quiet pleasure to know that her wounds affected him so deeply, and she would have liked to tell him that each wound was proof of how much she loved him, but she didn't want to remonstrate with him or sound like she was complaining. She was aware that he knew.

There was no more mention of their talk last night, but Abigail spent much of the day turning the matter over in her mind. She had pledged herself to him, and could thus hardly refuse his request that she have sex with another man without changing the nature of their relationship, but then, she couldn't escape the feeling that things had already changed just by the Doctor's even broaching the subject. It seemed to indicate some subtle change in his feelings toward her, and Abigail spent much of the day trying to determine just what that change meant. Perhaps she had been too submissive to him, too passive and retiring, such that he had come to take her for granted.

In any case, she was sure she hadn't heard the last of the matter. She was no longer the innocent she had been when she came to the Doctor's house, and she found that she was curious. She was curious to see just how the Doctor would arrange what he had in mind, and she was curious too to see how she would respond.

By dinnertime, Abigail was quite comfortable with Darcy, and was flattered to be with two such handsome and courtly companions. All three of them went in to dinner together, the men in tails and Abigail in a peach-colored gown adorned with roses at the bust, and, of course, her choker. This time, the pearl was replaced with a jet-black stone, and the Doctor told her that the black stone was a sign of her submission to him. She imagined that he thought it would remind her of her place when and if the time came.

Meals for the first-class passengers were sumptuous affairs, with three wines and numerous courses, and by dessert, Abigail was quite flushed and feeling flirtatious herself. Her knowledge of the Doctor's intentions gave an added level of interest to the normal dinnertime conversation and badinage, every joke and glance having a new and exciting meaning, and she found herself appraising Darcy and imagining what it might be like. By the end of dinner, she had come to realize that perhaps it was not the act itself that gave her such profound reservations, rather it was how she would feel about herself afterwards. That was where things got difficult.

It was a striking anticlimax, then, when the Doctor bid her retire early so that he and Darcy could play some cards and catch up on old times, but her disappointment notwithstanding, she did as he asked. She excused herself to the men's gracious good nights, went to the cabin and brushed out her hair. She kept her gown on, thinking she might be called on later that evening. She picked up her book and read by the light of the gas lamp.

The next thing she knew, the Doctor was shaking her awake. "Abigail? Wake up, darling. You must wake up."

"What is it Lucien? Is something wrong?"

"Come, Abigail." He helped her to her feet. "You must come with me."

"Why? What's happened, darling? Something's happened."

He put his hand on the cabin door and then stopped. He ran his hand through his hair as if in doubt, and then turned to her.

"You are mine, are you not, Abigail? You obey me in all things, is that not correct?"

"Yes, my lord. Of course. Whatever you request of me, you know that."

She thought she knew what was afoot. Still, he seemed truly agitated and upset, not at all how she expected he'd be.

"Darcy has called me on a point of honor," he said, keeping his eyes down. He spoke with his face toward the door. "It was foolish of me to let myself get involved with him this way, but he has always been able to bait me, and I always rise to the bait."

She went to him and pressed herself against his back. "But what has happened, darling?"

He took a deep breath. "You know how proud I am of you, Abigail, and Darcy is, after all, an old and trusted friend, though a devious one, damn him! I told him about our relationship, omitting the details, of course, and he contends that you are gulling me, that you are playing me for a fool, that no woman would obey a man in all things and so he proposed a test, a wager."

She waited expectantly. He seemed to have a difficult time finding his words.

"There's no need for such stories, Lucien. I knew you intended for this to happen. It's Darcy, isn't it? He's the one."

He looked at her in confusion for a moment. "Our conversation about your sharing yourself with another last night? Yes, I admit I had thought of Darcy in that regard, but I didn't intend for it to happen like this. I know what a step this is for you, my darling, and I intended to bring you to this slowly. But the man trapped me by my honor and called my hand."

"And so now I must redeem your honor by paying with my own?"

He picked up her dressing gown from where she'd thrown it on a chair. "No, Abigail, it's not like that…"

For once, she didn't let him finish, but opened the door and stepped out into the passageway. She was awake now, the anger and hurt had returned, and with them a desire to hurt him as well. She was suddenly eager for this to happen.

He caught her by the arm and stopped her.

"Abigail. I've told you many times that I would never force you to do something you didn't want to do."

She met his gaze. "I know."

He stood there, holding her arm, waiting for her to refuse, waiting for her to object, but he waited in vain. She just stood with her back straight, looking at him as her silence grew louder and louder until there was no mistaking what it meant.

"Very well," he said finally.

If he'd thought she wouldn't do it, he had been mistaken, and he followed her now as she led the way through the silent passageways back to Darcy's suite, her head held high. Outside the door, he stopped her.

"I'll be with you the entire time. There will be no intercourse. I've told him as much."

Abigail hardly heard what he said, but her face flushed red all the same as the enormity of what she might be doing struck her again.

The Doctor knocked and Darcy opened the door. He was wearing a red velvet robe and a white silk scarf and slippers and he greeted them warmly before giving the Doctor a knowing look that Abigail caught out of the corner of her eye.

Darcy offered them drinks and bade them sit, but the Doctor and Abigail remained standing uneasily in the middle of the floor in the dim light of the one kerosene lamp. Darcy shrugged and sat down on the small sofa and picked up his brandy. "It was most gracious of you to come, Abigail. I really didn't mean for Lucien to trouble you. I trust we didn't pull you away from anything?"

Abigail found that her throat was dry. "It's no trouble," she said politely.

"Good. I'm glad."

Abigail was nervous but her pride was up, and now that she was here, she wanted to get it over with as quickly as possible, whatever it might be. Lucien, however, seemed strangely at a loss. She stood before Darcy, her head erect, her hands clasped in front of her, though she couldn't meet his eyes. Even in the lamplight, Darcy could see her nervousness, and he was struck again by how lovely she was, even in her distress.

Seeing that no one knew how to begin, he said, "Lucien tells me that you obey him in all things. Is this true?"

She didn't move her eyes from the floor. "Yes," she said softly. "He is my lord and master, whatsoever he wishes of me I will do."

"And you would obey him even if he told you to give yourself to another man?"

"Yes." She choked back the lump in her throat. "Yes, I would. If he told me to."

Darcy looked at the Doctor and raised his eyebrows. He was impressed, but the Doctor was too angry and upset to enjoy his moral victory over his friend. He knew what must come next. Darcy would never be satisfied with a mere answer. He would need to see for himself.

"Well, we shall see, shan't we?" Darcy said. "Proceed then, by all means, Lucien."

The Doctor knew that there was no turning back. He stood behind Abigail and began to unbutton her gown, and she lowered her head, not looking at anything as she felt his fingers, his familiar fingers, working at the buttons of her gown, removing her clothes as he had so many times, but this time exposing her to another man's eyes.

"I want you to know, darling, that whatever happens, my love for you will not change," he whispered to her. "I take full responsibility for what is about to happen. You are entirely blameless."

"My lord…" Abigail began. She wanted to reassure him, but the words stuck in her throat.

And then she felt the bodice of her dress slipping from her chest.

She restrained herself from instinctively putting her hands up to hold the top of her gown in place, and she felt the dress fall from her breasts, exposing her naked body down to her waist. She felt both men's eyes on her and she blushed deeply, growing almost faint.

She heard Darcy's sharp intake of breath at the sight of her breasts, full and round, her nipples innocently erect in the golden candlelight, and she stood there unmoving under his gaze, trying to keep her pride intact. Her embarrassment was tempered somewhat by seeing the look on Darcy's face as he stared at her. Clearly, he had not really expected her to be so bold, nor had he expected the sight of her breasts to be so arousing. The erotic tension in the room was palpable as Abigail felt both men's eyes on her.

"Magnificent!" Darcy breathed, sitting forward on the sofa. His admiration was honest and heartfelt, his appreciation genuine. Abigail could feel his gaze like heat on her flesh, and despite her efforts at self-control, her breathing increased under the intensity of his gaze. She felt her nipples begin to grow turgid and erect, and she cursed her body's own betrayal.

The Doctor, too, was overcome by her vulnerability, by her attitude of patient submission. Automatically, he took her breasts in his hands and pulled her back against him possessively, his lips going to that soft spot just below her ear, as if they were alone.

"Abigail," he whispered. "Abigail, forgive me, but it must be done."

Now that her breasts were exposed she looked defiantly at Darcy. The Doctor had taught her never to be ashamed of her body, that there were few men who would not grow weak at the sight of her beauty, and she thought perhaps Darcy would be satisfied with her present humiliation and that would be the end of it. But what she saw in his eyes told her that her ordeal was only beginning, that he would not stop until he had seen everything.

She leaned back against Lucien, seeking shelter from the lust she saw in the stranger's eyes, but there was no shelter to be had. The Doctor's warm hands hid her breasts from Darcy's gaze, but then the Doctor began, perhaps unconsciously, to massage them, demonstrating not only her nakedness and the firm, sensuous resilience of her breasts, but the secrets of their lovemaking as well. Abigail whimpered in embarrassment that anyone should see how he pleasured her, how easily he commanded her body. The kisses he lavished along the side of her neck became more fervent in response to the feel of her femininity in his hands, and Abigail realized that he was growing aroused and, to her horror, that somewhere inside, she was beginning to feel the same stirrings of an excitement so illicit she dared not even think about it.

He turned her face back to his and he leaned his face forward and kissed her deeply, and the passion in his kiss took her breath away. How could he be so stimulated by this horrible humiliation? How could he put his passion for her on display before a stranger's eyes?

Worse, how could her body respond like this, for there was no denying the thrill she now felt as he kissed her and stroked her breasts, finding the nipples and rolling them softly between his fingers. She was torn between her natural modesty and the excitement of his touch, and what made it worse was the knowledge that the passion they shared was being witnessed by another man. Without thinking, she automatically reached back for the Doctor's manhood as she had so many times before when he'd held her like this.

"No," he said.

Abigail caught herself, hoping Darcy hadn't noticed.

The Doctor reached into his pocket and pulled forth a length of rope. Quickly and expertly he bound her wrists behind her, rendering her totally defenseless, totally at his mercy and at the mercy of this stranger who now shared her intimate secrets. Still, she did not protest. She was his. If he wanted to show her off, it was his right and she wouldn't interfere.

Darcy got up and came to her, his gaze alternating between her eyes and her breasts. His eyes flicked up over her shoulder and looked at the Doctor inquiringly, and Abigail felt rather than saw the Doctor nod. Darcy hummed softly in appreciation as he hooked his thumbs in the waist of the gown and worked it down over her hips as Lucien continued to hold her against himself, lost in the heat of his own intense desire. He held her tightly, his hand firm against her cheek pressing her head back to take his passionate kiss, as if trying to keep her from seeing the desecration of her body that was happening at Darcy's hands. She felt Darcy pulling her dress down, exposing her naked stomach, her hips, and she groaned in abject shame as she felt the garment slip from her thighs and slide down around her ankles, leaving her only in her silk stockings and her choker, naked in the presence of these two virile men.

"Gorgeous," Darcy breathed. His eyes fixed on her shaved mound and he could not tear them away. He fell to his knees in front of her, reached up and put his fingers lightly on her hips as if framing a work of art. "Just gorgeous."

She tried to protest, tried to tell the Doctor that she was now naked and he must make Darcy stop, but he seemed oblivious to all but the feel of her breasts in his hands and his tongue delving hungrily into her open mouth, smothering her sounds of entreaty. His passion was making her dizzy, carrying her along with him and making her nipples harden even as she blushed from her nakedness.

Darcy was on his knees before her as if in worship, and she felt his hands as he traced the contours of her hips and thighs, trying to soothe her with soft words and murmurs of appreciation. His touch was like acid against her skin, and like acid, it left a fiery trail wherever he touched her. She whimpered when she felt his lips on her thighs, warm and imploring, and she knew she must not, she could not let him go any further. But Lucien held her face to his, a slave to his savage kisses, and before she could free herself, she felt Darcy's hot breath on her shaved skin, and then the lewd caress of his lips on her naked sex, kissing her. A sob tore from her throat, but still the Doctor held her helpless, held her still for his friend's depredations of her naked body.

Her cries were muffled, swallowed in Lucien's mouth. Did he want to shame her like this? Did he enjoy sharing her with another man? She didn't want to think of it, and indeed, all thought was growing impossible as Darcy's mouth licked and sucked the smooth columns of her thighs beyond where her stockings ended. He was on his knees, his tongue soft and sinuous as he traced out the bare skin around her cleft, teasing her, tormenting her, and then his long, muscular tongue worked its way between the wet lips of her sex and plunged inside.

Abigail was lost. She could not resist what he was doing to her. The unbearable physical pleasure that spoke directly to her body with no concern for what she felt, spoke in such a way that her body betrayed her utterly and eagerly answered him, her hips pushing forward for more of his warm and wonderful tongue.

She tore her face away from the Doctor's grip for a moment and looked down at the man kneeling before her. She could look down between her breasts and see his face upturned, eyes closed in bliss, his long wicked tongue curved up into the hot slot of her pussy. Then the Doctor took her face in his hand again and pressed her back against his chest so he could kiss her, leaving the image of Darcy feeding between her legs etched upon her mind.

It was as if the two men were fighting for possession of her — Lucien's hot and passionate kisses reminding her of all they shared together, Darcy's tongue and mouth calling to the sexual animal that hid in her body. Tears rolled down her cheeks as she fought for the control that was rapidly slipping away from her while the two men fought for her, each demanding that she yield herself to him.

And behind this was the shameful knowledge that a stranger's touch could bring her such terrible pleasure. She groaned into the Doctor's mouth, groaned in shame at herself even as her body opened itself to Darcy's obscene licking and sucking, pushing herself at him, her thighs trembling and wet with his saliva and her own lewd secretions.

Darcy was moaning himself at the feel of her softness on his tongue. He licked her with long, obscene strokes, pushing his face into her and luxuriating in the richness of her lubrications, tasting her, urging her on, drawing the pleasure from her body as he drew her juices into his mouth. She began to shudder as she felt herself falling into a maelstrom of wild sensations and raw, conflicting emotions.

Finally, the Doctor released her face and she tore her mouth from his, sobbing in despair at her body's wicked betrayal. She had betrayed her love, betrayed her honor, and yet the feel of the two men making love to her made her burn with a lust she had never known before. The Doctor was achingly hard and pressing against the crack in her buttocks. Darcy's robe was open and flung back and she could see him take his long heavy cock in his fist and begin to masturbate as he fed at her sex like a wild bear at a tree filled with honey.

It was madness. And yet, she felt a shuddering thrill at the thought that her mere body could elicit such wild and wanton behavior from these two men of the world. Their cocks were hard and aching for her, filled with cum for her, and that thought filled her in turn with lust. Would both men orgasm from the thrill of her body? Was she such a slut that the mere touch of her against their hands and mouth could bring them to climax? Her own flames of lewd pleasure were raging out of control as Darcy continued to caress her most intimate place with his obscene tongue, his slurping and moaning sounds loud in the stifling air of the cabin.

She felt like a complete whore — she was one. The sight of these two strong and sexual men consumed by their lust for her naked body, reduced to lapping at her pussy and pressing their cocks against her, gave her a feeling of strange and sinful triumph. She writhed in the Doctor's embrace, pushing her loins out at Darcy's sucking mouth, spreading her thighs for him, and her moans and entreaties were as mindless and inchoate as the gales of salacious desire that racked her frame. Her bound hands scrabbled behind her until they took hold of the Doctor's cock through his pants, turgid and monstrously erect, and she squeezed it hard, making him groan as she reveled in the feel of his potent thickness. She could picture his big shaft, almost feel the clear fluid she could feel running over her fingers — even taste the hot musk of his semen on her tongue.

Oh God no! she thought dimly. *Please! Not that! Not in front of them!*

But her body again refused to listen. She was going to orgasm, suffer the ultimate indignity, the humiliation of coming from their depraved attack. She gasped and shuddered and her nipples hardened painfully.

"Oh God, no! Lucien! Oh, I'm going to come! Stop! Please! Don't make me…"

But there was no stopping them and she knew it. Darcy shoved his tongue and even his nose into her, losing himself in her femininity, and the Doctor's fingers found her nipples, those orgasmic triggers he knew how to use so well, and bore down on them, sending honey-sweet spears of pain through her breasts. Her resistance faded, melted away and she shoved herself against Darcy's face and let herself come, her hips jerking in hard, sharp spasms against his sucking mouth, coming so hard, it set the room spinning around her. She heard Darcy cry out and she knew he was coming too, coming from the sheer pleasure of feeling her gush onto his tongue. Her head swam, and had the Doctor not been there to hold her up, she surely would have crumpled to the floor.

What was she? Whore? Lover? Lady or slave? At that moment, she didn't know, and feelings of shame and hot desire consumed her so that she hardly knew herself where she was or to whom she belonged. She was caught in a storm of emotions from which only a man's hot embrace could promise any shelter. Let it be the Doctor or even let it be Darcy, but let it be someone. She needed to be fucked. She felt like she might die.

She looked savage, almost dangerous. Her hair had fallen from atop her head and wild strands hid her face as she panted for breath, her naked breasts rising and falling. The Doctor held her tight, afraid to let her go, afraid that perhaps this time he'd gone too far, pushed her over an edge from which there was no coming back. She trembled in his arms like a wild animal, her breath hissing through her teeth.

He said nothing. He reached down to untie her hands but she said "No!" and he stopped.

He knew what she meant. She was afraid to have the use of her hands back, afraid that she might be unable to stop herself from taking what she so desperately needed. He quickly threw her dressing gown over her, picked up her gown from where it lay on the floor, and guided her to the door.

Darcy was still on his knees on the floor, a puddle of semen before him, more semen dripping from his knuckles. He looked up at the two of them.

"God, how I envy you, Lucien!" he breathed.

The Doctor led her roughly down the darkened passageway, pulling and pushing her as she staggered along, her hands still tied behind her, half-sobbing in her lust and confusion. The boat was throbbing with the sound of the big paddle wheel as he led her down the stairs and to their cabin. He opened the door, pulled her inside and immediately turned around, put his arms around her and pushed her back against the wall, his mouth covering hers. He pushed the cloak from her shoulders and filled his hands with her naked buttocks, pulled her to him as she kissed him savagely, biting at his mouth in a frenzy of confused emotions. She didn't want to stop, didn't want to think about what had just happened, didn't want anything but the hardness of his body and the fierceness of his passion burning away her shame.

He backed her up until her bottom hit the top of the dresser, and then he lifted her on top of it, never breaking the kiss. He got his trousers down and his big cock free, and with one lunge, he filled her with it, making her sob with relief. Her long stocking-clad legs came up and embraced his back as he began to fuck her. No tenderness, no preliminary, just an animal need to make her his again, to reclaim what he had almost thrown away.

Abigail was hardly lucid but she threw herself against him, desperate to be his once again. She sobbed as he fucked her, the overwhelming emotions she felt coming out in hot tears that rolled down her lust-contorted face even as she urged him on with the most obscene language.

"Yes! Fuck me! Fuck your whore! Harder! Harder! Hurt me with it! Oh God!"

Her language excited him even more and as his hips slammed into her, he reached beneath her, found her anus and forced his finger into her, filling her with masochistic joy so that she screamed into his mouth.

He too was close to tears, his chest bursting with emotions he couldn't comprehend. He kissed her, licked her, bit at her, all the while moaned her name, "Yes, Abigail, my darling, my beloved! You're mine! Mine always! Mine forever! Now take it, darling! Take my hard cock! Fuck me, darling, fuck me!"

She didn't know who she was any longer but she didn't want to think of that now. She knew she was his, no matter what happened, no matter what might ever come between them. She turned her face to the side and whined as she felt a new orgasm building inside her, this one for him, for her lover and master.

* * * * *

"Explain? I don't know if I can explain it," he said.

It was late, very late, and their room was all dark but still they didn't sleep. It had been a night of tears and kisses, questions and rapprochements as Abigail struggled with the knowledge of what she'd done, what she'd become.

She couldn't deny that she had enjoyed it—or, rather, that her body had enjoyed it—and the Doctor had worked long and patiently to soothe her conscience and assure her that she had done nothing wrong. She had been following his commands. His feelings for her were unchanged.

"But how will I live with myself? Knowing that I'm capable of that kind of betrayal? Is that what you want of me, Lucien? To be a whore for your amusement?"

He sighed deeply and sat up. He'd been reclining against the headboard, pillows propping him up, and Abigail had been lying with her head on his chest, her eyes red from crying.

"Perhaps. There is an undeniable thrill I get from seeing the way men look at you, knowing that your heart and your body are mine. And there is a wonderful thrill at seeing you being pleasured by another man, though I can't say why."

He ran his hands through her hair, then caressed her cheek with the backs of his fingers. Abigail took his fingers and pulled them to her lips, puffy now from crying.

"I need to know that you're mine by choice, Abigail. I need to know that you've known other men's love, and that I'm still the one you want. Not just because you're used to me or you know me. I need to know that you choose me, every day, and for that, you must know what other men's love is like. Does that make any sense to you?"

She looked at him searchingly and for a long moment, he was silent. Then he continued, "And I have to show you that these things you feel, the things you do that move me so much, they're part of you, Abigail. They come from you, not me. I may bring them forth from you, but they're a part of your true nature. They're nothing to be ashamed of. As long as your heart belongs to me, and mine belongs to you, there's nothing to be ashamed or frightened of."

His words were soothing, but there was still so much she didn't understand. All she knew was how she felt in her heart, and for now, the fear was gone, leaving only the familiar sweet ache she always felt when he was with her.

"I love you so much. I never want to lose you." It was all she could think to say.

He gave a little laugh of understanding and kissed her head, then leaned back and was quiet for a time, lost in thought. Then he slid out from under her and got to his feet, leaving her alone in the bed. He went to his valise where he kept his business papers, and she watched curiously as he took something from inside.

"I was going to wait." He came back to the bed and sat down. "I wanted to wait until some night when we were on deck and the stars were out and the moon was right. But now I see that waiting is foolish. I don't want you to be afraid of losing me, nor I of losing you. And I'll never love you more than I love you now."

She looked down into his hands and saw a small box of midnight-blue velvet. He opened it and even in the darkness of their suite, the diamond gave off a flame of multicolored light that made her breath catch in her throat.

"Marry me, Abigail, and we'll never think of losing each other again."

Chapter Thirteen

Abigail owned no jewelry but the choker the Doctor had bought her, so the ring she now wore on the third finger of her left hand was an unfamiliar weight, but one she welcomed. The Doctor was amused at how she had suddenly developed the habit of straightening her hair with her left hand when people were about, or holding her parasol over her shoulder with her left hand uppermost, so she could catch the reflection of the flashing diamond out of the corner of her eye. She was quite sure that everyone else could see it too, and of course, that was the whole idea.

It wasn't really the ring. It was what it represented, that she was going to be married to the Doctor, that he had asked her to be his wife and that she—after she'd regained her voice—had agreed. It was something she'd never even dared let herself think about, but now that she was engaged, she seemed to be a different person. From her new vantage point as his fiancée, she could look back on who she'd been and see the uncertainty she'd learned to live with, the knowledge that despite his confessions of love and his displays of consuming passion, in practical terms, she'd really been nothing more than his mistress, whose status could've changed at his slightest whim. She hadn't known how insecure and racked by doubt she'd been, how high she'd gone without a net. Now his proposal of marriage made everything all right, and she could look down now without fear and marvel at how far she'd come.

Abigail's elation was so great that it even drove thoughts of last night out of her mind—a significant feat since the experience had left her terribly shaken. She suspected that it had been her uneasy feelings over that *ménage à trois* that had prompted the Doctor to make his proposal early, several days before he'd intended, but that didn't bother her. He'd obviously meant to pop the question somewhere in the next few days, and whether now or later was beside the point.

In any case, everything had changed so much that when she and the Doctor joined Darcy and his companion for lunch the next day, Abigail found that any residual embarrassment she felt about last night's encounter was dispelled by the warmth of Darcy's sincere expressions of happiness and his very real desire for their joy together.

Darcy's companion was an elegant blonde lady named Virginia Cecil, the wife of a wealthy land speculator who was currently in Oklahoma territory, laying claim to as much property as he could, now that statehood seemed likely. Mrs. Cecil was obviously unsuited to frontier life and so had elected to spend her time amidst the civilized amenities of London and Paris, from which she was now returning to her home in St. Louis. She was older than Abigail, quite worldly and knowing, and while her manners and conversation were above reproach, she still carried an exciting hint of continental decadence and of the Parisian demimonde and art set.

Mrs. Cecil made no secret of the physical nature of her attachment to Darcy, and Abigail suddenly found herself in the unusual position of now being the virtuous one—a legitimate fiancée rather than a romantic lover—and she was surprised to find herself envying them and almost resenting the role of wife-to-be, with all its implications of stodgy domesticity.

As Virginia talked on about the romance and excitement of bohemian Paris, Abigail found herself sneaking surreptitious glances at the married couples around her, and she couldn't help notice the stolid, impassive faces, the lack of conversation, the looks of general boredom, if not thinly disguised hostility. She dearly wanted to be the Doctor's wife, but as lunch progressed, she found herself just beginning to worry about what marriage and commitment might do to the sexual passion and desire upon which their relationship was based.

The Doctor noticed Abigail's thoughtfulness at lunch, and he asked her about it as they strolled the deck after leaving Darcy and Virginia at the card room.

"Will you grow tired of me after we're married?" she asked him by way of reply. "I've seen it happen with so many other couples. I would die if it happened to us, after what you've shown me. Truly, I don't think I could live without what we have now."

"It won't happen with us, because I'm taking steps," he said. "All the training, the things I'm teaching you. The boredom you mention that sets in after some years of marriage—for boredom is what it is—has its roots in complacency and laziness. Complacency sets limits on our freedom, and laziness keeps us prisoner. Together, they destroy a couple's passion because they make everything so tediously predictable. Once you know your mate and have found their limits, there's little one can do to keep the freshness alive, and the bonds of love become bonds of servitude.

"We will have no limits, you and I," he added. "That's why I'm having you do what we're doing."

He was leaning on the rail and now he looked up at Abigail. She gave him a smile, but he saw that she wasn't quite convinced. Still, the sight of her in her white dress with the light of the sun filtering through the white parasol moved him deeply, and he felt a sudden pang of desire for her.

"Never mind that now." He gave a dismissive laugh. "Tell me though, now that we are engaged, do you find your feelings about last night have changed?"

"Why should my feelings have changed?"

"I assumed that a significant part of your uneasiness came from feeling that I was giving you away to other men. That you felt it tempered my commitment to you."

She was reluctant to broach the subject again. The fact was, that despite her ease at lunch, toward the end, she had found herself thinking again about Darcy on his knees before her, his thick cock in his hand, masturbating as the Doctor held her tight, a prisoner to another man's lust. The thought of her reaction to that lust still filled her with shame, but she was aware now of some other feeling in there as well, something dangerously exciting and forbidden that seemed to offer an antidote to her present fears.

"Is that what you think?" The ring on her finger gave her a new and unaccustomed boldness. "Don't you think that my own self-respect and sense of integrity might have something to do with it? The trust I had in you?"

Her words came out with an unexpected sharpness, and the Doctor looked at her. "You find that trust betrayed?"

"Well, I do wonder whether this is how you intend to keep the freshness in our marriage. By whoring me out to other men."

She was sorry as soon as she'd said it, but she could hardly take it back. She felt his eyes upon her, and she had no choice but to stand by her words, harsh as they were. Something was nagging at her, and she didn't know what it was.

"When I pledged myself to you, Doctor, I pledged myself to *you*. I did not know I would be shared with all and sundry, merely for your amusement. I entrusted you with my dignity and with my reputation. I…"

"Stop." He stood up from the rail. She saw that she had gone too far. The ring on her finger had made her perhaps too bold, and she felt the sudden surge of anger inside him.

"You forget yourself, my dear," he said, biting out the words. "Your pride has gotten the better of you. I've told you that my feelings for you after last night are unchanged. If anything, they are deeper than before. Your dignity is uncompromised, at least for me. I can see though, that's it's not the same for you. This sense of being ill-used, this fit of self-righteousness, is out of place and does you no credit."

She opened her mouth to speak but he cut her off.

"You must learn, my darling, that you are not your body. I can command your body, I cannot command your feelings, nor your spirit. It is your spirit that I love.

"Men may have several lovers. It doesn't seem to affect their feelings of dignity. Why should it be different for a woman? Is your person so much more valuable than mine? Are you so much more delicate?"

"It's different for a woman," she said.

"Yes. That's what we always hear. And why should this be? Could it just be another word for selfishness? For the power a woman exercises over a man? Yes, I shared you with another. I watched as another man gave you pleasure, and it was terribly arousing, wonderfully gratifying to me. And I daresay it was arousing to you as well, and I wonder if that's what's at the bottom of this. That it's not I who betrayed you, Abigail. It's yourself, your own pride.

"You pledged yourself to me, did you not?" he went on. "And yet, here I find your pledge was false. Here I find you choose not to give me everything after all. You cling to your pride, to your petite bourgeois notion of 'self-respect' and modesty…"

He stood back from the rail, words failing him. He looked at her for a moment, and the anger in his eyes sent a thrill of fear through her body. She wondered how this beautiful day had suddenly led to this, but at the same time, there was something gratifying in his anger. It gave her a sudden thrill she hadn't experienced since he'd first put the ring on her finger. She welcomed it.

"Come," he said suddenly, and he stood aside for her.

She knew where to go, and she walked ahead of him down the stairs to their cabin, willing herself to go slowly. She had to fight an urge to run, though whether she meant to run from him or toward him she didn't know. Her mind was suddenly a whirl of confusion and excited dread. His anger, she realized, was the same as his lust. For her, they were one and the same, and she longed for that hot rage.

"Lock the door," he said when they were inside. "And remove your gown."

Had she provoked him on purpose? She didn't know. All she knew was that some part of her thrilled to have her master back. She'd thought she'd lost him.

She disrobed under his gaze with trembling fingers, feeling more vulnerable and excited than she had in weeks. Still, she wasn't fast enough, and before her gown was fully undone, he reached out and took her wrist, pulling her toward him as her dress fell around her shoulders. Then his lips were on hers and his hands were on her body with an urgent savagery that left her breathless. Yes, she wanted this. She needed this from him. It was as he'd said, he owned her body—it belonged to him. Certainly her breasts and her lips were of no use to her. It was his hands and his desire that made them worth anything at all.

When he broke the kiss, his eyes were still smoldering, hot enough to cause a delicious melting feeling in the pit of her stomach, and farther down.

"The leather corset with the rings," he said sharply, standing in the barred sunlight that came in through the blinds over the windows. "Put it on."

She knew the one he meant. It was of sturdier leather than the others, set with lacing and metal rings around the waist. Abigail ruffled through her drawer, stepping out of her dress and underclothes as she did. She dared not anger him further. Already he was looking through his collection of crops and whips, and she knew she'd best not delay.

"Turn around," he commanded when she presented herself to him. The corset was set with laces in the front and back, and she could not reach the back laces herself. He'd only had her wear this particular garment once, and then he'd left the back fairly loose. He'd been much calmer then, more willing to be gentle.

Now he pulled the laces tight, tugging on them with impatience, cinching her in tightly so that the top of the garment dug into her full breasts right across the sensitive discs of her nipples. She could feel the anger and strength in his hands as he bound her in, and when she gasped, he took advantage of her sharp intake of breath to make the laces even tighter, until the leather creaked. It was like the embrace of a boa constrictor, tighter than her own skin. The corset nipped in at her waist and exaggerated the voluptuous spread of her hips, pushed her breasts up and out not far from her chin, turning her into a caricature of a woman, exaggerating her feminine ripeness.

He spun her around and pushed her back against the wall, then pulled her head back to accept his raping kiss. His hands squeezed her breasts painfully, and Abigail felt the wetness gush helplessly between her legs. His wildness infected her, and when he dug his fingers into the soft flesh of her sex and found her already swollen and wet, she snarled and bit his shoulder.

"Little minx!" he spat. He pulled her away from the wall and spun her around again so that her back was to him, pulled her arms back and tied her elbows so closely together that her breasts half-spilled over the top of the restricting garment. From the waist up, she was totally immobilized, her chest forced out by the unnatural constriction of her arms. He turned her roughly back to face him and sucked and bit at her proffered breasts as she mewled in excited helplessness. He grabbed at her hair, pulling the pins from it so that it spilled wildly down over her shoulders. He gathered it in his hands and pushed her back against the wall again.

"No!" she exclaimed, "No!" when what she meant was "yes". His excitement and rage thrilled her. She was totally helpless in his grasp and it drove her wild with desire for him. She wanted to be hurt, punished, whatever he wanted to do to her.

He pulled her away from the wall and pushed her down on the bed, upsetting a smoking stand and sending it crashing to the carpeted floor. With her arms pinioned so cruelly behind her back, she fell on her chest and face. She turned her head to the side for breath and at that moment, he slapped her naked bottom hard, catching her by surprise, making her yelp in shock.

"Get on the bed. Lie flat and spread your legs!" he hissed at her, and as she crawled awkwardly onto the bed, dragging her breasts across the cover, he went to his valise. He took two pieces of rope, tied one around each of her legs, just below her knees, then he retrieved a sliding steel spreader bar from the case and locked it open.

In order to attach the bar to the rope on her legs, Abigail had to get on her knees, her face on the mattress, her bottom in the air. He got her collar from the top drawer of her bureau, sat down on the bed and put it around her throat, moving her hair out of the way in order to buckle the collar around her neck. As soon as she felt the cool leather against her skin, the reassuring weight of the metal rings, Abigail closed her eyes in pleasure. How good it felt, more natural than the ring on her finger, as if she'd been undressed without it. She felt herself tremble in anticipation.

"This is how you women are, isn't it?" He worked at the buckles. "You act as though butter wouldn't melt in your mouth, as if your reputation is beyond price. And then in the privacy of your bedroom with your lover at your side, the things you want to do and have done to you would shame the very devil himself. Wouldn't they, Abigail? Wouldn't they?"

She didn't answer. She was on fire for him but she dared not give in and show her desire. Kneeling on the bed with her naked breasts crushed beneath her and her ass in the air inflamed her, spoke to something deep and needful in her nature, something wild and dangerous that could only be set free when she was tied and helpless like this.

He pushed her over, got up and came back with a length of silver chain that he attached from one knee, up through her collar, and down to the other knee, forcing her knees up against her chest, making it impossible for her to lower her legs. She couldn't move at all now, and he had to bodily pick her up and set her back on her knees, her chest and face pressed into the bedcover.

Abigail was breathing hard, panting with anxiety and desire. In all the times he'd tied her up for his sexual pleasure, she'd never felt so helpless or been made to feel more submissive. It wasn't just the way she was bound with her arms trussed behind her. It was the excruciatingly snug grip of the leather corset as well, holding her stomach in and forcing her breasts and hips into lurid prominence, as if she were nothing but a leather-wrapped sex toy. She could feel how swollen and shamefully wet she was—with her legs held open, there was no way she could disguise it—and she knew that he could see it as well. She knew he could see because he sat down on the bed and leaned forward, running his hands up the insides of her thighs and over her naked bottom, soothing the spot he'd just spanked. Then he dipped down and ran his thumb slowly along the length of her slit, testing her.

"Wet," he said with lewd satisfaction. "Soaking wet. You love this, darling, don't you?"

Shame and excitement fought within her, and before she could even think to answer, he slapped her ass again, leaving the red print of his hand on her skin.

"What else do you have that you've been holding out on me, Abigail? Your pride? Your precious self-respect? You're as excited as you've ever been, aren't you, my darling? Just waiting for me to take it from you. To take everything from you."

She wanted to cry out, *Yes! Take everything from me!* For she knew he already owned all she had to give. Yes, she was a whore for him, willing to do anything he wanted, willing to be plundered and used for his pleasure, willing to put up with anything in exchange for the hot rage of his lust. All she wanted now was for him to confirm it by giving her the punishment she desired, the punishment she deserved for being such a whore for him.

He got off the bed and she didn't have to watch him to know that he was going for a whip. He chose one from his case and swung it experimentally through the air, and she could tell from the sound alone it was a crop, long and supple. She closed her eyes, almost swooning in expectant excitement.

"Don't make a sound." He knelt on the bed. "Not a word."

No, no, she wouldn't. The door was louvered, the walls were thin. The sound of the thrumming steam engines was not loud enough to drown out any screams, whether of pleasure or pain. Abigail held her breath and concentrated on making him lift his hand, raise the crop into the air. She saw it in her mind's eye, hovering over her naked buttocks. She could see it trembling in the strength of his grip, his anger and desire. She pushed her ass up back to him, wanting it.

Whapp!

The pain seared through her and Abigail bit her lip to keep from crying out in joy. She could feel it—his lust, his rage and need for her in the lash of the crop on her eager flesh. Nothing had ever felt so right.

Slapp!

He hit her again and Abigail sobbed into the duvet, hot tears of gratification squeezing from between her lashes.

The Doctor put his hand on her smarting flesh, feeling her where he'd whipped her, then used his thumb to open her and smear her excited juices over her exposed labia, shaming her with her own arousal. He pushed his thumb against her and it slipped easily into her wetness, stretching her open. His other fingers curled up outside against her shaved mound while his thumb pressed down against her inside wall, looking for the bundle of nerves that was clustered there, right beneath the tip of his thumb. He found it and bore down, stroking with his thumb even as the lash began to fall again against the pale and trembling whiteness of her ass.

It was like nothing she'd ever experienced before—a new kind of sexual arousal. The sensations from the place he was touching inside her were bizarre and unfamiliar, a profound and disquieting kind of pleasure as if he'd somehow found a direct link to her sexual core, more general and less distinct than the sensations she was accustomed to, but even more intense. And meanwhile, the crop punctuated her growing rapture with sharp stripes of brilliant pain, mixing heaven and hell inside her, as he drove her into the arms of her slutty and shameful desires, whipping all her defenses away, exposing her to her bare soul of subservient sexual desire.

And then his thumb was gone. She felt him move on the bed behind her and she took advantage of the lapse of sensation to turn her face to the other cheek, where she could see herself in the dressing mirror, trussed up on her knees like a piece of poultry, her bottom thrust lewdly up into the air, without dignity, without escape.

The Doctor was watching her face in the mirror too, lust incandescent in his eyes. He gave her just a moment to catch her breath, and then she saw him reach out a finger and felt it press against her defenseless anus.

"Ahh!" she cried, forgetting her pledge to be silent.

He had touched her there before, had even inserted his finger during sex, but she knew that this time would be different. He had never given her bottom this kind of single-minded attention before. She knew what was coming, and rolled her head back to hide her face in the duvet so he wouldn't see her excitement and shame.

He got off the bed and came back with a jar of some sort of ointment. He scooped some up with his fingers and spread it over her anus, working it around and dipping inside her, making her breath catch in her throat. It was cold and greasy, yet soothing at the same time, and the feeling of his fingers working smoothly into her rectum felt terribly lewd and degrading even as it called forth feelings of a deep and primitive pleasure.

"No..." Abigail groaned, and was rewarded with another sharp slap on her buttocks that tore her mind suddenly off the weird sensations of being so rudely violated.

He slid another finger inside, and now she could feel them moving within her, even hear the thick, viscous sound as they slid in and out of her rectum. There was nothing she could do to stop it. Her arms were pinned behind her and her thighs kept wide apart by the steel bar between her knees and by the chain that ran from her legs to her leather collar, keeping her hog-tied on hands and chest and knees. She had no choice but to put her face down and take it, feel what he was doing to her, the pain of being stretched, the nagging pleasure at the base of her brain that raised goose bumps on her neck and breasts. She knew what he was going to do and she wanted it. She only prayed she would be able to stand it.

"That's two fingers," he said. "That's enough."

He slowly removed his fingers, leaving Abigail with confused feelings of loss and relief. Quickly, he stripped off his trousers and shorts. She couldn't keep her eyes from his cock, huge and erect, his balls hanging free, big and heavy with semen. He had never looked so much like an animal as he did now in the subdued daylight of the cabin—like a wild stallion, hard and virile, his muscles swollen and his cock rampant and aroused. He climbed up on the bed behind her and got himself in place and she felt the hair on his body pressing against her whipped and sensitive ass. He was just like an animal—like a hairy and rutting goat, a wild bull.

"This is what you need," he said as he got himself in place. "This will take care of your pride. This will remind you of whom you belong to!"

Abigail held her breath as she felt the knob of his cock slide down the crease of her ass, looking for her opening. She was already dilated from his fingers, and his shaft naturally lodged against the tight ring of muscle and lay there warm and throbbing, the head velvety soft over the steely tautness within. She gritted her teeth and clenched her eyes tight as she felt him take her buttocks in his big hands and spread her apart, and then he pressed against her with all the force in his body, implacable, ineluctable. She felt herself give.

He slid inside with a groan, throwing his head back in triumph. Abigail's jaw dropped at the unbelievable sensation.

She forgot herself and sobbed, "Oh God!" as her toes dug into the cover of the bed in an instinctive attempt to escape. But once he was inside, it was not as bad as she'd feared. She felt him there, throbbing softly, filling her with a pressure that was both obscene and wickedly pleasurable.

With the head of his cock now inside her, he seemed temporarily satisfied and his forward pressure relented, allowing her a moment to adjust. She cracked her eyes open and looked in the mirror and saw him in his flush of male victory, powerful and triumphant, his spear lodged in her virginal ass. She saw the strength in his shoulders and arms, the corded muscles of his thighs. He looked like something out of mythology, like Neptune rising from the waves, and despite her discomfort, she thrilled at her lover's power and overwhelming masculinity, almost as if she shared in his carnal triumph over her obsequiously kneeling form.

Her vicarious thrill lasted only a moment though, because he put his hands on her hips and began to push into her again, holding her still, forcing his way into her body, taking possession of her. She bore down—she didn't know what else to do—and somehow that made his entrance easier. She felt his hard rod slide into her ass, filling her with sensations that were both obscenely thrilling and terribly degrading. Hot spears of feeling tore down through her legs and up her spine, into her breasts, a lewd and maddening sensation.

He gave her time to get used to it. He let her body adjust to being so completely conquered, and when he felt her begin to relax and tremble with renewed lust, he began to fuck her, slowly, barely moving, his thick cock slipping in then out of the tight clutch of her rectum. Each withdrawal made her feel as though he were pulling her insides out with him—each slow, insistent push filled her again with his hard male flesh.

The corset crushed her in its embrace, his cock filled her, and the ropes and chains held her tight. As he began to move inside her, Abigail was consumed with a raw need to be fucked like this, to be conquered and taken, to be owned and possessed by him.

He grabbed her hair and pulled her face to the side.

"Let me see you, you gorgeous whore!" he gasped. "Let me see everything you feel with my big cock in your ass! Do you like it? You love it, don't you? Tell me how you love it, Abigail! Tell me!"

She couldn't speak, couldn't bear his eyes on her. She knew her face was a mask of obscene and degraded pleasure and yet she couldn't possibly control it, couldn't keep from showing what she felt. She did love it. She loved being owned and used by him, and he was right—she had no more pride. She was his totally. Everything she had was his.

He reached around her, found the sodden flesh between her legs and dug his fingers in, looking for the center of her pleasure. He knew how she liked to be touched, knew what drove her wild and what brought her release. He forked his fingers around her greasy little clit and began to slide them back and forth in time to his big shaft sliding in and out of her stretched ass.

Abigail's head swam. She wanted to scream but she had no breath. She snarled like an animal, egging him on, her teeth exposed. She began to pant in quick shallow breaths, overcome with sensation.

He felt her body begin to twitch and spasm as it always did before she came. He pulled her hair back from her red and sweating face so he could see her as she succumbed to her orgasm, as she surrendered to the maelstrom of release caused by his cock in her ass. He was close, holding on only so he could time it just right. Time it for when she was about to peak, for when her breathing stopped, for when her whole body went tight...

"Ahhh!"

She screamed so loudly he had to clamp his hand over her mouth, and as he did, he let himself go, pulling himself from her ass and driving his cock up the crease between her buttocks so that it stood up like a fountain. He leaned back, his face a mask of furious ecstasy as his cock jerked and geysered, jetting his hot cum a foot into the air to land on her hair, her bound arms, her back, the leather corset, one gush after another, with all the force of his shattering release...

Chapter Fourteen

It was a mystery to her.

She loved him with a love that almost frightened her, and yet when they made love, it seemed to be his anger that thrilled her. She realized now that she had goaded him earlier that afternoon. She had spoken with the full intention of bringing forth that side of him that she loved so much, that sexual animal that bound her and used her and took from her whatever he wanted. She was afraid of losing that part of him, losing him to the tedium of marriage.

Yet, why did she find this violence, this cruelty, so terribly exciting, so wonderfully fulfilling?

She would have liked to talk to him about it, but whenever she tried, the Doctor would go off into discussions of Mr. Darwin's ideas and the theories of some obscure Dr. Freud of Vienna—the male's desire to conquer and the female's to be conquered, if only symbolically. Theories were all well and good, but they didn't help Abigail understand the feelings she had inside, and this was her main concern.

But if the Doctor was unable to help her, Abigail found an unexpected confidante and kindred spirit in the person of Mrs. Virginia Cecil, who seemed to have a genuine fondness for her and who was always willing to talk and, more importantly, to listen.

From the first, Virginia had made no secret of the fact that her feelings for Abigail went beyond being sisterly. In Paris, Virginia had affairs—affairs with men, affairs with women, affairs with both, and from their first conversation together over tea and cakes in the salon, Virginia had quite openly expressed her sexual interest in Abigail and had, in fact, invited Abigail to share her bed. To her own very great surprise, Abigail had taken no great offense, had not even found the idea disconcerting, certainly not as disconcerting as she had found the experience with Darcy. If anything, she enjoyed basking in the older woman's lavish attention, and was not above occasionally playing the flirt herself at Virginia's expense. Virginia was so worldly and sophisticated that Abigail found her attentions extremely flattering. She said nothing to the Doctor about it, of course—it was her own little indulgence, a secret between her and Virginia.

That changed the day the steamboat docked at Vicksburg. Virginia was arranging Abigail's hair that afternoon in her suite of rooms, showing her the latest Paris style, when they crossed over that indefinable line between friendly affection and something more potent.

Mrs. Cecil had been brushing out Abigail's hair, talking of Paris and of Natalie Barney and her lesbian lover poet, Rene Vivien, the scandalous theatrical productions they had staged, their provocative public behavior in the salons. Abigail was leaning back, eyes closed, adrift in a sensual trance that came from having her hair attended to, soothed by the rhythmic tug and glide of the brush, half-listening to Virginia's hypnotic words, when the older woman suddenly stopped, leaned over, and pressed her warm lips to the side of Abigail's neck.

Virginia's lips were gentle and undemanding. The kiss was more like a compliment than it was anything overtly sexual, an appreciation of Abigail's feminine beauty, though it clearly hinted at things far beyond friendship. Abigail, eyes closed in a semi-trance, didn't mind at all. She let her head loll to the side and accepted the kiss as her due, sighing in pleasure. She felt her nipples begin to peak from the sheer sensuality rather than from any sexual arousal.

"Such a beauty," Virginia said softly, stroking her hair. "What they would do to you in Paris, I can just imagine."

Abigail smiled, her mind still afloat in a sea of hazy sensuality. Virginia slipped her hands down over the front of

Abigail's gown and took her breasts in her hands, admiring their weight and firmness. Her lips went back to Abigail's neck, tender and worshipful, and now Abigail could feel the older woman's desire. It was so different than a man's urgent need, slow and languid, promising a deep and gentle fulfillment if only Abigail would surrender.

"I would adore you," Virginia said as she kissed her way up to Abigail's ear. "I would take all night with you. I would show you what love can be like."

Abigail was near melting, her blood like warm honey in her veins. The woman's touch was so sweet and undemanding, so easy to accept.

"No," Abigail said reluctantly. "No, I can't, Virginia."

"Ginny," the older woman corrected. "But you want to. You know you do."

Abigail smiled. "Perhaps I do. But wouldn't that be betrayal? I am engaged."

"Betrayal?" Virginia laughed. "Then ask him. If the Doctor is anything like other men, I doubt he'd feel betrayed to find us in bed together. Go ahead and ask him." She bent over and kissed Abigail's ear, then ran her tongue around the rim. "Ask him and then come back and tell me how he looks when you do. But come back alone this time. Come for tea. I'll wait for you."

As she walked back to her cabin, Abigail thought about how much power there was in being sexually desirable. Beauty and wealth, brains and talent, all the world admired those— people fought and clawed for them. But this sexuality...it came so easily to her, and she was quite amazed at what an advantage it was to be desired.

Back in their own cabin, the Doctor's face was much as Mrs. Cecil had imagined it as Abigail told him of her encounter, and his look of incredulity and excitement made her beam with secret delight. Of course, he was wildly aroused by the thought of Abigail having sex with another woman—she entirely expected that. What really delighted her was that this was something she had done on her own. She had seized the erotic initiative, something she knew that he had doubted she could do, and, since he wasn't invited to her soiree with Mrs. Cecil, he would be the one on the outside this time. It would be a perfect payback for what he'd made her do with Darcy.

"Virginia Cecil? A lesbian?" he asked, his journals he'd been reading quite forgotten. "I would have scarce believed it, although I should have known had I given it any thought. Of course, London, Paris, it makes perfect sense. The set she ran with is quite bohemian, very radical in their habits. But you, Abigail, weren't you scandalized? After your reaction to Darcy…"

"Not at all." She turned away from him and removed her hat so as to hide the smile on her face. "It's quite different when it's another woman. There's none of this business about fidelity and ownership. It's very sisterly, really."

"Sisterly?" he echoed.

She threw herself on their bed, quite delighted with his discomfiture.

"Well, yes. It's much easier to accept a woman's touch. For me, at least. After all, didn't you tell me that there was no real difference between a friendly embrace and making love? 'It's only a matter of degree' you said. I remember it exactly."

"Well, yes, I suppose I did. But you must know that she doesn't mean to be satisfied with a friendly embrace. Do you know anything about Sapphic love, Abigail?"

"Not really. No more than what my desires tell me. But I'm not a child anymore, darling. I know what adults do."

"And?"

"And I find it quite exciting. Flattering, really, but exciting too."

She sat up and began to rearrange her hair. It needed no arranging, but fixing her hair lifted her arms and brought her breasts into prominence so that he could have a good look at her. Teasing him was an unfamiliar experience, but it was wonderful fun. He was so helpless.

The Doctor stared at her for a long moment, then dropped his eyes back to his scientific journal and looked at it as if it were written in Mandarin Chinese.

"Shall you see her again?" he asked. "In an amorous sense, I mean."

"Yes, I intend to see her for tea, after a short nap," she said sweetly. "But that's what I wanted to ask you about, darling. You are my master, after all, and I do belong to you. I would need your permission."

"Yes, well… Yes. I'm all for it." He tried to keep the eagerness out of his voice. "I think it's an important part of your education. Yes."

He shifted in his seat. "Unfortunately, I have business in Vicksburg this afternoon, so I won't be able to accompany you."

"Why ever should I need your company, my love?" she asked innocently, picking up her hat and taking it to the closet.

"Well, if Darcy's going to take part…"

"Darcy is not involved. This is between us girls. No men are invited."

She emerged from the closet and saw the hangdog look on his face. Really, he was just too predictable.

"Don't fret, my lord." She came over to his chair and caressed his face. "If it works out, I'm sure you'll get your chance."

* * * * *

In truth, Abigail couldn't say whether she decided to accept Virginia's invitation because of her own desires or whether it was just to make the Doctor squirm. Probably it was a bit of both. She truly liked Virginia. The woman was beautiful, cultured, sensuous, and wealthy — and very well-connected to boot. Plus, Abigail was quite simply curious. She was quite sensitive to a woman's beauty and bearing, and had often wondered of late what it must be like to make love to a woman. And then, it just seemed so deliciously wicked.

Virginia had the largest cabin on the ship, a full three-room suite on the upper deck. Abigail presented herself at Mrs. Cecil's door at 4:00 p.m. and was met with a gracious welcome. She didn't have to say why she'd come, it was perfectly understood.

"Come in, come in," Virginia said as she showed her in. "Darcy's playing cards, and I told him I don't want to be disturbed. We have all afternoon. Sit, darling, sit. I've brought my brush. Let me do your hair again. You do like it so when I brush your hair, and I love to see the look on your face. It will help relax you, too."

It was the perfect suggestion, because Abigail was more than a little nervous now. The Doctor had left for his business appointments most reluctantly, after making her promise to tell him everything when he got back, and his eager excitement had rubbed off on her, making her anxious and causing her to suddenly doubt the wisdom of what she was about to do. She trusted Virginia, and she was sure that the older woman would stop whenever Abigail said the word, but still, this was a big step for her.

Virginia served her French absinthe, and after two glasses, Abigail's anxiety lessened and she felt a delicious lethargy settle into her limbs. As before, Virginia spoke to her softly as she brushed her hair, talking of the delights of lesbian love, speaking slowly, hypnotically.

"When a woman makes loves to a woman, it is done quietly, with tranquility and consideration. We know how to draw forth the pleasure that we have locked inside, how to coax out the deepest feelings and most delicious sensations. We take our time, we do not hurry. A lingering kiss, an hour upon the breasts, soft, tender kisses on the abdomen, slowly calling Venus from her depths, slowly joining her in her dance of delight, spiraling, arousing, opening one another like the petals of the rose, to drink the dew, imbibe the nectar, to drift off down the river of joy, the lotus land of bliss…"

The brush in her hair, the caressing words, the warmth of the liquor—they all worked to put Abigail in a sensuous and languid mood. She felt nothing like the need she felt with the Doctor, the urge to be taken and used. Instead, she felt herself falling into a kind of sensual enchantment, lulled by Virginia's hands and voice.

When Virginia's lips came down on hers, as soft as the rose petals she'd alluded to, Abigail closed her eyes and let the woman take her away. The kiss was sweet and generous, free of any invasive tongues or scratchy beards. Instead, Virginia kissed her lips with tiny kisses, savoring her. Abigail was conscious of Ginny's French perfume, the soft caress of the older woman's lips, the taste of her as they kissed. At first, Abigail resisted instinctively, but Virginia's lips were sweet and insistent, and soon she felt herself respond to the erotic urging. What did gender matter anyway? It was love that mattered, love and desire.

Abigail opened her eyes slightly and saw Ginny's eyes closed in pleasure. She was so much more gentle and accepting than a man. Abigail felt herself sink into the chair. She parted her lips and gave herself over to Virginia's love.

It was so much sweeter than with the Doctor, much more prolonged. The kiss stretched into an infinity of tenderness. Ginny's tongue was sweetly inquisitive, a gentle bee in the flower of her mouth. Abigail wasn't even aware of the older woman's fingers on the buttons of her dress until she felt the softness of Virginia's hands on her breasts, heard Virginia moan with pleasure as she lowered her face to kiss Abigail's nipples and run a teasing tongue around them.

The chair creaked softly as Virginia got to her knees at Abigail's feet and lowered her mouth to Abigail's breasts, kissing and sucking tenderly, massaging them in a way that brought a deep, sweet pleasure to the younger woman's body. As she sucked her nipples, Ginny's hand slid up under Abigail's skirt and found the soft flesh at the top of her thighs. Abigail moaned and opened her legs, but Virginia denied her what she most wanted, content to just tease, stroking lightly at the inside of her thighs, ever closer to Abigail's center but never getting there.

"Mmmm, Virginia…" Abigail sighed. "That's so lovely…"

"Yes, my baby," the older woman answered. "Just relax. Let me love you."

The long, slow, kissing continued, the teasing of her legs. Virginia's hand even dropped down between Abigail's buttocks to tease her there, causing Abigail to hunch lower in the chair and spread her legs in lewd invitation to the invading fingers. That feeling of slow languor began to fade, replaced by a sweet sexual urgency and impatience. Abigail's breasts felt heavy and full—she felt tight and congested, and she began to ache for a stronger touch. She had soaked through her drawers, and as Ginny continued to tickle her thighs under the humid tent of her dress, Abigail's hips began to pump slowly in a shameless imitation of the coitus she desired.

It was sweet to lie there and be loved like that, to be the passive one and let Virginia be the aggressor. It absolved Abigail of guilt, but it also deprived her of any way to control the action. She was ready for something more than foreplay now, she was ready for the real thing now, but her entreaties to Virginia had no effect.

"Please, Ginny, touch me now!" she moaned, writhing in the chair. "I need it so, please!"

Virginia only smiled and gave Abigail's nipple a little tug with her teeth.

Abigail began to twist in the chair. She opened her legs wide, took Virginia's wrist and pushed her hand against her aching sex as she ground her hips salaciously, groaning in pleasure at being touched at last. Virginia's eyes were hot with lust as she watched the girl shamelessly trying to work herself off, and Abigail, conscious that she was being watched, let herself go, putting on a show, letting Virginia see just how hot she was, how badly she needed relief. She went so far as to caress her own breasts, rolling her nipples between her fingers, and as she did so, she watched Virginia's face. It was exciting to see the fever in the sophisticate's eyes as Abigail acted out for her.

"Ooh, you are a little slut, aren't you, Abigail?" Virginia asked in a low voice. "A naughty little slut, just like me!"

"Are you a naughty slut?" Abigail asked her, looking straight into her eyes and shuddering as Virginia's fingers found her clit. "A big girl like you? Are you bad too?"

"Yes, I'm bad," Virginia whispered hotly, rising up to kiss Abigail's lips. "I'm very, very bad. I'm going to show you how bad…"

Ginny stood up and Abigail watched as the blonde took a few steps back and then removed her dress. Beneath it, she wore only a black corset, decorated with little yellow bows the exact color of her hair; her pubic hair slightly darker. She wore black French stockings that went to mid-thigh, the same as the Doctor had bought Abigail, held up by black garters. Her shoes were French too, and quite smart, with very high heels.

Virginia picked up her dress and draped it over a chair. "Now, you."

Abigail looked at her for a moment, her gaze hot. This was it, the moment of truth. Already she was feeling it again, that sexual wildness, that need to be bad, to show Virginia just how base and perverse she could be, to let her slutty side out. The fact that she was with a woman suddenly seemed to make no difference at all.

Abigail stood up tall, shoulders subtly back so that her breasts stood out, showing off her proud, tight bottom. She felt very sexual, very desirable, and she knew that Virginia wanted her, wanted her badly.

Abigail undid the buttons and removed her dress, letting it slide to the floor. She wore only a silk chemise and knickers in the modern style, snug and gauzy. She stood there looking at Virginia for a moment, then removed both undergarments and laid them aside. Virginia's eyes ran up and down her body and fastened on the smooth skin of her pubis, where a bare gleam of moisture could be plainly seen.

"Beautiful," Virginia breathed. "You are a whore, just like me. Aren't you?"

"Come and find out."

Virginia came to Abigail and put her arms around her, and Abigail reciprocated. Their kiss was hot now, and passionate, mouths open, nostrils flared, hands searching, tongues contending for some sort of dominance. Abigail was no longer satisfied with playing the passive role. There was something about seeing Virginia unclothed, something about the look of desire in her eyes that made her suddenly want to be aggressive. They kissed and Abigail felt Ginny's breasts against her own, a curious but not unpleasant sensation, nipples sliding against each other. She felt the older woman's pubic hair on her own naked flesh and ground against it.

Still kissing, Virginia pushed Abigail back into her chair and got down on her knees between the girl's legs. She took Abigail's breasts in her hands and squeezed them as she kissed Abigail's mouth with lips that were urgent and impatient. Virginia's corset still concealed her breasts from Abigail's searching hands and Abigail struggled to free them, but then, Ginny broke the kiss and straightened up, still on her knees. As Abigail watched, Ginny lifted her breasts from their confinement and then pulled the top of the garment down, letting them stand free.

Abigail leaned forward, took Virginia's breasts in her hands and began to kiss them.

"Oh yes, baby, yes!" Virginia hissed, looking down and caressing Abigail's face. "Bite them now. I like that. Bite them."

Abigail found herself growing inflamed. She kissed and bit the older woman's breasts, digging her teeth into the soft, perfumed flesh. Every bite brought a moan of passion from Ginny's lips, and every moan drove Abigail higher in her frenzy of lust. Virginia's breasts were so sweet, so warm and soft in her mouth, and the thought of what she was doing was so obscene, that suddenly, without thinking, Abigail reached around and slapped Virginia hard on the ass.

"Oooh!" Virginia sobbed. She threw her head back and shuddered, tried to cover the sob with a throaty laugh, but there was no hiding the fact that the slap had deeply aroused her and cracked her composure. Abigail could feel her tremble with excitement.

Abigail slapped her again and this time there was no laugh, just a hot gasp and a mewl of surrender. Virginia was losing her self-possession, and her body jerked with a little spasm of involuntary pleasure. Abigail recognized the spasm—a little frisson of pre-orgasmic excitement, a brief flash of overexcited nerves.

"Oh yes!" the blonde gasped. "Hit me again! Oh God, baby, I love that!"

"Yes?" asked Abigail, taking her lips from Ginny's breast. Her eyes were glowing hot with desire. "You like that? You like being spanked?"

She slapped Ginny again, then again and again.

Virginia's eyes were closed, her head back, her mouth open in sexual rapture.

"You like that?" Abigail asked her again. She realized that she suddenly sounded just like the Doctor. Those were the very words he said to her. "Are you a naughty little girl? Do you need to be spanked?"

"Oh God!" Virginia groaned. She reached for her own breasts and squeezed them hard.

Abigail felt a sudden surge of sexual excitement and physical power. She knew just what Ginny was feeling, that helpless desire to be used, to be spanked, abused, made the victim of another's lust. Seeing the older woman like that brought out something new and unexpected in Abigail—a desire to hurt her, to give her just what she wanted.

Dimly, she realized that this was what the Doctor must feel when he used her this way—the feeling of power, of overwhelming desire, and then she stopped thinking about it. The present was too real, the feelings too strong. She knew everything that Ginny was feeling, and now she knew what the Doctor must feel as well.

Abigail got to her feet, took Virginia by the arm and tried to lift her up, just as the Doctor had done to her so many times. But she wasn't the Doctor and she didn't have his strength.

"Come on, up!" she snapped at the blonde. "Get up, darling, up!"

The sound of her own voice barking orders gave her an eerie thrill.

Virginia got to her feet, totally submissive now, betrayed by her own desires, her half-lidded eyes glowing with hungry anticipation. Though she and Abigail had compared notes on sexual experiences, they had always been vague and never detailed. Abigail had no idea that this was what Ginny wanted, she had no way of knowing. She only knew it was what she herself wanted right now. She'd been played with and aroused for the better part of an hour and she ached for release, any kind of release. Her need made her boldly assertive.

"Here!" Abigail pulled Virginia over to a writing table that stood by the chair. "Stand here and lean over the desk."

Virginia obediently set her hands on the mahogany desk and leaned forward, spreading her legs, her breasts hanging pendulously over the polished surface, her ass jutting out. Abigail's hand already hurt from hitting her and she looked around for something else to use. Her eyes fastened on the hairbrush.

"Oh yes!" Virginia cried, as she followed her friend's eyes. "Oh, Abigail, please!"

"Shut up!" Abigail barked, then jumped at her own words. She might have laughed in embarrassment had she not been so terribly aroused.

She got behind Virginia, placed one hand on the small of the blonde's back, and slapped her ass with the hairbrush. The sound was like a gunshot in the room and Virginia squealed. The brush left a fat red welt. Virginia sobbed and fell forward, catching herself on her forearms.

"Yes, do it!" Virginia gasped, "Beat my ass. Make me feel it!"

Abigail hit her again, then again, her own lust rising with every stroke.

Virginia began a constant keening moan, punctuated by a little yelp whenever the brush landed. Her head was down, her fat tits pressed against the desktop, her fingers clawing at the smooth surface. With each blow, her ass quivered and she slid a little further along the desk.

Abigail wanted release. She needed release. She needed for someone to come—whether herself or Ginny hardly mattered. She reached around Virginia and without a second thought, pressed her fingers into the woman's pussy, the first time she had ever touched another woman's sex. Virginia was soaked. Her clit was turgid and erect, larger than Abigail's, a sweet pearl of pleasure.

"Oh God, oh God, I'm going to come!" Virginia wailed.

The brush came down, Virginia's buttocks quivered from the blow. Abigail's fingers worked in the blonde's cunt in violent, insistent circles, demanding that she orgasm. Two more blows and Ginny collapsed on the desk, crying out as she spasmed in violent release, her open mouth pressed against the desk.

Abigail didn't let her rest. She pulled Virginia's still quaking body away from the desk and climbed onto it herself, lying on her back and opening her legs. Virginia knew what to do. She bent over and put her mouth between Abigail's legs, dropping to her knees as the girl closed her thighs around the blonde's head.

Virginia's mouth and tongue worked on her as the blonde sobbed and moaned in the echoing throes of her orgasm. Abigail dug her fingers into Ginny's hair, holding her tight against her and rubbing her crotch against the woman's face. Her relief was immediate. As soon as Ginny's tongue parted her labia, Abigail felt herself rush up toward her climax. She felt wicked, obscenely depraved, but also wildly powerful, and to the heady rush of sexual fulfillment, there was the added thrill of knowing that she could do this. She could love and be loved by a woman, and if she could do that, there was nothing she couldn't do. She was free, wonderfully and totally free, and as if in celebration, her body arched off the desk as her orgasm ripped through her, complete and devastating, pleasure burning in every nerve of her body.

Now it was her turn to scream, and she bit the back of her hand to stifle her cry of release as she arched her back and her pussy spasmed and clenched at Virginia's tongue. The orgasm was intense, going on and on as her whole body jerked and convulsed atop the desk.

The next thing she knew, she was lying on the desk, her belly quaking still with the force of her come. Virginia was kissing her and sobbing, her tears hot against Abigail's skin.

"Oh, Abigail, Abigail! Oh, that was so good, baby! That was so good for me! That was so good…"

Abigail raised her hand and began to stroke Virginia's head, soothing her, calming her, while steeling herself now for the remorse and guilt she was sure would come, the bitter ashes of her perverted lust.

But as she stroked Virginia's hair, she caught the brilliant flash of the diamond on her finger, felt the weight of the ring on her hand, and she remembered everything.

Wait 'til she told the Doctor…

* * * * *

"I crossed some barrier today," Abigail said. "Of that I'm sure. I daresay you would have been proud of me."

They were standing at the rail outside their cabin watching the moonlight on the banks. This seemed to be their favorite place for conversing lately. Something about the steady progress, the way the banks slid away behind them, made talking easy, and they had been standing here ever since the steamboat left Vicksburg, as Abigail told the Doctor exactly what had transpired between Virginia Cecil and herself.

"I am proud. Fantastically proud. But what barrier is that, my dear?" He had listened raptly, the excited smile on his face impossible to conceal.

"I've made love with a woman," she said. "Don't you find that extraordinary? Now I don't think there's anything I can't do."

He put his arm around her and pulled her close.

"I do find it extraordinary," he said. "But then, I find you extraordinarily extraordinary."

He kissed her and Abigail smiled, quite pleased with herself.

"Now I suppose you'll want me to arrange another session with Ginny so that you can join in?"

"Oh, I don't know," he said. "I would have liked to have seen you two together, just as it excited me to see you with Darcy. But you seem to have done very well without me."

"But you do want to be there with us, don't you? You did tell me that every man yearns to have more than one woman at once. Virginia was very curious as to how you were as a lover, so I imagine she's quite looking forward to it."

He took his arm from around her so he could look in her eyes.

"Well, I'm sorry, but I'm not particularly interested in Virginia Cecil. I'm grateful to her for giving you such pleasure, and I would like to see you with her, just because it excites me wonderfully to see you get so sexually aroused. But really, you're the only woman I'm interested in."

Abigail looked at him blankly for a moment.

"You're serious?"

"I'm serious. Now come to bed and let me show you how serious I am, my extraordinary little slut."

Chapter Fifteen

The Opera House in St. Louis on a warm night—a sea of expectant faces, dinner jackets and gowns in every color imaginable, sparkling with the brilliance of the women's jewelry as the thunderous applause died away, ebbing in excited anticipation of the start of the next and final number. The cream of St. Louis society was assembled like jewels in a velvet box to hear Damiano Della Pavia, the dashing violin virtuoso who now stood illuminated in the glare of the arc lights. All eyes were upon him as he glanced at the conductor, his bow hovering over the strings of his Amati as he prepared to step into the allegro of Brahms' Violin concerto in D.

From their booth in the first balcony, Virginia Cecil and Abigail Du Pre leaned forward in their chairs. Both women looked especially fine, Mrs. Cecil in a black velvet gown that set off her fair complexion and golden blonde hair, Miss Du Pre in burgundy-colored silk with a shawl embroidered in the Chinese style. Mrs. Cecil wore an elaborate diamond necklace, while Abigail, her hair up in a fetching French twist, wore only a matching velvet choker adorned with an ivory silhouette set against an onyx background—white against black, innocence defined by experience. Abigail had borrowed Virginia's opera glasses so that she could get a better look at the young prodigy on stage, and she held her breath to steady them as she studied him closely. She had been studying him all night—his long hair, his soulful eyes and expressive face, his extraordinary hands—for she was looking at the man who she was to seduce that very night—Damiano Della Pavia, twenty-two years old, the toast of three continents. The arrangements had already been made.

The ladies' escorts, Mr. Darcy deLongville, and Dr. Lucien Trier, both in formal wear, relaxed in their chairs as Della Pavia tore into the music. That is, they relaxed as well as they could given the nearness of these very attractive women and their knowledge of what the night had in store for them following the concert.

The Doctor was Abigail's lover, her sexual master and teacher as well as her betrothed, and Abigail wore the symbol of their engagement prominently on her left hand. Their relationship was unique in that Abigail had come to him as chattel, as mere property paid to him in satisfaction of her cruel and uncaring father's long outstanding debt. The Doctor had introduced her to a world of sexual experience the likes of which Abigail had never imagined, but one she had rapidly made her own.

She had discovered in herself a capacity for pleasure and a talent for pleasing others so pronounced that she now considered sex her true calling. This was not to say that she had become in any way vulgar in her behavior or deportment, but she now realized that she was blessed with a rare gift for sexual pleasure. It was her shameful but exciting secret that within her genteel and refined exterior, she concealed a heart capable of the most consuming passion, a heart she felt that only the Doctor with his ropes and whip could summon forth.

The Doctor disagreed that he was the sole cause of this side of her, and this was what the Doctor was trying to teach her now—that it was she who controlled her passionate nature, not he. He was trying to accomplish this by arranging an assignation between Abigail and another man. The Doctor thought it essential that Abigail know another's caress, not only to show her what she was capable of feeling, but to show her that she was capable of physical pleasure even when there was no very strong affection.

His earlier attempt to share her with another man had not gone well. Abigail had finally responded—had, in fact, climaxed with unusual force as the Doctor held her and smothered her protests with kisses as Darcy, on his knees before her, used his tongue to bring her to orgasm. But this had left her with a nagging feeling of betrayal, despite the Doctor's repeated rationales and explanations. Things had changed, though, and now, having conducted her own lesbian affair with Mrs. Cecil, Abigail had a new perspective on the use of her body as an instrument of pleasure. The Doctor too had reconsidered, and had decided to change his approach, seeking out a man who appealed to Abigail, and giving her the opportunity to seduce him herself.

The music ended with a fine cadenza, the orchestra silent as Della Pavia stood alone, his bow flying as the notes burst from his violin in rapturous brilliance that brought some of the more emotional members of the audience to their feet with shouts and whistles, wholly unprecedented, as they cheered him on. He responded with such astonishing virtuosity and passion that when at last the music ended, the house reacted with an instant of stunned and perfect silence. The applause that followed was like a clap of thunder after the lightning had struck, but long and sustained, making the very balconies tremble, and there was no doubt that the audience would not be satisfied with anything less than several encores.

Abigail found herself on her feet along with all of them in the box, her heart in her throat and tears brimming in her eyes at the man's almost supernatural mastery of his instrument, and as he bowed low, his hair almost sweeping the floor, she wanted him as she had wanted few things in her life. She loved the Doctor, but this man had captured her heart.

"Are you staying?" Darcy asked the Doctor, raising his voice to be heard over the applause and shouts.

"For one or two encores perhaps, yes," the Doctor replied. "Are you leaving?"

"Yes, I think so," Darcy said, helping Virginia with her cloak. "Going to get back to the hotel and take off my monkey suit. We'll see you back there."

The Doctor saw them out—the boxes on this level were private—then locked the door after them before rejoining Abigail.

"Darcy's not one for music, I'm afraid."

"I can't imagine that," Abigail responded. "To be unmoved by such playing, such passion. I pity him."

The Doctor looked at her with a bit of fire in his eyes as on the stage below, Della Pavia quickly tuned his violin, holding it under his chin, and then raised his bow and nodded to the conductor. The audience quickly grew silent as the first notes of the encore began.

"Oh, I would spare my pity." The Doctor moved his chair closer to her. "Darcy finds his deepest pleasures in gambling, in games of chance. To each his own."

"And you, my dear?" she asked as he put his arm around her. "Where do you find your pleasure?"

The Doctor laughed. "You should know me by now, darling. I'm surprised you even have to ask."

Yes, she did know him, she knew him well. But still, he had the power to affect her as if she'd never been touched before. As Della Pavia's violin soared above the orchestra in a strain both beautiful and bitter, Abigail felt the Doctor's hand boldly slide up under the skirt of her dress in the darkness. Once she would have been scandalized by this, but now she couldn't repress an indulgent smile. It thrilled her to be desired, and to be desired so much that he would risk public scandal just to satisfy himself, just to touch her. After a moment's resistance for appearance's sake, she parted her legs slightly to give him access to what he desired. She was naked beneath her dress, of course, and her fingers tightened on the wooden arms of her chair as he found her bare flesh.

The melody swirled around her, sweet and cloying, as Abigail closed her eyes and felt his fingers working between her legs, teasing her. He almost always desired her to be naked beneath her outer clothes, such that her nakedness became a matter of familiarity to her. But now, with his warm hand upon the inside of her thigh, she remembered it all over again, how exposed she was, how wicked. His fingers were on her flesh, urging her, coaxing her. She was enjoying being a grand lady tonight, her hair perfect, her gown magnificent, but she knew that he was trying to call forth that shameless and wanton slut that she carried inside.

And she couldn't resist him—she never could. She tried, concentrating on the music, running her eyes over the dim forms of the listeners stretching away in the darkened balcony, but his fingers spoke to something deep inside yet always near the surface these days. At last she closed her eyes and let her head fall back against the chair. Her body slid imperceptibly down and she sighed deeply as she felt herself grow wet beneath his touch.

All those people in the boxes, she thought, could they see her? Could they guess what her lover was doing to her here in this public space? Could they sense her nipples hardening within the bodice of her gown, or read the look of rapt concentration on her face?

The music was lush and delicious now, the orchestra singing back to the violin while the violin soared, weightless, just out of reach. Abigail had been excited, sexually aroused ever since dinner in the fashionable restaurant where the Doctor and Darcy had finalized the arrangements for her encounter with Damiano, whom she'd met earlier that day. Now all the excitement was building to a feverish level in her body and she felt her breasts grow heavy, her loins ache with that sweet sexual hunger that the Doctor's fingers fed at present, but would not satisfy.

With a barely perceptible moan, Abigail gave up and turned to let her face rest against his chest, seeking refuge there, as if throwing herself on the mercy of the enemy. She raised a hand and caressed him through his shirt, then slid a finger inside against his warm, muscular body. When his fingers parted her labia, she dug her nail into his skin in warning.

"Oh, Lucien, please," she moaned. "Please stop. It's too much…"

"My delicious whore," he whispered. "Should I make you come? Should I make you climax in front of all these people?"

Such a lewd and delicious thought. He could do it too. He had that kind of power over her.

"Oh, my lord…" she sighed as he slid into her.

"Would you cry out, love? Would everyone turn and look at you, coming like a common slut on my finger? Should I tell them about the other man who's going to fuck you tonight? Will they all see what a whore you are beneath your fine gown and jewelry?"

She was long accustomed to this kind of talk from him, these terrible words, and she knew they belied his own lust and were not meant literally. He knew exactly what he was doing and the shame his words provoked only inflamed her. Even in the darkness, he could see her flush, her lips grow swollen with desire. He was her master and she could not tell him to stop, yet she wasn't at all sure whether she could control herself either. There was a real chance that she would betray herself, make a sound, a moan that would be overheard and bring all the opera glasses up to their dark box.

His fingertip slid up and down in her wetness, finding the nub of pleasure at the head of her labia and toying with it, pressing against it with a rhythm he knew she could not withstand. Her breasts rose and fell with her rapid breathing.

A rapid crescendo and then the orchestra went silent, leaving Della Pavia's violin soaring through the air, taking her with him on his river of sound. The Doctor didn't stop, didn't let up, pushing her, insisting that she come.

Her fingers tightened on the chair and she slid lower. Her legs fell open as she instinctively tried to assume the coital position in preparation for her impending orgasm. He wouldn't do this to her, would he? Make her come here in the Opera House? But what he said was true. She was a slut. She loved his fingers there, loved feeling her vulnerability.

He makes me such a whore! she thought. *Why do I love it so?*

That delicious tension, the unbearable ache began between her legs, and Abigail felt herself grow dizzy as the music suddenly thundered around her.

"Oh... Oh..."

And then the Doctor's fingers abandoned her, leaving her hanging, like an unresolved chord. Abigail realized that the music was over and she was left with nothing but her need, her body continuing to pulse, her hips fucking at nothing. With a finish as swift as the cut of a knife, the concerto had ended and the audience was roaring its approval, and the Doctor applauded with fingers still wet with her arousal—the fiend. She had built to a near orgasm along with the orchestra, and while the music had gone on to its climax and resolution, she had not. She was still quivering, her body trembling for release.

"Come," he said to her, acting as if nothing had happened. "It's time for us to go. Lord knows how many more encores they will have. The man plays like Orpheus himself!"

He helped her with her wrap and led her from the box, out into the corridor and toward the grand staircase as the house still shook with thunderous applause. Abigail's legs were trembling, she was wet and she could feel it as she walked, and as she looked down from the staircase, she caught sight of the eager pucker of her nipples through the thin fabric of her dress. She pulled her shawl up to hide them.

The lobby was crowded with those still hoping to squeeze their way in for the final encore while others stood to talk in inconvenient knots, barring the progress of those trying to leave early to reach the coaches waiting outside. Abigail's body felt alive with sexual desire and ached from unsatisfied need. She looked down on the crowd like a queen from on high, feeling the potent power of her own sexuality.

The Doctor had skipped down a few stairs ahead of her and now, seeing she wasn't with him, turned and looked back up at her, curious. "What is it, darling?"

"Nothing," she said, trying to clear her head of the salacious thoughts that now came to her unbidden. She took his hand and began to descend, but he stopped her and gestured to the crowd.

"Yes," he said, reading her mind as he so often seemed to do. "All of them. You could have any man you wanted. Any one of them."

His words gave her a brief chill. All her life she had been ignorant of sex, of its power and its hold on people. She had imagined that men chose girls based on their character and reputation. Now she knew that was all false. A new world had opened up for her, a world in which she had an intoxicating power and presence, and she knew that the Doctor's words were true. She was a desirable woman and any man in the lobby would be hers if only the circumstances were right. She was indeed a queen, and they all her subjects, vassals to their desires.

She would never admit it. She rearranged her wrap in preparation for the street. "Do hurry, Doctor. These crowds oppress me so."

* * * * *

The Doctor had given much thought to his failure in introducing Abigail to the experience of another man's love, and he'd decided that his mistake had been to compel Abigail to share herself with Darcy without obtaining her prior consent. This time he wanted her to manage the seduction on her own. He would bring her together with another man, and then let her handle things as she desired. In his search for a lover for Abigail, the Doctor had been looking for someone who was handsome and desirable, and who could sweep Abigail off her feet and then entirely disappear. Della Pavia had been the perfect choice—young, dashing, prodigiously talented, and with a reputation that suggested that he would be perfectly amenable to the kind of casual tryst the Doctor had in mind.

It helped too that Abigail had a weakness for music and musicians, and was especially enamored of men's hands, which she found highly erotic. When they had seen the notice in the Cairo newspaper announcing Della Pavia's upcoming concert in St. Louis, Abigail was amused, though in truth, she thought such an assignation beyond the Doctor's powers to arrange. She had been wrong. Both Darcy and Virginia knew people in the theater, before the footlights in Darcy's case, and in upper management in Virginia's. Between them, it was relatively simple to arrange for the Maestro to attend a late-night soirée. Virginia's Italian was good enough to make clear the implications of such a meeting and the sight of Abigail was enough to convince the young Maestro. He had come to the States from a tour of the continent where such things were not at all unusual.

As for Abigail, she had no idea what would happen, but she was ready to try. She'd been captivated by the romantic young prodigy with his long hair and soulful brown eyes, but it was the sight of his hands that decided it for her, graceful though masculine, and so expressive, even in the way he held his bow.

The four of them had taken adjoining suites on the uppermost floor of the Rickenbach Hotel — St. Louis' finest — and it was to their own rooms that the Doctor and Abigail now retired to find Virginia and Darcy already there. A cold buffet had been spread upon the table — oysters, poached salmon, ham and beef, cheese and pastries — with champagne cooling in buckets of shaved ice, wine and brandy for Damiano, should he prefer, although none of them was particularly hungry. Cigars and cigarettes had been laid out, and a small supply of brick opium procured from a local pharmacy, a particular vice that appealed to Mrs. Cecil, though one she indulged in rarely. In addition, the Doctor had concocted his own medicinal elixir designed to lower inhibitions and ease anxieties. He was very conscious of Abigail's uneasiness and did not want her to fail at her task, brought down by last-minute qualms or pangs of conscience.

As things now stood, there didn't seem to be much likelihood of that, despite the fact that it was nearly midnight and Della Pavia had still not arrived. They had reached the hotel with Abigail still in a high state of sexual arousal. The Doctor had seen to that, for in addition to his fiendish teasing at the concert, he had been inciting her further in the coach as well, kissing her, caressing her breasts, while spelling out for her in no uncertain language the things he hoped Della Pavia would do to her. It was a virtuoso performance of his own, whispered to the secret person she was inside, the person she was only for him, playing her desires against her sense of shame. After a few glasses of champagne and a dose of his elixir, Abigail was anxious to get started, anxious for anything.

Darcy, however, proved to be less patient, the more so since he had passed an interesting poker game going on in the hotel's card room. As soon as midnight came and went with no sign of their guest, he excused himself and left for the gambling salon downstairs, with directions that he be called should things get more exciting.

"It does get tiresome," Virginia said as the door closed behind him. "Being second to whatever deck of cards happens to be lying about. Gamblers are tedious lovers at best."

The three of them were seated at a round, cloth-covered table, each responding to the tension of waiting in their own way. Abigail was agitated, and fidgeted with a Japanese fan, watched by the Doctor, who seemed barely awake, hardly moving. Virginia was scraping opium from the finger-sized block with a penknife, preparing to fill the tiny brass bowl of her long, elegant Chinese pipe.

"My consolation." She sighed with resignation.

Once the tiny bowl was filled to her satisfaction, she lifted the chimney off a kerosene lamp, and turned the flame up, then tilted the bowl to the fire and sucked at it with genteel little breaths.

"Would you like to try it?" she asked Abigail, who was watching her in fascination. "It's not harmful, not as long as you don't overindulge, and it would do wonders to settle your nerves. Isn't that so, Doctor?"

"There's nothing wrong with my nerves," Abigail said, conscious now that she had been staring. She quickly looked away. "Well, perhaps there is a little anxiety, I suppose. Much as anyone would feel with something like this hanging over their heads. Something not entirely pleasant."

Virginia inhaled, held her breath for a minute, then discharged two long plumes of smoke through her nose with a long and contented sigh.

"Not entirely pleasant?" Virginia echoed. "Half the women in St. Louis would die to be in your shoes, my dear, myself included. I only hope that there's enough left over for me. How I adore musicians! Such sensitivity!"

The Doctor was sitting between the women, his fingers forming a steeple as he watched Virginia smoke. He was thinking about opium, its sedative properties as opposed to its well-known propensity to deaden the desires of the flesh.

"Perhaps you might try the pipe," he told Abigail. "It might do you good."

Abigail sighed in exasperation, but in fact, she was curious. It seemed as though lately, she was curious about everything she had once looked away from as being forbidden, if not depraved. Besides, the Doctor was looking at her with a look that told her he found something arousing about the pipe, though she couldn't imagine what. She was determined to go through with this silly seduction, just to show him she could do it, and she wanted to show him that there were other things she could do as well.

"Very well." She sat up. "I shall. What must I do?"

The first time she coughed terribly and was obliged to take a sip of water, but then, once she knew what to expect, she took the next three drafts without trouble, as she and Virginia shared the bowl, passing the pipe back and forth with an increasing sense of intimacy.

Aside from feeling very pleasantly relaxed, she noticed no pronounced change in herself, but then as Virginia cleaned the pipe, she was suddenly aware of how lovely Virginia and the Doctor's voices sounded, how very musical and full of warmth. She looked at the paisley cloth covering the table, and wondered why she hadn't noticed it before, the colors were so exquisite, so sensuous — reds and purples she could almost taste, greens and blues that had an entrancing richness and depth she had never appreciated before. And the pattern — so deliciously cunning and filled with hidden meanings and delights for the eye. There were stories in there, stories of profound import and brilliant wit. Whoever had made this cloth had been a wonderfully accomplished artist. She had never seen anything so beautiful.

She looked around and the room itself seemed transformed, the shadows so rich and mysterious, the colors vibrant and unusually vivid. She didn't feel intoxicated. It wasn't like liquor. It was as if scales had fallen from her eyes and a fog had been drawn from her mind so that she saw things as they really were for the first time. She had never felt so alive, her senses so acute.

Abigail's eyes were captured first by the brilliance of Virginia's diamonds, and then by the gorgeous texture of her black velvet gown. It was a blackness deeper than the night sky, yet warm and luxurious, against which Virginia's skin positively glowed with a soft and inviting vitality. She only had to look at that skin to feel its softness and warmth beneath her fingers, that wonderful feminine mystery.

She looked into the woman's face and saw Virginia's eyes, half-lidded with sensual intoxication, reading her own. There was a wisdom and warmth in Virginia's eyes that she'd never seen before. She felt like the woman was seeing right into her soul, and it thrilled her.

"Doctor, would you mind if I kissed her?" Virginia asked slowly, her eyes still locked on Abigail's. "Would you mind very much if I kissed her lips? Because they call to me."

Abigail heard her words and felt them spread throughout her as if each word were a pebble thrown into a still pool, the meaning like ripples spreading to every corner of her mind. She felt her body respond, felt her own eagerness for the lewd sensation of Virginia's loving touch.

"Doctor..." Abigail began, but then words failed her. Her voice felt as though it were far away, and her lips and mouth were not suited for speech now — but for something else.

"Abigail?" he said to her, but her eyes were on Virginia, beckoning her, trying to pull her across the table. Abigail knew dimly that she needed his permission, though she couldn't at the moment recall why, and yet it seemed so long in coming. Everything was happening so slowly.

"Please tell her yes," Abigail said at last, hardly aware of it. "Please tell her yes, she may kiss me."

The black velvet dress approached her and she was suddenly enveloped in the smell of Virginia's perfume, which evoked a flood of memories and meanings and sensual delights that all but made her groan aloud. Abigail closed her eyes and tilted her head back for Virginia's kiss and the feel of the woman's lips on hers was simply the most erotic thing she had ever experienced in her life — soft, warm, alive with love and desire. Abigail opened her mouth and moaned as Virginia's tongue slid slowly across the soft inside of her lower lip. It wasn't just the sensual pleasure of the kiss, it was the feel of the older woman's love and desire for her that caused Abigail's body to feel as if it had suddenly burst into sexual bloom, needing to be touched and embraced, penetrated and possessed.

The two women were so lost in their kiss that they hardly heard the soft knock at the door, discrete and tentative.

"Enter," the Doctor called, not moving his eyes from the two women.

Della Pavia walked in, his violin case in his hand. It was darker in the room than it had been in the hallway and his eyes took a moment to adjust. He saw the women and his eyebrows went up and his expression suddenly warmed. He looked at the Doctor and smiled with pleasure.

"*Buona sera*, Signore Doctor. I am so sorry I am late. I was detained. But had I known…"

He spoke with an Italian lilt, appending the whisper of a vowel to the end of each word. He took off his cape and laid it over a chaise, then stood there a moment, straightening his clothes as he watched the women kiss.

"But this is beautiful," he said softly, so as not to break the mood. "And in Chicago, too…"

"St. Louis," the Doctor corrected him.

"Of course, of course, forgive me, St. Louis," he said. "But one doesn't expect… In Paris, yes. Roma, London… But in St. Louis?" His smile grew and he shook his head in appreciative wonder.

"Ladies," the Doctor said. "Our guest has arrived."

There was no hiding the scent of the opium smoke in the air, and it was obvious that both women were under its spell, but if Della Pavia noticed he didn't seem to care. Virginia broke their kiss and managed to stand up—the look of pure carnal desire was plain on her face. Then she focused on the young man and regained her composure. She smiled credibly, not the least bit embarrassed at being caught in a Sapphic embrace.

"*Buono sera*, Maestro." She languidly extended her hand.

Della Pavia took her hand and kissed it. All the while his eyes were on Abigail, who now stood and looked at him in the full flush of her sexual heat, all inhibition gone.

" Senorita Du Pre. I am once again enchanted."

Abigail was obviously intoxicated, and her movements as she stood had a slow languor that held both men's eyes—the Doctor gauging her willingness and Della Pavia eager to get started. She felt the Doctor watching her as Della Pavia kissed her hand, his own dark eyes boring into hers. Between the opium, the liquor, and her own erotic arousal, Abigail was ready for anything.

Dr. Trier stood up and took Mrs. Cecil by the arm.

"I believe we'll be in the card salon, should you need us for anything." He kept a firm grip on Virginia and steered her toward the door. Abigail didn't even acknowledge their going—she had eyes only for the young Maestro.

Already, pangs of jealousy were clutching at the Doctor as he saw the look that passed between his fiancée and her new lover. At the door, he made the mistake of stopping and taking one last look back, just in time to see Abigail take a deep breath and step into the other man's embrace.

The Doctor hurried Virginia down the carpeted hallway, heading for the stairs—afraid that if he stopped, he wouldn't be able to keep himself from going back and calling a halt to what he had so carefully planned. He had not anticipated this sting of petty jealousy and it took him completely by surprise.

Inside the room, Abigail almost swooned into Della Pavia's arms. The drug made every sensation sharp and exquisite. She was already in a state of high arousal, so the touch of his lips on hers was thrilling, and as he kissed her, he stroked her face with those remarkable hands.

Abigail took his hand in hers and stared at it, fascinated. His fingers were strong yet long and elegant, and she marveled at what wonders lay in them, what secret knowledge.

He kissed her again, crushing her to him and she had to open her mouth to his passion. As she did, the realization of what she was doing suddenly came to her, sobering her, and she felt herself inwardly draw back.

This was not the Doctor. This was not the man she loved and trusted, that she would give her life for. It was someone she didn't know, an artist, a genius, but not someone she loved. She pulled her face away under the pretext of drawing breath and turned her face to the side in sudden confusion. Della Pavia's lips were on her throat, where her collar should have been, and his hand was on her breast. She felt her body respond—she could hardly help it—but she couldn't let herself go. She would do it, she'd said she would, but she knew then that she couldn't let herself go.

He stood away from her and gave her a look that she knew instinctively he'd used on other women before, dark and seductive. Despite herself, Abigail felt her body respond, but she couldn't help but notice that he was still barely more than a boy. Under all the genius and the affected manner of a great artist, he was hardly of an age to shave, and for all his show of Mediterranean fire, she knew that she had nothing to fear from him. He could not command her passions the way the Doctor did, nor could he even hope to take her to those places she'd already been. It occurred to her that she was probably much more experienced in sex and passion than he was, had gone further and knew things beyond his imagining. The Doctor had taught her well, and Abigail was now the maestro.

He undressed quickly, expecting her to do the same. Although her mind was clearer now, she was still possessed of that opiate languor and he was naked before she had her dress off. Touchingly, he kept his socks on.

She knew now what it would be like, already knew with perfect clarity that it might be good with him, but it would never be what she thought of as making love. With the security of this knowledge, she took off her clothes. His eyes went to her shaved mons and she saw them widen with feral intent. Despite her sudden diffidence, the look on his face satisfied her pride — he found her beautiful. After that, there was really nothing more that she wanted to know from him.

He went to her and kissed her again, his body cool against her heated skin. He led her to the bed and laid her down on it, covered her naked body with his and began to kiss her. His kisses were warm, ardent, his eagerness gratifying, and she couldn't deny that it felt good to be kissed like this — but she sorely missed her ropes. With her limbs free, she felt as though there was something more she should do with her hands — touch him or caress him. Instead, she laid one arm on the pillow over her head, draped the other across his shoulders and let him have his way. He seemed to expect no more — in fact, he seemed barely to notice her at all. He was too engrossed in the pleasures of her breasts, and his hand moved without preliminaries to her sex and stroked her there impatiently.

The thought of those hands on her brought the return of her wetness, but he was too eager, too impatient. She thought she should touch him, take him in her hand, but she had no desire to and he didn't press her. In fact, Abigail felt as though she needn't be there at all. She looked down at the top of his head where he worked at her breasts, moaning with desire, and then her eyes began to wander around the ceiling. Her mind was much clearer now, the fumes of the opium chased away by her initial excitement. What he was doing felt good, but still, she was strangely uninvolved. She felt almost indulgent toward him, and in a very short time, Della Pavia had positioned himself between her naked thighs, prepared to take her.

Abigail stopped him, her hands against his chest. She sat up and retrieved a lambskin condom from the table beside the bed and presented it to him very matter-of-factly. The young Italian looked at it with surprise and, she thought, a little distaste, but she held it up like a shield between them, smiling sweetly, and with an impatient shrug, he relented. The condom reminded them both that this affair was carnal, not affectionate. Once it was on, his entrance was sure and swift, an act of impatience rather than passion. There was no denying the fact that he felt good and that Abigail was still afire with need for release, but it wasn't the deep, profound satisfaction she felt with the Doctor. Della Pavia wasn't the answer to all those questions her body always seemed to ask, not like the Doctor was, but he felt good all the same. He was, after all, the toast of Europe—Paganini come again—the secret romantic desire of thousands of women, and now he was here, expending his passion upon her. As he adjusted himself between her legs, moaning with pleasure, Abigail realized that it had happened, that she was now fucking another man—one she didn't love.

He was on his knees over her, his lips at her ear, and she could hear his labored breathing and sighs of salacious enjoyment as his thin, boyish hips began to rise and fall, driving his cock into her. She had no urge to respond and her passion remained untouched. Her body responded to the feel of his cock inside her and she took what pleasure she could from that, blotting out any idea of shame, trying to concentrate on the physical sensation. This was what the Doctor had wanted, but as Della Pavia fell into his rhythm, rocking on top of her, she realized that the Doctor had been mistaken. He had no doubt expected to shame her with her pleasure, show her what she was capable of feeling at another man's hands, but she knew now that whatever erotic benefit she obtained from this coupling was negligible. Her own worst fears were unfounded. She was not a whore. Della Pavia could fuck her all night and get no more response out of her than he was getting now. She was pure—her heart belonged to only one man.

With that realization, she felt a thrill of triumph and relief. The Doctor had been wiser than he knew when he'd told her that her spirit could not be touched by anything she did, and she had no cause for shame, her body would not betray her. She almost laughed with relief, and a smile spread on her face.

Della Pavia noticed the change in her and saw the smile, a sign he mistook for an indication of her growing arousal. He smiled too and he began to fuck her faster, and Abigail, secure in her invulnerability, now let herself go. Her knees fell apart, her hips lifted to him, and she let herself luxuriate in the sensation of being fucked by the young stranger, owing him nothing.

He was, after all, a genius, and the fingers that coaxed impossible beauty from the strings of his violin now toyed with her breasts or traced the shell of her ear, as if she too were an instrument upon which he could play. But how he worked at her! Gasping and panting, his hips pumping blindly. Lost in the haze of his own desire, he seemed oblivious to her and his movements were clumsy and ultimately selfish—the rabid pumping of a man with a whore. Abigail realized that he was intent only upon his own pleasure, that she might be asleep or doing sums in her head for all he cared. The need that throbbed inside her remained untouched, and she knew she'd find no release with him.

Della Pavia was reaching his crescendo, so when a knock came at the door, shy and soft, she heard it but he didn't. Abigail turned her head in time to see the Doctor step into the room, looking miserable — as abashed and tentative as a schoolboy, all but wringing his hands.

Abigail had the wicked thought of putting on an act for him, of throwing her head back and filling the room with the sounds of a woman in sexual transport, but the Doctor looked so despondent and worried, she didn't have the heart. Besides, the effects of the opium were still with her, and the idea of simulating any emotion she didn't feel seemed quite beyond her.

Della Pavia was almost there. His thrusts were deep and brutal, his moans loud in the room. The Doctor stood captivated, unable to watch and unable to look away. Abigail might not be at the same level of excitement, but it was impossible to be unmoved by the young man's ecstasy, and her face and chest flushed pink with sexual pleasure as the Maestro thrust deep and hung there quivering. She felt his cock jump and lurch inside her, spitting its seed into the restriction of the condom.

"Eh? *Dios Mia*!" he said in alarm as his spasms subsided and he saw the Doctor standing there in the shadows. "Signore..." he began.

"Oh, never mind that," the Doctor said, trying to calm him. "This is no badger game, nothing like that. Er, look...it's *bono*, okay? *Capice*? Okay?"

"Okay? Good. Not mad? Good." Della Pavia sighed with relief as he rolled off Abigail, keeping a wary eye on the much larger Doctor. Now that he had come, he seemed even younger, very much a boy in a man's bed.

As soon as he was off, Abigail got to her knees. The hazy gleam of the opium was still in her eyes, and she was radiant with her sexual glow. It brought out the light sprinkling of freckles on her breasts and chest, making her look wonderfully young and fresh to the Doctor—far beyond the reach of any kind of degradation or debauchery. And now, her innocence was enhanced by her touching enthusiasm and satisfaction.

"There, Doctor," she said, totally unashamed of her nakedness, the womanly thrust of her breasts. "I've done it. I hope that was to your satisfaction."

Della Pavia stripped off the condom and threw it aside, wrapped himself in his opera cape and grabbed for his shoes. Abigail realized that he must be accustomed to making this kind of exit. The sight of the two grown men, one filled with contrition and worry, the other hopping around naked trying to get his shoes on, made her smile to the point of open laughter.

"Are we done?" she asked with open delight. "I hope we're not done, because I'm certainly not finished yet."

Chapter Sixteen

Abigail fell back onto the empty bed, completely at ease with herself, amused at the two men's discomfort.

"You can't mean to leave me like this. I still need to be finished. It's not fair that you men should have your satisfaction so quickly, with not a thought to the lady's."

As she watched them, she slid her hand down over her belly, parted her legs, and boldly began to masturbate. Her long, slim fingers parted her sex-slick labia and ran up and down her wet crease.

Della Pavia's jaw dropped. The Doctor looked at her and licked his dry lips. Abigail had been afraid that he perhaps had already satisfied himself with Virginia, the consequences of which she didn't care to contemplate. But it was obvious from the look on his face and the bulge in his trousers that he hadn't, and now his ego fought it out with his lust and his desire to assert his possession of Abigail once again.

For her part, never had Abigail felt so wickedly uninhibited and free, so imbued with the power of pure, raw female sexuality. She looked at the two men, one her betrothed, the other her casual lover, and she reveled in her sexual power over them. One was paralyzed by his own pride and confusion, the other rendered temporarily impotent by his recent experience of her body. In a three-way tug-of-war, Abigail had emerged the victor, and she lay on the bed playing with herself, taunting them with what they couldn't have.

Or so she thought. Her taunting was not without real effect on herself and she needed some sort of completion, needed it badly. Her selfish little body was not amused at the men's predicament and reacted to her own caresses by causing her hips to roll lewdly in a private sexual dance, as her eyes closed and lascivious visions writhed in her head. She hummed her song of sexual pleasure, soft moans escaped from her lips, telling the men just what she was feeling, what she wanted. Her fingers felt very good, and she was close. Let them watch—she had nothing to hide anymore. They both wanted her, and this was what they wanted. Her spell of her sexuality hung in the room, more potent than the dissipating pall of opium smoke.

It was more than the Doctor could stand. He ignored Della Pavia, crossed the room swiftly and swept Abigail into his arms with wild passion, sobbing with relief as he bore her back down onto the bed. He kissed her hungrily even as she continued to play with herself, and his kiss was filled with that savage possessiveness and desire she needed so badly—the Doctor's rough male hunger. She loved teasing them, but how much better it was to surrender, to give herself to his consuming passion, to let his need take her away.

Such power and desire in a kiss! Such terrible hunger. Abigail moaned into his mouth, tasting her victory as she brought herself to the very brink of orgasm again, then stopped, ready for him. He was half-undressed, his jacket half off, his clothing a mess. He pushed her hand away and replaced her knowing fingers with his own, crude and brutal but charged with such lust and raw possessiveness that he brought tears of gratitude to her eyes. And then he was between her legs, and his cock was inside her, where Della Pavia had just been, claiming her, dominating her, owning her.

Now there was no faking. She felt him hard and hot inside her and she came with a deep, stubborn violence, crying out and sobbing in her joy as she bore down on his thick, naked cock. He grabbed her wrists and held her down on the bed the way she liked—made her a prisoner of his lust as his hips rose and fell with angry intensity, bruising her, showing her there was no escape.

Abigail responded with unusual fervor, wanting Della Pavia to see, wanting her love for this man to be witnessed. She wanted to show him how it was done, how a man took his woman.

"Mine! Mine! All of you! Mine!" the Doctor gasped as he drove into her. She felt him tense, all the muscles in his body going rigid. All that strength, all that savage passion, so hard, so powerful, and all for the sweet, subtle throb of his flesh shoved deep between her legs as he jetted inside her, all his hot anguish and need, all he had to give.

* * * * *

"It was a case of the biter bit." They lay in the immense four-poster in the bedroom, the door closed, the one lamp on the bedside table trimmed down to a feeble glow. "I knew it as soon as I left the room. The jealousy I felt was just terrible, Abigail, all the more so because it was so unexpected. And yet, I knew it was something I had to do—we had to do. Why I cannot say exactly, but I knew it."

Abigail stirred in his arms. She had thrown on a nightdress for modesty's sake, thinking it strange that she should still feel uneasy in her nakedness when she had just revealed to the Doctor and Della Pavia so much more than any gown could ever conceal. Her head was on his chest, listening to his slow and steady heartbeat as she enjoyed the feel of his fingers combing gently through her hair. She had already told him what it had felt like to her to make love to another man, sparing him nothing despite the anguish she saw in his face.

"It was nothing, really," she had said. "I was strangely uninvolved, as if I weren't even here. He is a lovely man—a boy, really—but all his passion was saved for himself. I'm afraid that his talents do not extend far beyond his music, for he played me rather clumsily."

"He didn't make you sing for him? Like a violin?"

Abigail looked at him and smiled. "He did not. Oh, he felt good enough, and my body responded." Here she felt him tense. "But that's as far as it went. I don't think I would have climaxed, no matter what he had done." Feeling she had perhaps let the

Doctor off too easily, she added, "However, I would not be averse to doing this again—perhaps with another partner, one who was more mature, more patient and knowing. I might grow to like it. With your permission, of course."

The Doctor sat up, uneasy, and Abigail regretted her teasing.

He got out of bed, went to the window and stood there in his dressing gown, looking out onto the quiet streets, clearly troubled.

Darcy had returned from his card game some time ago, which was what had driven the Doctor and Abigail to seek privacy in their own bedroom. Darcy had lost, having run into a table of players as sharp as he and not to be outdone by his riverboat tricks. He had been in a dark mood and ready to take out his frustrations on Virginia. Della Pavia's presence had given him a pretext for the kind of perverse sexual gratification he desired, the sort of thing that appealed to Virginia as well, whose tastes in these matters ran darker than Abigail's. For some time there had been an absence of noise from the parlor next door—a very suggestive absence of sound.

"My lord?" Abigail asked as she went over to the Doctor. "I'm afraid I have displeased you?"

She touched his arm but received no response—clearly, he was very troubled by what had happened. After a moment's silence, Abigail slowly got down on her knees before him, bending her head and bowing submissively. In truth, she felt elated, entirely victorious, but she would not let him see that. His plan had been silly after all, but she would not tell him that either. They both knew now. She waited there for his pleasure, feeling his eyes upon her.

"This is hardly fitting," he said at last. "I hardly feel like your master at the moment. I'm not sure who controls whom anymore. I'm afraid I've gone too far, Abigail."

She looked up at him and said, "No, my darling, don't feel that way. You are my master, because I give myself to you. From the start, I've given myself to you and nothing has changed. What you want is what I want and if you desire me to be with other men, then I'll do it. But I'll only do it because you want it."

He wanted to speak but said nothing, though she could feel the emotion in his body even as she knelt at his feet. He reached down and picked her up, made her stand so that he could embrace her—a fierce embrace, passionate and possessive. She felt him suppress a sob of emotion.

"Oh God, Abigail…"

He buried his face in her hair and held her there with his wonderful strength.

She waited until his grip had relaxed. "All my life I was raised to defer to men," she said, feeling that some words were needed. "And all my life I resisted inside. Forgive me, darling, but men are vain, petty creatures for the most part—full of themselves and their own importance. Still, I did as I was expected, acting the lady, keeping my thoughts to myself. And now I find in you the one man to whom I want to defer, whom I want to serve and whom I want to be used by. In your love, I find my release and my fulfillment. I find more things than I have ever dreamt of."

He released her and pushed her away to arm's length so he could look at her. She saw the brightness in his eyes…tears.

He swallowed thickly. "And in you I find the one thing I cannot possess, cannot control. You bring this out in me, Abigail, from the first you've brought out this animal in me. All this time—all the things I've done with you—they were my attempts to own you, to possess your spirit, your essence. And yet, no matter what I do, you slip through my hands. You're incorruptible, pure, and so terribly beautiful that you bring me to despair. I tie you in chains, beat you, do everything I can to degrade you, and yet still you elude me and still I pursue you. Is this what love is? To be constantly chasing something you never can have?"

He crushed her to him again, his grip ferocious, trembling. Overcome with emotion, Abigail grabbed his hair in her small hands and forced his head back that she could kiss him. She pushed her tongue into his mouth in abject surrender, trying to suck the breath from his body or give hers to him. She felt so frail in his arms, and now she wanted him so badly.

He released her and she fell again to her knees, reaching for his dressing gown, fumbling to get her hands on him.

"My lord, my lord," she gasped, "Let me, please. Please let me put you in my mouth! Or take me. Take me as you did before. I need you so much!"

"No." He pushed her away, collecting himself with difficulty. "No. Not now."

He was uncertain, racked with emotion. She had rarely seen him like this—so beside himself—and she realized now why he needed the ropes, the ritual of the whip. It was a matter of control, of mastering the demons of his own passion. She realized this and it gave her a sudden chill to think of him out of control, what that terrible strength and need could do to her if he should ever let it all out, unchecked and unrepressed.

"We have guests." He straightened his robe and retied the sash. "We're being most remiss in neglecting them."

"Yes, my lord. I suppose we are."

Abigail collected herself as well, eager to let the moment pass. He had opened himself to her in a way he never had—more than she had a right to expect—and she was willing to let him go now, to assume their familiar roles where they were both more comfortable.

And in truth, she was eager to see what their friends were up to in the other room. She had no doubts now as to the Doctor's feelings for her or as to the nature of their relationship, and she had much to think about. But for now, she wanted to slip back into the world she had come to know so well—the world of unbridled sexuality, a world in which she was more and more comfortable with each new adventure and revelation.

"Well," Darcy said as they entered the sitting room. "Welcome to the party."

Virginia was on her knees, blindfolded, her arms spread out to the sides. Her wrists were held by ropes which traveled up and over the open French doors that led to the private veranda, so that she was framed by the dark night sky and the quiet streets of St. Louis. The curtains blew into the room on the faint, warm wind, licking at her like flames. She was stripped down to her corset, shoes, silk stockings and shoulder-length opera gloves. She still wore her diamond necklace and one bracelet, which even in the dim lamplight of the room flashed with cold fire.

Della Pavia was wearing only his trousers and was securing one end of the rope, attached to her wrist, over the door to a sturdy sconce in the wall, tightening it and bringing her hands up to the level of her head. As expected, Darcy had recruited him to help in his treatment of Virginia, and Della Pavia—though new to this—appeared to be a very enthusiastic student. His eyes were bright with excitement.

Darcy's jacket and tie were off, his shirt opened, but other than that he was fully dressed. He had a few whips and floggers laid out on the table amidst the empty glasses and the half-finished decanter of brandy. He was going through them when they entered.

"Are you here to play?" he asked the Doctor. "Or just to watch?"

"Watch," the Doctor said a little too quickly, Abigail thought, though she found it gratifying.

Darcy grinned. "As you wish. Mrs. Cecil's not adverse to an audience, are you dear?"

Although Virginia's eyes were concealed by the black satin blindfold, the excitement on her face was clear. Her lips were freshly painted and bright red, lewd in the lamplight.

"Is that you two?" she asked, her excitement making her forget her continental accent and revert to her natural Southern drawl. "Y'all come to watch what they're doing to me? Watch how they treat me. They're animals."

Darcy smiled and walked over to her as the Doctor pulled a loveseat out from the wall and arranged it so that it gave them an excellent view of what was to transpire. He took the comforter from the back and indicated for Abigail to sit.

Virginia's breasts hung naked over the top of her corset, the nipples pink and engorged with excitement.

"Animals," Darcy said softly, as he caressed her breasts with the crop. "Animals. Yes, I suppose we are. And you? What are you, Ginny?"

Virginia made no answer, so Darcy lifted the whip and tapped her nipple.

"What are you, hmmm? A dirty slut, I'd say. A hot little tramp."

He tapped her other nipple, and Abigail nestled closer to the Doctor. She had never witnessed the kind of play she and the Doctor engaged in, and the sight of her friend in ropes gave her a deep vicarious thrill. She felt herself grow wet. She had known for some time that Virginia's tastes in this sort of thing were different from her own, more extreme. Whereas Abigail accepted the names the Doctor called her as a sign of his own passion, she could sense that Virginia took a depraved sort of pleasure from the crude language and in being on display like this. Virginia was a powerful and formidable woman, accustomed to being catered and deferred to, but in her sex, she liked the tables turned. She liked to be degraded and forced to play the slut, and she apparently didn't mind others witnessing her loss of dignity.

Darcy, too, liked to be watched — especially when he had a woman like Virginia under his thumb. Together with Damiano Della Pavia, who was born to the spotlight, the three of them formed a perfect cast for some memorable sexual drama.

The Doctor spread the comforter over them. Under its cover, his hand slid up the inside of Abigail's leg and found the lips of her sex, already swelling with fresh excitement and moisture.

"Ahhh!" Virginia cried out when the whip came down on her left breast, then the right, expert, stinging little blows, kissing her flesh with sharp snaps of pain.

"Yes, I'm a slut," she said, answering Darcy's earlier question, proud behind her blindfold. "I'm a whatever you say. Now what are you going to do about it?"

He whipped her again, the crop just passing by her nipples, flicking it as it passed. She gasped, flinching in the ropes and trying to protect her chest.

Behind her, Della Pavia's erection was visible as he stepped out of his trousers, anxious for some contact. He got down on his knees behind Virginia and pressed her back against his naked chest. His fingers sought out her nipples, hard and erect after the whip, and he took them and rolled them between his fingers, making Virginia groan and writhe against him. He dropped one hand between her legs and Abigail could see him work his finger around in Virginia's pussy, those long, exquisite musician's fingers.

"Take this," Darcy said, throwing the crop to him. "And whip her ass. See how she loves it. She can come from a good ass whipping, can't you, darling? Especially when she has some nice hard cock in her mouth."

Darcy walked up to her, unbuttoning the fly of his pants as he went. Abigail couldn't see for sure, but she knew he had his cock out and was pushing it at Virginia's mouth. She could see her friend turn her head to the side in denial.

Della Pavia moved back, and still on his knees, began to rain blows on Virginia's naked buttocks—the dull, flat smack of the little leather paddle sharp in the room. With every blow, Virginia grunted, stubbornly resisting the pain and refusing to open her mouth. The young Italian was new to this, and his blows lacked Darcy's finesse. But then, Darcy had been whipping her sensitive breasts. Her behind was not so tender and could take the harder blows. With each lash, Della Pavia's eyes grew brighter, his grin more wolf-like.

Abigail could feel each blow, and with each one she felt her moisture increase. She reached beneath the afghan and pulled the Doctor's hand against herself, wanting his fingers inside her, wanting to feel like she too was a naughty little slut who needed a whipping. Through her own excitement, she couldn't help but notice that the men's sadistic pleasure looked very much like sexual lust, and Virginia, flinching at the cruel pain, looked exactly like a woman who was getting fucked — the same rapt concentration on her brows, her breathing loud, her nostrils dilated.

The whip fell fast and steady now, and with a final feral cry of surrender, Virginia opened her mouth and let Darcy ram his big cock inside. Her moans and cries were now muffled by the hard male flesh between her lips, but Della Pavia kept up the assault, transported by his feeling of power over the kneeling woman. With each blow of the crop, Virginia inched across the floor on her knees, tucking her buttocks in and thrusting her hips forward in a vain attempt to escape the wicked lash. Darcy's trousers slid down his hips with each thrust of his shaft into her mouth, and Abigail could see the muscles in his buttocks clench powerfully every time he sent his hardness sliding between Virginia's lips. Virginia's cries changed to a blubbering, frantic chant of lust and entreaty as her head began to bob forward and back, making her breasts shake on her chest. Darcy reached down and grabbed her nipples, pulling them out and using them as handles to pull her against his cock.

"Here it comes, baby! You hot slut! Suck my goddamn cock! I'm gonna come! I'm gonna come in your fucking mouth!"

Suddenly, all grew quiet. Della Pavia poised with the whip in his hand, knowing that Darcy was reaching his climax. Virginia froze, pulling hard at the ropes, only her loud, gurgling cry audible as Darcy gasped. For a moment, it was so quiet that

Abigail thought she could hear the Doctor's fingers sluicing in the wet trough of her own cunt.

Then Darcy moaned, a harsh, sharp cry, and Abigail saw him shiver. He must have pulled his cock from Virginia's mouth for an instant, for she heard the woman sob once quickly before her voice was cut off again as Darcy shoved his spurting shaft back once more into the warm suction of her willing mouth. His buttocks clenched in powerful spasms as he thrust his hips forward, pouring his seed into the slavering woman's throat. Virginia choked and gagged, her voice suddenly thick and bubbling from her mouthful of semen.

Darcy pulled his cock from her with a gasp, long strings of ropey ejaculate and saliva connecting his shaft to her still-seeking mouth before they stretched too thin and broke across Virginia's chin and breasts. His legs propelled him shakily back to a convenient chair, where he fell exhausted.

Della Pavia lost no time in taking Darcy's place. He came around in front of her and slid his erection into Virginia's accepting mouth. In her attempt to escape the lash, Virginia had pushed her hips far forward. She now leaned back in the ropes as Della Pavia straddled her thighs, a foot on either side, and bucked his loins forward, holding her head in his hands, muttering and cursing in Italian and broken English.

Abigail held onto the Doctor's strong arm, almost hiding behind it as she peeked out at her friend's ravishment at the hands of the young virtuoso. She could feel everything that Virginia was experiencing, for she knew the feelings well — the debased excitement of being used so cruelly for a man's pleasure, the thrill of surrender to such all-consuming lust. She knew the feelings but she had never seen them acted out before, and she found herself sharing the man's urge to control and dominate the helpless woman, even as she herself felt the deep need to share Virginia's shame and degradation.

Abigail's excitement was reaching a high and unsustainably fervid pitch and she had a sudden urge to throw the blanket aside and let them all see her orgasm, let them see the Doctor's fingers playing inside her, show them what a shameless slut she was too. She wondered briefly at her reluctance to do so. They had all of them seen her naked, she had no need to be modest, and she realized that she had no scruples about showing them her body. It was that vulnerability at her moment of orgasm, her helplessness that she still wanted to conceal. That was saved only for the Doctor—only he could see her like that—her naked self, some sort of holy of holies for which he was the only priest.

A quick, pre-orgasmic temblor spilled through her body and she increased her grip on his arm. She was close—soon she would have no choice and they would all see. She grabbed his hand and pushed it hard against her, working her clit against his fingers, her nipples painfully hard, wishing she had his teeth on them to give her that sharp bite of pain that she longed for.

Della Pavia released Virginia, and with his cock absurdly hard and erect, went to his violin case and took out a bow. He glanced up to see that the others were watching him, and he smiled. He walked behind Virginia and reached over her shoulder. Holding one breast in his left hand, he ran the tip of the bow down between her legs and began to rub her with it, playing the frog of the bow in the swampy wetness of her excited cunt.

"Oh God! Please!" Virginia cried, thrusting her hips even further forward, pushing her clit against the bowstrings. "Oh my God!"

Della Pavia grinned, and Abigail felt a new gush of wetness flood from her.

"Ecce!" the young man said. "A 'cello, eh? A 'cello!"

He laughed, and ran the bow up and back with delicate movements of his hand. His fingers stretched out, holding his bow just as he did when that beautiful music poured from his instrument. But this time, it was Virginia's ragged gasps and moaning sobs that issued forth as he ran the strings over her sex, bowing her with languorous legatos and maddening tremolos. The strings of the bow were briefly visible as they passed through the fleshy cleft of her distended labia, while her hips began to buck wildly, totally beyond control, the bow speaking directly to her overstretched nerves.

Abigail watched Virginia intently, knowing her friend was going to orgasm, seeing how Virginia had lost all shame, all inhibition, even her sense of self, and had turned into nothing more than a bundle of sexual nerves. Virginia arched her back, pressed her head back against Della Pavia and instinctively turned her head and opened her mouth wide, searching blindly for his cock to suck on as she came — the final bit of degradation she needed.

How beautiful she looks! Abigail thought as she felt her own orgasm begin. No doubts, no thoughts, nothing but sensation, taking her away, setting her free...

Virginia's scream might have been her own. It was loud and wild, raw with the force of her climax, and at that very moment Abigail dug her nails into the Doctor's muscular arm and climaxed as well. She let go and felt herself dissolve and seem to flow out of herself, gushing joyously into her lover's hands, giving herself to him totally.

Chapter Seventeen

The river at New Orleans brings down all sorts of things from the north—tree trunks and hen coops, empty bottles and bits of crates, and even as she watched, a bouquet of flowers still wrapped in a faded blue ribbon, spinning slowly in the muddy water. They might have been the sign of an unrequited love, thrown away in despair and bitterness. Or they might have served their purpose and brought tears of joy to a woman's eyes somewhere upriver, perhaps lost over the side of a bridge in her rush to meet the love of her life, careless, overwhelmed with happiness.

Abigail chose to believe the latter, chose to believe that all hearts finally found their homes, no matter how odd and unexpected those homes might be. She watched as the big riverboat—the *Maid of Missouri* this time—found its clumsy way home to the dock. It bumped up against the quay with the big stern wheel backing and churning up masses of white foam, checking its way against the river's constant flow.

She scanned the decks, crowded with passengers ready to disembark, looking for him amidst the confusion of the dock men heaving lines and making them fast to the bollards, tying them off. Home at last, tied safe and snug. As the last line was snubbed off and the boat emitted one long, final whistle, she saw him, dressed in white, making his gruff and impatient way down from the second deck through the crowds of passengers, a suitcase in each hand.

She had to stop herself from calling out to him like an excited child, reminding herself that she was a married woman now and that a certain amount of decorum was in order. He disapproved of public spectacle—unless he were the one in charge of it—but now, when his eyes finally found her in the crowd, his face lit up in a broad smile. He pushed his way through the crowds, using his luggage to force an opening.

"Abigail!" he exclaimed, dropping his suitcases and taking her in his arms.

For a moment there was just him, enfolding her in his arms, pressing her against the strong, hard familiarity of his body, the smell of the sun on his clothes, his cologne. He stepped back and looked at her, pleasure obvious on his face.

"Welcome back, darling. My lord."

His smile broadened as he looked at her, then he turned his attention to old Barrows, who stood motionless beside the gig, waiting to take the Doctor's bags and stow them away.

"Barrows, I hope you're well? You shouldn't have troubled yourself in this heat, though. You could have sent one of the boys."

Barrows gave the smallest of smiles in acknowledgment, his way of saying that it was no trouble at all. What a contrast between the old inscrutable half-breed with his leathery skin and Abigail, all peaches and cream in her dress of spotless white, her complexion like honey.

She watched him surreptitiously as he chatted with the old half-breed. This had been the Doctor's first trip away, a three-week jaunt up the river on business. She couldn't help but think back to the last time she'd been on this dock, when they'd returned from their own riverboat trip, a trip that had changed her life. She was hoping now that the river had worked some similar magic, some small miracle that might rekindle the fire they'd had before when they'd come back from St. Louis, ready to be wed. It wasn't that the flame had gone out, not by any means. It was just that she'd noticed a diminishment in its intensity, perhaps the first signs of that wan domesticity that suffocated the passion out of so many affairs once they were sanctified by marriage, smothered them in familiarity and complacency. That troubled her. She wanted to be his lover and his slave always, welded to him by that same incandescent passion they had shared before. She would be his wife, of course, and the best one she knew how to be, but in private she longed to feel that storm of desire and passion he could unleash in her. She needed that. It was what gave her life its savor. No, more than that. It's what gave her life its meaning.

But she was the Doctor's student, and she had learned well from him. She hadn't been idle in his absence, but had used her time alone to develop a friendship with Virginia and her particular circle of friends. Abigail was eager to tell the Doctor what she'd been up to. She didn't though, because she wasn't entirely settled in her mind about what she'd done, and she wasn't at all sure of how he would take it. At the moment, he seemed distracted, perhaps tired.

"My dear?" The Doctor called her back from her reverie. He stood by the shay, prepared to help her aboard.

Abigail collected her wits, gathered up her skirts and took his hand, leaning on him as she took the big step up and into the carriage. He sprang up behind her and settled himself in the seat as Barrows strapped the other luggage on behind. The shay had no top, so there was no question of his becoming intimate with her as they rode along, as he had liked to do so often in the past. Instead, he asked about her health and other domestic matters, and what news there was.

"Virginia's at the Carlisle," Abigail said, holding her hat in place against a mild gust of wind that met them as they turned down Crescent Street and away from the river. "She's been a real godsend, and if it weren't for her and Lyle Fourchette and his friends, I don't know what I would have done while you were gone."

"Lyle Fourchette?"

"Oh yes. I'm so eager for you to meet him. With Darcy away, he's been mostly escorting Virginia. A very sophisticated gentleman, with a very exciting circle of friends. Most wonderfully wicked. I know you'll like him. I never knew such interesting people lived in New Orleans. Outside of you and your friends, of course."

"Darcy is back now," the Doctor said. "I came downriver with him. He sends his love."

"How sweet. But I hope he's not still carrying a torch for Virginia. She seems quite enamored of Lyle's circle, and one can hardly blame her. You know how she likes to play the field."

He looked at her carefully now, judging her. "This Lyle Fourchette seems like quite the character. I daresay you've been seeing a lot of him and his friends during my absence?"

"Well, darling, you did want me to expand my own horizons, and you urged me not to sit at home while you were gone, did you not?" She spoke rapidly, afraid that perhaps she had given the wrong impression. "It was nothing more than a few dinners, a night at the Opera or two. I felt sure you would have approved, been proud of me even. Besides, I really was acting more as an observer, not a participant."

She waited for some sign of approval, but it was not forthcoming.

"In any case, you'll meet them soon enough." She primped her hair in her nervousness. "I do hope you don't mind terribly, darling, but I took the liberty of arranging a soiree for this evening, a kind of welcome home party."

"Oh?" He looked tired, but he smiled.

"Yes. I do so want you to meet Lyle and his circle. Hannah and the staff have everything well in hand. Just a small dinner, no more than a dozen couples. I'm sending the servants away. Perhaps you could invite Darcy if he wouldn't be put out, what with Virginia being there and all."

She waited for him to take the hint, but he either missed it or deliberately chose not to notice.

"That's very bold of you, Abigail, don't you find?"

"I hope not, my lord," she said quickly. "I only did it for your pleasure. I thought it would please you."

His face was noncommittal, and Abigail hoped that he was just tired and not himself. Arranging this party had not been easy and she knew she had taken a grave risk in doing so without his knowledge or permission, but she felt she had to do something about the distance that was opening up between them, and she thought that this might do it.

But there was more to it as well. Abigail had become more familiar with Lyle and the members of his group than she had perhaps let on. It was nothing serious, no real feelings were involved, and she was certain that it was of no consequence. It was really nothing more than what he'd encouraged her to do on her own. But still, taken with her uneasiness about their relationship, she found it worrisome, and she didn't like the feeling. She knew she should tell him, but this hardly seemed the time.

"You're very quiet, my lord," she said, aware of her own silence. "If I've done wrong, I apologize. If you wish, I'll beg off and cancel the whole thing. They'll understand. I'll tell them I'm ill."

He smiled, but it was an indulgent smile. "Not at all," he said. "I commend you on your initiative. It sounds like a wonderful idea and I'm looking forward to it. I'm just tired now, but I think a nap and a bath will do me wonders. Just sleeping in my own bed again."

The shay stopped where a large farm cart blocked the intersection, loaded with cabbages and onions. The driver had stopped to talk to a lady leaning from a balcony, and now, as he started the horse again, the cart lurched forward, dislodging a cabbage, which rolled into the street like some grim omen.

"I stopped in St. Louis and saw Professor McMahon at the university there," the Doctor said, seemingly from the blue. "I sat in on one of his physics lectures and I've been thinking about it ever since."

He turned to her. "Are you familiar with the idea of inertia? In the sense of physics, I mean."

"No, my lord. I've never really had a head for science at all, as you know."

"It's very simple, really. Inertia is an object's mass multiplied by its velocity—its speed. But what it means in practical terms is that it's a measure of an object's resistances to change in speed or direction, either of which is considered an acceleration in the language of physics."

"I see." She wondered where this was going. "That sounds fascinating, darling."

He went on, seemingly talking to himself now. "When you travel along at a constant velocity, you can't really tell that you are moving without looking at the world outside. If this shay were entirely closed so that we could not see outside, and if we were traveling at a constant speed in the same direction—with no bumping or rocking to and fro, of course—we could not tell that we were moving. We wouldn't know whether we were moving or standing still."

Abigail nodded politely, more confused than ever.

"But we would sense an acceleration," he continued. "If we changed direction or speed, if we slowed down or sped up, or turned a corner, we should be able to feel that. So you see, we only perceive accelerations. Changes in speed or direction. We only sense the change."

The cart passed. Barrows flicked the reins and the horse started forward, driving Abigail back into the leather seat.

"I've been thinking that it's much the same with our emotions and passions. One hardly knows it when one is consistently happy, or even in love for that matter. However, we do know when something suddenly makes us happy, or when we are falling in love. We feel the emotional acceleration."

He turned to her. "It's the change we feel, do you see? It's the change in our emotional state that we're aware of. Without that emotional acceleration, it all feels the same. We hardly know whether we feel anything at all."

* * * * *

She waited on him when they reached the house. She saw to his refreshments and drew his bath, asked if he would like her to wash him, or whether he wished for her to ready herself for his pleasure. She was willing to do anything for him, but he was very tired and wanted only to sleep, so Abigail sat by him and rubbed his back as she knew he liked until he had fallen asleep in their bed, still wearing his robe from the bath. Then she tiptoed out, closing the door behind her.

There was no doubt in her mind now that something was wrong. It was not like him to resist the pleasures she offered him, especially after a prolonged absence, and her spirits fell. It couldn't have come at a worse time, too, just when she needed to busy herself with the last-minute arrangements for the party. She was very nervous about this, not only about his reaction to her new friends, but about the success of the party itself. Lyle's crowd was very sophisticated and worldly, decadent even, and Abigail so wanted their approval.

The moon was full and low in the sky, as fat and romantic a moon as anyone could ever have wished for, oozing its pale, buttery light across the dark shadows of the lawn. The windows of the mansion were all open, the French doors too, allowing the curtains to billow gently in and out as the guests passed languidly from the one room to another, or stepped out onto the veranda for a breath of air.

The women wore their best and finest, and the men were splendid in their tailcoats or evening wear, though some women were already losing items of their dress, or splitting off into small select groups where they donned clothes deigned to enhance their sexual charms or announce their particular fetish. Virginia had brought back an interest in masks from her time in Paris. The fashion had been adopted by Lyle Fourchette and his friends, and so many of the guests wore elaborate harlequin masks adorned with sequins and lace.

The dinner party had slipped effortlessly from brandy and after-dinner cordials into parlor games and now into something darker and more intimate, something more like the entertainment Abigail knew the group favored. There had been little overt sexual contact yet, but now couples had paired off or formed small groups. Cuffs and chains and whips had appeared and clothes were coming off, and the sharp slap of a crop could be heard from the upstairs library, followed by a woman's thrilled gasp and a man's salacious laugh.

Abigail floated through the dim, candlelit rooms in her satin gown and shoulder-length gloves, her collar around her neck. Her own mask was adorned with black sequins and elaborate plumes, and while there was no concealing her identity, she did enjoy the bit of anonymity it gave her.

She was a little drunk, and flushed with excitement. She should have been pleased with the way the evening was going. The Doctor had seemed to like Lyle, had laughed at his jokes and had been a most gracious and thoughtful host. He had gotten on famously with the ladies and their escorts, and had obviously enjoyed himself during the game of Charades and the much more risqué bout of "Secret Desires" they had played. She had seen his eyes light up when Lyle had asked his permission to take things to the next level and she was sure the Doctor found some of the women there to his liking, but then his enthusiasm seemed to wane, and she had lost track of him. He had watched intently as Virginia had been stripped and tied over the dining room table, and she'd seen that hungry gleam in his eye as Lyle had used the whip on her, bringing her to a writhing orgasm as the others looked on with bated breath. That had served as the signal for the couples to find their own privacy, and now the party had dissolved into knots of people and couples scattered about the house. The Doctor seemed nowhere to be found.

At this point, she was uncertain of how to proceed without his guidance. She thought he must have found some woman to his liking and perhaps taken her to some private spot. That was his prerogative as her master, and she was determined to ignore the jealous feelings that nagged at her—if only she could find him, or identify the missing woman. So it was that she now searched the mansion room to room in search of him.

At the door to the library, she was startled by a tall, exotic woman in a merry widow with long, wild black hair—Esmeralda Desjardin—a high-Creole lady who was Lyle's occasional lover but who really belonged to no one but herself, a fact she made abundantly clear. With her powdered face and crimson lips, she looked like the queen of the damned and dissolute, a look that suited her. If Lyle's circle could be said to have a Mistress, Esmeralda was she, and her wickedly libidinous behaviors put her head and shoulders above the others in the group.

"Esme," Abigail asked when she had gotten over her fright. "Esme, have you seen my husband? Have you seen the Doctor?"

"Husband?" Esme echoed. "What a strange word. No, I haven't darling, but whatever do you need him for in any case? I just know that you're really looking for me now, aren't you?"

Esme had played with her before. At one of Lyle's afternoon teas, Esme had stood behind her and kissed Abigail's neck and massaged her breasts as the other guests engaged in their own brand of group sex in the parlor, right before her eyes. Esme had made it clear then that she was interested in even more intimate play whenever Abigail was of a mind for it.

She blocked Abigail's way now, put her hands on Abigail's hips and held her there, staring into her eyes. "Wherever he is, I'm sure he's enjoying himself, darling. Isn't it time we did the same?"

Esme leaned over and kissed her on the mouth, and despite her preoccupation, Abigail felt her body respond.

"No, Esme, I really have to find the Doctor…"

"Oh hush, Abigail, really. Don't you think you've been carrying on with that married woman business long enough? We all know how loyal you are, what a good little wife. Now it's time to share. You've been teasing us for weeks."

"Esme…"

But the taller woman's fingers were already at the bodice of Abigail's gown. The dress was so tight that she scarcely had to touch Abigail's buttons before they popped open on their own, exposing her naked cleavage first, and then the flat discs of her areolas as Esme parted her gown. She ran her fingers inside the dress to caress Abigail's nipples while she stopped her protests with an ardent kiss.

"Well, Abigail! I see you've decided to join in at last."

It was Lyle, still dressed, wearing a red harlequin mask and holding a glass of brandy in his hand.

"Esme," he said, acknowledging the other woman and nodding in greeting. "I'm glad to see you've started. It's a wonderful party, Abigail, you've really outdone yourself. A perfect place for your coming out."

"My coming out?" Abigail was somewhat flustered to be caught in such a flagrant lesbian embrace. "But this was really a coming-home party for the Doctor—for you to meet him—and now I've lost track of him."

"Oh, he seems like a big boy and I'm sure he's around somewhere, probably with one of the girls," Lyle said. "And shouldn't you be taking advantage of his absence now?"

"That's just what I was telling her," Esme said.

"Good," he replied. "You've been a part of our circle for what? Two or three weeks now. Isn't it time that you did more than just observe or steal an occasional kiss?"

As he said this, he insinuated himself close to her, so that the three of them formed a tight little group. He slid his hand beneath Esme's so that he was holding Abigail's breast, and the three of them joined in an openmouthed kiss, Lyle and Esme's tongues both seeking out Abigail's passive yet willing lips.

Lyle was tall and thin, and his skin bore the marks of a fearful case of childhood smallpox, which gave him a sinister appearance and a sense of evil that Abigail always found exciting. The Doctor might be given to rages of lust, but Lyle had an aura of perverse wickedness about him that Abigail found difficult to resist. Now, with his tongue sliding across her lips and his long fingers on her nipple, and with the soft pressure of Esme's breasts against her own, she began to fall under their spell.

No doubt the Doctor had disappeared on purpose, intentionally trying to ruin her party, and Abigail resented that. She put one hand on Lyle's shoulder, the other on the back of Esme's neck, and she extended her tongue, licking them back, hoping that perhaps he would see her and be scandalized.

The three of them stood like that, swaying slightly in the doorway, as the sounds of the other guests' acts of love and surrender reached their ears. The orgy was now underway, and the sounds of laughter and conversation had been replaced by the occasional lewd sounds of lovemaking, soft groans and entreaties.

"Where can we go?" Lyle asked her softly. "Let's get started."

Abigail stepped back and took a breath. Yes, she was ready for this. Her master had taught her well, and she had learned her lessons. If he was unwilling to give her what she wanted, then there were plenty of others here who would.

"This way." She led Lyle and Esme to the locked dungeon room at the end of the hallway.

She didn't notice Lyle's surreptitious signals to other men they passed on the way, but by the time they got to the dungeon and Abigail unlocked the door, there were two other men with them, Victor Montgomery and Immanuel Van Zandt, two of Lyle's particular cronies.

Once inside, it took only a moment to light the wall sconces and the candelabras, and as soon as they were lit, she was gratified to see the looks on the men's faces as they stared about at the dungeon room. Even Esme seemed impressed as she walked among the bondage equipment, the harnesses and chains, looking at them with a professional's respect.

"Whatever is this?" She fingered the chains that held the hammock chair suspended from the exposed rafters.

Abigail went to the sash against the wall and pulled it. The chair fell from the ceiling with a dramatic clanking of chains, and then hung there rocking and undulating slowly, straps swinging, like a menacing spider.

Esme and Lyle exchanged a meaningful look, his brows rising with interest.

"How lovely," Esme drawled, hiding her excitement. "Perhaps you'd show us how it's used, Abigail?"

There was no sign of the Doctor, no one to give her permission. Lyle and Esmeralda and the two men were looking at her, and Abigail had to make her decision.

For three weeks she had kept these people company and watched their perverse games and decadent pastimes. She had let Esmeralda kiss and fondle her, had let others explore her body, but always with limits, always with the awareness that she belonged to someone else. But always there had been the understanding that at some point, she would join them and become more than just an observer. She had taken up with them because she'd been lonely, and because she believed that the Doctor wanted her to, but she couldn't deny too that they excited her, that they appealed to her own increasingly lascivious nature. Now it was time to pay. She would have preferred that the Doctor were here to watch her, to see how well she had learned her lessons, but with or without him, it was time to pay.

"Certainly," she said, unbuttoning her gown. "Watch me."

They did watch, entranced, as Abigail took off her mask, slipped off her gown and stepped out of it, revealing herself—naked but for her black satin corset, her opera gloves and her collar. The corset stopped at her hips, and her bare and shaven sex was clearly visible. The half-cups of the bodice supported her breasts but left her nipples exposed, now visibly turgid and hard with sexual excitement.

Abigail felt herself swell with sexual energy as she always did when she revealed her body to her lovers. She felt ripe, sexy, and desirable to both men and women, and it gave her a delicious feeling of power to be looked at the way her guests looked at her now.

She let them look as she picked up her gown and threw it over a chair, then walked to the hammock and climbed in.

"Those straps go around my thighs, and you must place those stirrups under my feet." She settled back into the black leather sling. The hammock was still set from her last use with the Doctor, so that both her hips and her head were at the level of a man's crotch, a fact not lost on those present.

Lyle was standing by the wall-mounted wheels, inspecting the apparatus. "And this must control the height of your hips, and this your thighs. How very ingenious. Marvelous engineering, don't you find, Esme?"

But Esme had gone to the big wooden armoire and opened it and stood looking at the collection of whips and harness gear, manacles and sex toys. She found a black rubber phallus attached to a leather strap, a dildo, one the Doctor had never used because it was expressly intended for a woman to wear. A smaller, ancillary dildo hung from the base of the shaft, meant to be inserted in the user's vagina. Esme stared at the assemblage for a moment before whipping the broad leather belt around her hips and buckling it in place, cinching the straps tight for a snug fit.

"Yes. Marvelous," she said, staring down at her new phallus. "Let's see how well it works, shall we?"

Abigail knew what was coming, and she felt her body quake in delicious anticipation. Esme was beautiful. Even with the artificial cock jutting from her groin, she was a fine figure of a woman—thin, long-legged, and blessed with full, enticing breasts that trembled with each step as she cat-walked over to Abigail on her sharp heels. And more than that, she had that air of a sexual predator, a woman who took her pleasure from men and women alike, and now she intended to take her pleasure from Abigail.

She stood between Abigail's spread legs, leaned forward and ran her hands over the girl's body, from her hips up to her chest. Her long fingers spread over Abigail's breasts and then dug in, squeezing them, then slid up to take the girl's nipples between her fingers and roll them from side to side.

Esme stared into Abigail's eyes to gauge her reaction to this bold violation, and she was surprised to see Abigail staring back at her, daring her to do it, impatient to get started.

"Why don't you boys get comfortable?" Esme never took her eyes from her victim. "Take out your cocks. Let us see how hard we can make you, right, Abigail? Should we let them watch?"

"Yes," Abigail said. "Let them watch."

The feeling of being helplessly exposed in the hammock, the naked lust on Esme's face, and the sight of the men staring with almost comical intensity all combined to make Abigail tremble with desire. This was new to her, this desire to be watched, but it was terribly exciting. She knew Esme would make her react, would draw forth that slut she was inside. She had seen Esme's passion before, for both men and women, and now she shivered with eagerness to be the target of that lust.

Esme grasped hold of the chain that supported Abigail's shoulders, and she leaned over and kissed her, tenderly, but with such heat and desire that Abigail moaned up into her mouth and her thighs gave a little convulsive twitch of anticipation. The brunette let go of the chains with one hand and pulled down the bodice of her merry widow, letting her breasts spill out so that her nipples pressed against Abigail's eager buds. She rolled her chest against Abigail's as she kissed her, and their nipples skated against each other's skin.

"I always knew you were a little whore," Esme whispered to her. "Are you going to show us now how hot you are? Are you going to show us what a whore you are?"

Abigail was breathing deeply as Esme straightened up and ran one red-lacquered nail down Abigail's body, over the black corset, across her pale skin, and down to the girl's naked slit. Abigail gasped as Esme opened her up and slid a finger inside.

"Wet. You're already wet, Abigail. You're excited, aren't you? Have you ever been fucked by another woman?"

"No," she breathed. "No. You show me. Show me what it's like."

Esme laughed with wicked delight. She removed her finger and stood up, then sank to her haunches so that her face was at Abigail's crotch. She threw a glance at Lyle, who had already unbuttoned his trousers, and then she opened her red lips and extended her tongue toward Abigail's pink and exposed flesh.

Abigail jerked in the chains and cried out when Esme licked her. The touch was like an explosion. She grabbed the chains over her head and levered her hips up at Esme's mouth, at the same time glancing at Lyle, seeing his eyes wide, a lewd smile on his face. She had a wild urge to shove her cunt up into his face as well, let him have a good, close look. Let him see her woman's desire. Let him see that she was just as bad as he thought — even worse. As always happened, her own sluttiness gave her a feeling of wonderful power.

Esme moaned into Abigail's pussy as she licked her, the sound muffled by the wet and swollen flesh sliding across her lips. To her right, Victor had dropped his trousers and had his cock in his hand, openly masturbating. Immanuel's pants were open, and he was taking off his shirt, his eyes locked on the two women. It wouldn't be long now.

Abigail knew that they all meant to fuck her, and the thought excited her terribly. She had let a man have her when she hadn't particularly wanted to, because the Doctor had ordered her to. But now she had no qualms. She wanted this. The men's cocks were hard for her, and she couldn't wait to feel them inside her, fucking her, or in her mouth, spurting their hot semen across her face. Lyle had been right. It was her coming-out party. After today everyone would know what a wild little slut she was, everyone would get hard when she walked into a room.

"Oh yes! Suck me! Suck my pussy, Esmeralda, you slut!" she cried out. Knowing that the men were watching her made her hot, made her want to hold nothing back, and she ground her wet and hairless labia against Esme's sucking mouth, pushing her wet lips against the woman's eager face. Lascivious chills ran down her back, the smooth muscles on the insides of her thighs standing out as she worked.

Esme suddenly stood up and wiped the smeared lipstick and Abigail's secretions from her mouth with the back of her hand. She parted her legs and half-squatted, her hips thrust out lewdly, fumbled between her legs and inserted the smaller dildo into her own wet sex. She gave a low, choked groan as the little cock sunk between her shaved lips and disappeared inside her. Then she recovered herself and shuddered, took the black rubber phallus in her hand and slid the head up and down Abigail's wet and glistening slit.

"Are you ready, darling?" she asked. "Are you ready to get fucked?"

Without waiting for an answer, Esme took a stance, spreading her feet for balance. She pushed her thin hips forward, grasped Abigail's thighs and pulled the hammock back against her, impaling the girl on the hard artificial cock with lascivious glee. Abigail wailed as the thing filled her, spread her open. It was harder than a man, and it had been weeks since she'd had anything inside her. It was cold, but it warmed up quickly, and it felt horribly lewd and wonderful, impossibly good.

Esme's arms strained, her buttocks clenched as she shoved the dildo into Abigail and watched the girl's face, watched that girlish, angelic look dissolve into a mask of hot, whorish lust. Abigail had a natural, open innocence, and seeing the look of carnal pleasure on her sweet features made Esme growl with desire to despoil her, to see the little vixen come.

"Oh yes!" Victor cried. "Fuck her! Fuck the little tramp!" He was fisting himself violently now, his legs bent, his balls swinging freely as he rapidly pumped his long cock, transported by the sight of Esme's artificial phallus distending Abigail's naked pussy, now wet and drooling with the clear oils of her animalistic arousal.

"Go ahead, you sorry son of a bitch!" Esme snapped at him, her words punctuated by her savage thrusts into Abigail. "Spill your seed all over your hand, you miserable cocksucker! Let me see you come like a little schoolboy for me!"

Victor gasped as a pre-orgasmic spasm of pleasure ran through his body, and Esme quickly lost interest in him. She had figured out how the hammock worked now, and she reached down and grasped Abigail's breasts and used them to start the hammock swinging, forcing Abigail to swing up and back on the black rubber dildo. Once a rhythm was established, she found she no longer had to swing Abigail at all, that she could keep the hammock going by thrusting her hips, and she began to fuck her with vicious little thrusts. The dildo in her own pussy was giving her dirty little thrills of its own as it thrummed and squished inside her, and her breasts jiggled from her ragged breathing and the force of her thrusts. She brought one hand down to Abigail's pussy, and her fingers slid along the slick flesh until she found the other girl's clit, which she began to rub and tease.

"Oh God!" Abigail cried, arching out of the hammock, pushing her cunt onto the punishing instrument. She reached up and grabbed Esme's exposed nipples and squeezed them between thumb and forefingers, paying the woman back for the degrading pleasure she was receiving, and she pressed her elbows to her sides to make her own breasts stand out, her nipples hungry, aching to be touched. Her belly trembled with little shocks of pleasure each time Esme's fingers rubbed against her clit, and her brow furrowed with concentration as she felt herself climbing swiftly toward a hot, shameful orgasm. She knew she would come in front of all these people, that they would see her helpless in her greedy pleasure, all her sluttiness revealed, but she didn't care. She wanted them to see. She wanted them to see that she was every bit as depraved as they were.

Lyle laughed with salacious delight. He'd removed his clothes but left his sequined mask on, and his erection was long and hard, standing up out of its tuft of black pubic hair. He came to Abigail's head, which was at the perfect level to take him in her mouth, took his cock in his hand and rubbed its seeping head against her lips.

"Come on, Abby darling. Come on now, sweetie. I know you've been wanting this since the first time you saw it. So open up, baby. Open up and take old Lyle inside."

She did want it. She wanted all their cocks, all their hot semen. She let him turn her face to the side, and she opened her mouth willingly as she felt his hot flesh slide over her lips. It filled her mouth with male musk, with the weight of male potency. She took his balls in her hand as she washed him with her tongue and began to suck on him, her cheeks hollowing. He was heavy on her tongue, delicious—she could feel him trembling with his urgency to ejaculate.

"Yes, baby!" Esme breathed, her eyes drinking in this obscene cocksucking. "Yes, yes…"

Nothing excited Esmeralda like seeing another woman's degradation, her slavery to her own carnal pleasure. She continued to drive the artificial cock into Abigail with sharp little strokes—a woman's version of a man's brutal fucking—and with each stroke, the phallus inside her own body rocked against the sides of her pussy, fucking her as she fucked. Esme felt high, drunk with power. She dug her nails into Abigail's softly yielding breasts. She found Abigail's clit and pinched it, let it slide greasily through her fingers.

Victor rushed over, the muscles in his jaw twitching visibly as he clenched his teeth trying to hold back his orgasm. He pushed his jerking cock against Abigail's throat and she reached for him with her free hand, but he brushed her away, too intent on his own masturbation. She threaded her hand between his legs and grabbed his ass, rock-hard as he prepared to spew his seed on her. In her excitement, she slapped his ass, grabbed it and dug her nails into the hard muscle, trying to squeeze the cum out of him.

And here was Immanuel, hard as a rock, completely naked, crowding in to rub the head of his prick against her silky breasts, leaving a trail of sticky wetness. She was surrounded by cocks, fucked by a woman, oblivious to the world outside as fires danced in her belly and sparks ran like short circuits in her limbs. She was going to come. They were all going to come.

"Look at her!" Lyle crowed, staring down at Abigail's feverish face as he rammed his cock savagely into her mouth. "Look at her suck my cock. She's ours now. All ours! What do you bet she comes home with me now, huh? Just wait'll she tastes the load I have for her! Little Abigail has found a new master!"

But Victor would be the first to go. His breath was whining through his teeth, and Abigail could feel his ass grow even tighter in her hand as his spasms of ejaculation took him. He cried out, hoarse and triumphant, and she felt the muscles in his ass clench rock-hard, felt his semen spurt against the skin of her throat, her cheek, burning her and filling her nose with the smell of male musk. He opened his mouth and groaned as he gushed the rest of his seed in rich dollops against the base of her throat, so that it ran in thick streams down the side of her neck.

She saw colors. She saw a world of cocks, all spurting, all ejaculating, bathing her with their molten seed, drowning her in the pearly viscosity of male cum. Lyle rammed his shaft into the back of her throat, held her head still and she felt him jump like a live thing on her tongue, jump and spit and spit again, flooding her with his essence.

Semen was in her nose, semen was in her mouth, her hair. She swallowed heavily as he poured his release into her face, jerking and babbling like a demented puppet. She heard Esme swear and wail as she began to slap and grab at Abigail's breasts, punishing her, driving her higher and higher.

Victor staggered away from her and Immanuel took his place. Lyle's cock had not even finished its thick discharge and was still pushing out the last remnants of semen when she abandoned him, turned her head away, coughed wetly, and searched hungrily for Immanuel's fresh, hard shaft. She knew that Esme was coming, banging into her with insane fury, but it was cum she wanted now, wonderful, thick male seed...

"That's enough!"

The Doctor's voice cut through the room like the crack of a whip.

"I said, that's enough!"

The hammock stopped and Abigail looked around in confusion. In two steps, the Doctor reached the hammock and pulled Immanuel from Abigail's side. She felt the loss of that beautiful male hardness in her mouth and heard rather than saw the Doctor hit him and then saw Immanuel stagger back and trip over a bench. Then the dildo was out of her and Esme was on her hands and knees gasping, her eyes wide with fear and interrupted passion and the Doctor was standing there looking at them all with black fury in his eyes.

"Out! Out!" he cried. "All of you, get out!"

"Now, look," Lyle said, gathering up his clothes. "There's no need for hostility here, friend. No one was forced into anything they didn't want to do..."

"Hostility be damned!" The Doctor grabbed Lyle by the back of the neck and pushed him violently toward the door with such strength that Lyle fell sprawling, his clothes still in one hand, his mask over his eyes like a demented raccoon.

"The party's over. I want all of you gone. Now. Get your things and get out!"

The men quickly gathered up their clothes as the Doctor turned his back on them all and got Abigail down from the hammock. He threw a robe across her shoulders and made her stand, and it wasn't until her feet hit the ground that she was able to realize what was happening and how truly furious he was. He was trembling and his face was dark with rage. He grabbed her arm so hard that she cried out in shock and real fear for herself. She saw the blood on his hand, the torn knuckle from where he'd hit Immanuel. He propelled her past the men, past Esme, down the hallway to the stairs.

Darcy stood by the front door, hustling the half-dressed revelers out, pushing them when they didn't move fast enough. Virginia stood in shame against the wall nearby, looking at the floor, holding her cloak tight around her shivering body, barely concealing her nakedness.

"Go up to our room," the Doctor ordered Abigail, pushing her bodily up the stairs. "Wait for me there. I may be a while. You are to wait for me there, do you understand?"

"My lord." She grasped at his sleeve. "I'm so sorry. I only thought…"

He looked at her and in his eyes she saw such a burden of raw hurt and pain that the words died in her throat. She could have accepted his anger, but this look of sorrow and anguish stopped her cold.

She felt a chilling hollowness inside her, and she turned and ran up the stairs, racing her tears to their bedroom.

* * * * *

It was some hours later that Hannah found her, after Abigail had wept it all out, crying until she could cry no more. Hannah drew her a bath and washed her, soothing her all the while. She didn't ask Abigail for the cause of the tears, and if she knew anything of what had transpired at the mansion, she didn't mention it. She treated Abigail with unusual gentleness, as if sensing the girl's shock. It was only when she sat Abigail down in her dressing gown, her hair still wet from the bath, and poured her a cup of tea that she said anything.

"Oh you poor thing," Hannah said. "I knew your party would wear you out. I told the Doctor he should have let me and

Barrows give a hand. I don't know why you got it in your head that you have to do it all yourself without anyone's help."

She stirred the sugar into Abigail's tea and handed it to her. Abigail took it numbly, in too much pain to say anything.

"But at least it was a nice party." Hannah went on. "The Doctor said they all had a very good time."

Abigail looked at her.

"He said that? The Doctor said that?"

Hannah arranged the teapot just so and straightened her apron before looking at Abigail, her eyes open and honest.

"Why, yes, he did. Right when we got in the cart for him to drive us back. He said it was a lovely party but that some of the guests let their drink get the better of them and began to misbehave, and that's why he ended it early. But you know, I always say it's not a party unless…"

"That's what he said? That some of the guests misbehaved?"

"Yes, ma'am. He said that some of them started to take some things that didn't belong to them, acting up and all and…Mrs. Abigail? Are you all right?"

"Yes, Hannah." She turned away to hide the fresh tears. "I just need to be alone for a bit. Thank you for everything."

Hannah quietly picked up the tray and departed, and Abigail drew her robe around her and went to the window, so ashamed.

Outside, the moon was high in the sky. It was late, the breeze had died, and the crickets had ceased their churring save for one lonely fiddler by the gate. She thought she could hear the Doctor bidding Darcy goodnight, thanking him, and then she did see Darcy's gig rolling down the drive, Virginia sitting beside him. They looked reconciled, and the sight of them together — Virginia leaning against him, Darcy's arm around her — brought tears welling again to her eyes.

She heard his tread on the stairs but she couldn't bring herself to face the door. She felt numb, as if she weren't there. She remembered that night so long ago when he had first come to her in this room, when she'd been his property, newly acquired, and she remembered how she'd shivered in fear and excitement at this new thing she faced. How far she had come, and how far she had fallen. She fervently wished she could go back to that moment, so she could feel like she stood at the beginning of something fresh and new again.

The Doctor walked in, closed the door behind him, and locked it. He looked tired and worn, though the rage still smoldered. His jacket and tie were gone. There was a bandage on his hand where he'd hit Immanuel.

There was a long moment when he didn't say anything, just stared at her, and Abigail couldn't meet his eyes. She just stood by the window looking out at the moonlit garden as tears fell from her eyes.

And then he came to her.

He crossed the room in two rapid strides, without warning, grabbed the lapels of her dressing gown and ripped them open, exposing her breasts as she stood there, too shocked to move. His eyes were wild with lust like she had never seen them before, almost insane with desire. Despite herself, she wailed in confused fear as he tore the robe from her body and threw her naked onto the bed, and before she could gather her wits at all, he was on top of her, holding her, pulling her hair, forcing her mouth against his. His hand found her breast and squeezed hard, hurting her, and he picked her up and threw her around the bed as if she were a child's toy, of no consequence at all.

He never hit her, never struck her, but his strength and his determination were ruthless, the violence of passion. Abigail, who only minutes before had been helpless in weeping, found herself fighting back. She fought with her teeth and her nails and her elbows and knees, fighting for she knew not what. She used her pitiful strength against him, trying to protect herself as best she could, and finding again that there was no protection, for he fought with all the fire of his desire for her, his terrible need to possess her.

He entered her savagely, ripping into her, bigger and harder than he had ever been. He held her hands in grips of iron and forced his way into her, hurting her just the way she wanted to be hurt, crushing her beneath him with the weight of his desire. Even in her panic and whirlwind of emotion, she opened herself to him, to his punishment and his rage, threw herself at him, biting and clawing, weeping and urging him on, begging him to destroy her. She screamed as he came inside her, screamed as he filled her with his hot, scalding seed, screamed and dissolved utterly into tears, clinging to him as though she would die without him there — as if without him there would be no her at all.

At last, exhausted beyond all effort, he lay half atop her, dripping his sweat onto her, his hand bleeding onto her naked breast, and Abigail lay there willing herself to be small, to be something that would fit against his heart.

He kissed her and stroked her tear-ravaged cheeks. "We don't need any friends. We don't need any toys or equipment or special clothes. We don't need any more games or lessons or anything like that. All we need is what we feel for each other. That's more than enough."

* * * * *

She sits by the river in her best yellow dress, a broad-brimmed bonnet on her head, her gloved hands resting on the handle of her parasol. Her tea is before her, but Abigail is watching the people as they promenade up and down in the street before her, men and women together, young lovers with their nervous caresses, old and wizened couples helping each other along. The men stop to tip their hats, the women to make their curtsies or bow graciously. They stop in the cafe and drink their coffee or lemonade. They remove their gloves or put them on, exchanging news of the world or gossip about their neighbors.

She wonders how many of them live with mystery so very close to themselves. How many of them have searched inside and found depths of feeling beyond what they can understand. She wonders how they manage to live without knowing of the incredible forces that lie so close to the everyday, and how they manage to live with them if they do know. How many — if any — have broken through the crust of what they think and found beneath it a realm that cannot be described, cannot be understood, but can only be experienced?

The Doctor is standing at the coach, helping Barrows load their purchases aboard. She sees by the wrapping on the packages that he has been to the corset shop, and the large pasteboard box could only be from the leather worker he frequents, a man who knows the Doctor's tastes and does exquisite work that fits her like a glove.

"Abigail? Abigail, finish your tea and let's go. It's starting to rain."

Already, large, warm drops of rain are beginning to fall, scattering the fashionable strollers, and the Doctor pulls his collar up, making a big show of getting wet. He's eager to get her home again, into the privacy of their house, where he can show her what he's bought for her today.

She feels a thrill in the pit of her stomach — familiar, yet always new. She finishes her tea, takes one more look at the people around her, then gathers her things and stands up.

The Doctor is waiting, and it's time to go home.

About the author:

Elliot Mabeuse is an award-winning author, critic, and porn theorist whose erotic explorations combine depth and insight with a singularly passionate intensity. His interest in the emotional and transformative power of sex gives his writing a unique flavor, and results in works of literate erotica that are sensual, humane, and deeply satisfying.

Retired from the chemical laboratory now, Doctor Mabeuse lives in Chicago where he pursues his interests in the transcendent powers of sexuality, religion, and the riddles of biochemistry.

Elliot welcomes mail from readers. You can write to her c/o Ellora's Cave Publishing at 1056 Home Avenue, Akron OH 44310-3502.

Why an electronic book?

We live in the Information Age—an exciting time in the history of human civilization in which technology rules supreme and continues to progress in leaps and bounds every minute of every hour of every day. For a multitude of reasons, more and more avid literary fans are opting to purchase e-books instead of paperbacks. The question to those not yet initiated to the world of electronic reading is simply: *why?*

1. *Price.* An electronic title at Ellora's Cave Publishing and Cerridwen Press runs anywhere from 40-75% less than the cover price of the <u>exact same title</u> in paperback format. Why? Cold mathematics. It is less expensive to publish an e-book than it is to publish a paperback, so the savings are passed along to the consumer.

2. *Space.* Running out of room to house your paperback books? That is one worry you will never have with electronic novels. For a low one-time cost, you can purchase a handheld computer designed specifically for e-reading purposes. Many e-readers are larger than the average handheld, giving you plenty of screen room. Better yet, hundreds of titles can be stored within your new library—a single microchip. (Please note that Ellora's Cave and Cerridwen Press does not endorse any specific brands. You can check our website at www.ellorascave.com or

www.cerridwenpress.com for customer recommendations we make available to new consumers.)

3. *Mobility.* Because your new library now consists of only a microchip, your entire cache of books can be taken with you wherever you go.

4. *Personal preferences are accounted for.* Are the words you are currently reading too small? Too large? Too...**ANNOYING**? Paperback books cannot be modified according to personal preferences, but e-books can.

5. *Instant gratification.* Is it the middle of the night and all the bookstores are closed? Are you tired of waiting days—sometimes weeks—for online and offline bookstores to ship the novels you bought? Ellora's Cave Publishing sells instantaneous downloads 24 hours a day, 7 days a week, 365 days a year. Our e-book delivery system is 100% automated, meaning your order is filled as soon as you pay for it.

Those are a few of the top reasons why electronic novels are displacing paperbacks for many an avid reader. As always, Ellora's Cave and Cerridwen Press welcomes your questions and comments. We invite you to email us at service@ellorascave.com, service@cerridwenpress.com or write to us directly at: 1056 Home Ave. Akron OH 44310-3502.

erridwen, the Celtic Goddess of wisdom, was the muse who brought inspiration to storytellers and those in the creative arts. Cerridwen Press encompasses the best and most innovative stories in all genres of today's fiction. Visit our site and discover the newest titles by talented authors who still get inspired - much like the ancient storytellers did, once upon a time.

Cerridwen Press
www.cerridwenpress.com

THE
☥ ELLORA'S CAVE ☥
LIBRARY

Stay up to date with Ellora's Cave Titles in
Print with our Quarterly Catalog.

To recieve a catalog,
send an email with your name
and mailing address to:

CATALOG@ELLORASCAVE.COM

or send a letter or postcard
with your mailing address to:

Catalog Request
c/o Ellora's Cave Publishing, Inc.
1056 Home Avenue
Akron, Ohio 44310-3502

Lady Jaided

The premier magazine for today's sensual woman

Lady Jaided magazine is devoted to exploring the sexuality and sensuality of women. While there are many similarities between the sexual experiences of men and women, there are just as many if not more differences. Our focus is on the female experience and on giving voice and credence to it. Lady Jaided will include everything from trends, politics, science and history to gossip, humor and celebrity interviews, but our focus will remain on female sexuality and sensuality.

Subscribe Online

Get 12 issues of Lady Jaided
mailed to you every month for only

$29.95

www.LadyJaided.com

Lady *Jaided* Regular Features

Jaid's Tirade
Jaid Black's erotic romance novels sell throughout the world, and her publishing company Ellora's Cave is one of the largest and most successful e-book publishers in the world. What is less well known about Jaid Black, a.k.a. Tina Engler is her long record as a political activist. Whether she's discussing sex or politics (or both), expect to see her get up on her soapbox and do what she does best: offend the greedy, the holier-than-thous, and the apathetic! Don't miss out on her monthly column.

Devilish Dot's G-Spot
Married to the same man for 20 years, Dorothy Araiza still basks in a sex life to be envied. What Dot loves just as much as achieving the Big O is helping other women realize their full sexual potential. Dot gives talks and advice on everything from which sex toys to buy (or not to buy) to which positions give you the best climax.

On the Road with Lady K
Publisher, author, world traveler and Lady of Barrow, Kathryn Falk shares insider information on the most romantic places in the world.

Kandidly Kay
This Lois Lane cum Dave Barry is a domestic goddess by day and a hard-hitting sexual deviancy reporter by night. Adored for her stunning wit and knack for delivering one-liners, this Rodney Dangerfield of reporting will leave no stone unturned in her search for the bizarre truth.

A Model World
CJ Hollenbach returns to his roots. The blond heartthrob from Ohio has twice been seen in Playgirl magazine and countless other publications. He has appeared on several national TV shows including The Jerry Springer Show (God help him!) and has been interviewed for Entertainment Tonight, CNN and The Today Show. He has been involved in the romance industry for the past 12 years, appearing on dozens of romance novel covers and calendars. CJ's specialty is personal interviews, in which people have a tendency to tell him everything.

Hot Mama Cooks
Sex is her food, and food is her sex. Hot Mama gives aphrodisiac a whole new meaning. Join her every month for her latest sensual adventure -- with bonus recipe!

Empress on the Mount
Brash, outrageous, and undeniably irreverent, this advice columnist from down under will either leave you in stitches or recovering from hang-jaw as you gawk at her answers to reader questions on relationships and life.

Erotic Fiction from Ellora's Cave
The debut issue will feature part one of "Ferocious," a three-part erotic serial written especially for Lady Jaided by the popular Sherri L. King.

ELLORA'S
CAVEMEN
LEGENDARY TAILS

Try an e-book for your immediate
reading pleasure or order these titles in print from

WWW.ELLORASCAVE.COM

ELLORA'S CAVE
THE BEST IN TODAY'S ROMANTICA™

ELLORA'S CAVEMEN

TALES FROM THE TEMPLE

Try an e-book for your immediate
reading pleasure or order these titles in print from

www.EllorasCave.com

ELLORA'S CAVE
The Best in Today's Romantica™

MAKE EACH DAY MORE *EXCITING* WITH OUR

ELLORA'S
CAVEMEN
CALENDAR

WWW.ELLORASCAVE.COM

ELLORA'S CAVE

ROMANTICA PUBLISHING

Discover for yourself why readers can't get enough of the multiple award-winning publisher Ellora's Cave. Whether you prefer e-books or paperbacks, be sure to visit EC on the web at www.ellorascave.com for an erotic reading experience that will leave you breathless.

www.ellorascave.com